BLOOD AND STONE

STONEHEART MOTORCYCLE CLUB
BOOK 6

EVIE MITCHELL

THUNDER THIGHS PUBLISHING

ISBN: 978-1-923610-10-1

Editor: Nicole McCurdy, Emerald Edits
https://www.emeraldedits.com/

Cover design: Megan Wade
Map design: Evie Mitchell
Images: Deposit Photo

To everyone who's ever fantasized about a grumpy biker president with silver in his beard and murder in his eyes.

This one's for you.

Also, to lawyers everywhere who've dreamed of telling their clients their legal strategy is shit.

Live vicariously, my friends!

And to Rooks.

Always.

ACKNOWLEDGEMENT OF COUNTRY

I acknowledge the Traditional Custodians of the lands on which I write, the Ngunnawal people, and pay my respect to elders both past and present.

I acknowledge the continued and deep spiritual relationship of the Australian Aboriginal and Torres Strait Islander peoples' to this land, and their unique cultural and spiritual relationships to the land, waters and seas, and their rich contribution to society.

Always was, always will be.

CONTENT INFORMATION

Please note the following content information include
SPOILERS for this book.

SPOILERS BELOW

Themes

**Note, this story contains numerous violent scenes.
Please check content information before reading.**

- **Violence:** Graphic violence, gunfights,
  kidnapping, death/murder (on page and off)
- **Assault:** On page beatings
- **Car accident:** Serious crash, hospitalisation,
  medically induced coma, emergency brain
  surgery (burr holes)
- **Domestic abuse:** including verbal and physical
  on-page violence
- **Child in peril:** A child witnesses abuse

- **Past trauma:** References to witness death (car bomb, including a child), parental issues, divorce, loneliness, and relationship breakdowns.
- **Medical trauma:** Detailed injury and recovery scenes, including medical drug use
- **Graphic consensual sex:** repeatedly. Like ALOT.

More information

If you have any concerns with the depictions in this story or would like further information before reading, please email Evie@EvieMitchell.com

END SPOILERS

BLOOD AND STONE

He's the president of the Stoneheart MC. She's the club's lawyer—and the one woman he's sworn to stay away from. When danger comes knocking, all bets are off.

JOSIE

I've spent years building walls. I've learned the hard way that caring too much is dangerous. Now I'm the Stoneheart MC's lawyer, and I've got a perfect system in place, keep my head down, do my job, and never let a client get close.

Especially not the motorcycle club's president.

Stone is everything I shouldn't want—commanding, protective, and far too easy to crave. Eight months ago, he pulled me close, then pushed me away.

Message received.

But when a hitman puts me in his crosshairs, Stone is the only one standing between me and a headstone. I'm terrified—but the way he looks at me now?

That might be the most dangerous thing of all.

STONE

I told myself Josie was too good for a man like me—a

man whose hands are stained with the business of the Stoneheart MC.

I was wrong.

Watching her walk away was the hardest thing I've ever done. Seeing her in the crosshairs of a cartel hit squad? That's where I draw the line.

They think they can use her to get to me. They don't realize that Josie isn't just our lawyer.

She's *mine*.

She thinks she's safe behind those legal briefs and her icy professional walls. She's wrong. She's under my roof for protection, and there's nowhere for her to run.

I should be focused on the war at our gates, but all I can think about is the woman in my bed. I've spent my life bleeding for this club, but if the world wants to take her from me?

I'll burn every bit of it to the ground to keep her safe.

Watch me.

Blood & Stone *is a steamy motorcycle club romance featuring a possessive president who's done fighting his feelings, a fierce lawyer who's tired of keeping her heart locked away, and a club under siege. With elements of second-chance romance, forced proximity, and the kind of love worth bleeding for, this story delivers danger, heat, and hard-won happily ever afters.*

If you love curvy heroines who fight back, protective heroes learning that strength means opening up, and a found family of lovable bikers who will ride to war for their own, this book is for you!

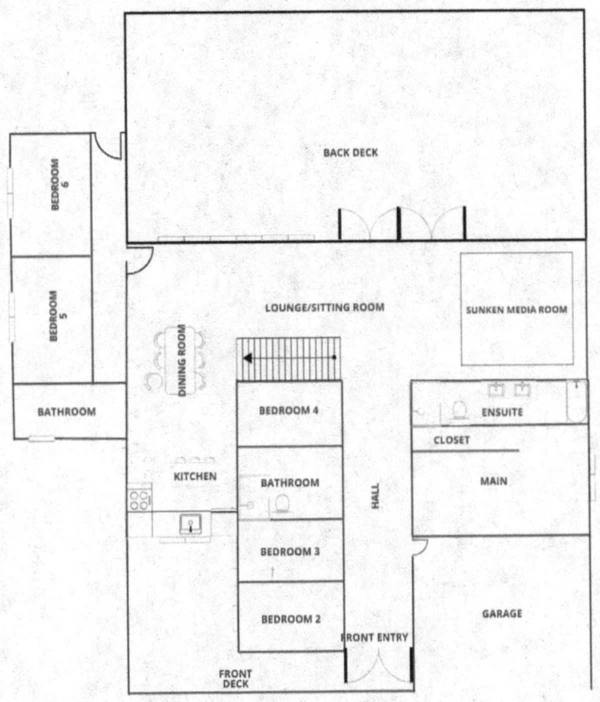

THE CLUB HOUSE

GROUND LEVEL

4 Acres
Land

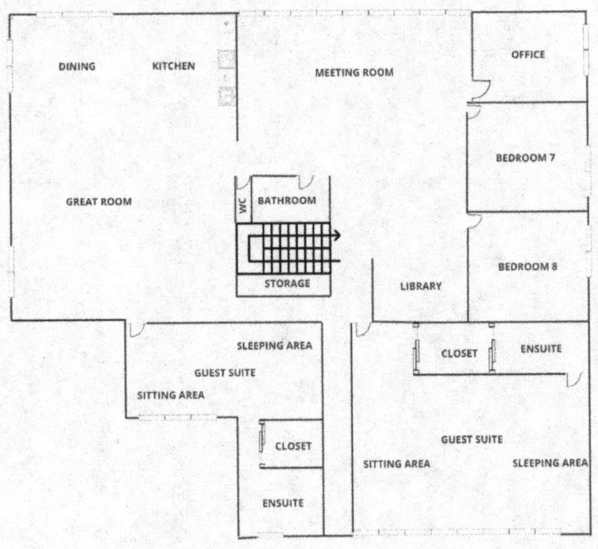

THE CLUB HOUSE

UPPER LEVEL

4 Acres
Land

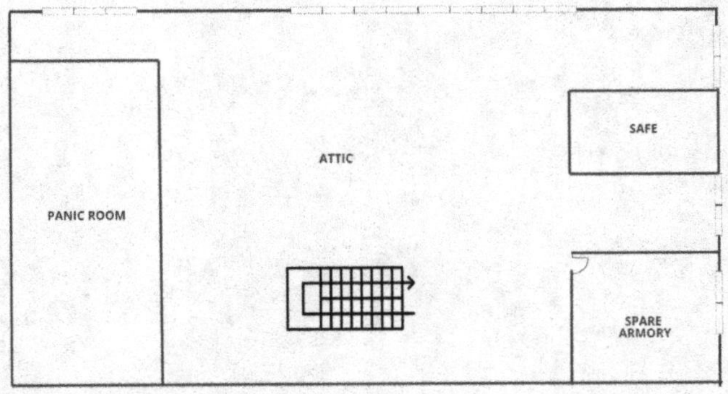

THE CLUB HOUSE
ATTIC

4 Acres
Land

THE CHAPEL

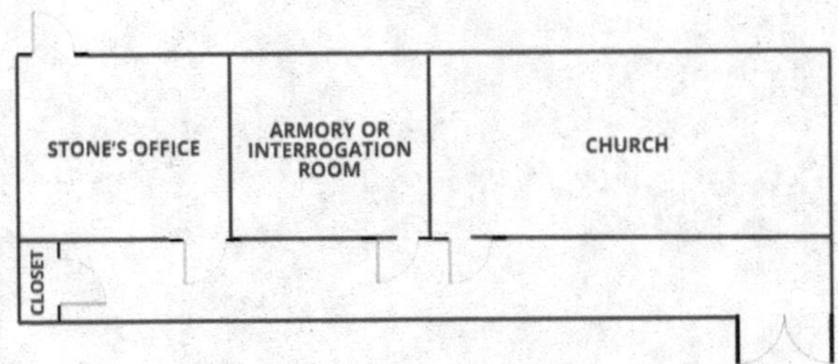

THE BARRACKS
GROUND FLOOR

THE BARRACKS
LEVEL 1

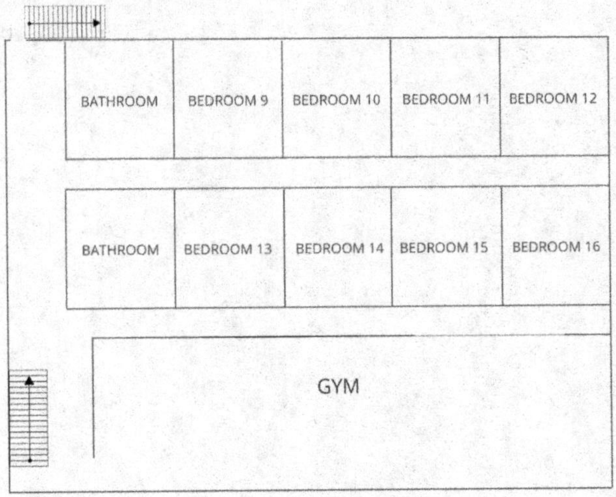

THE BARRACKS
LEVEL 2

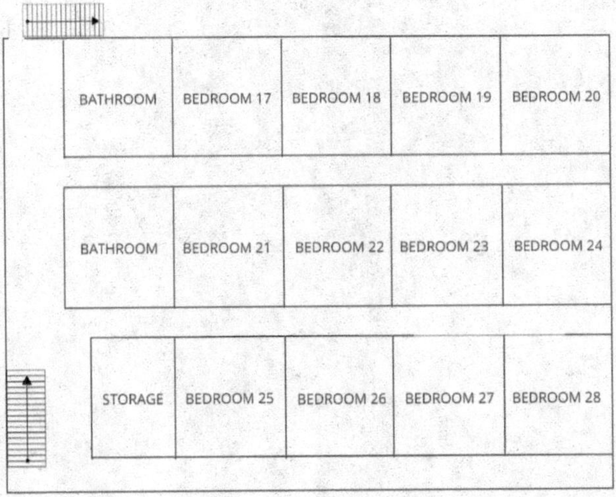

| BATHROOM | BEDROOM 17 | BEDROOM 18 | BEDROOM 19 | BEDROOM 20 |

| BATHROOM | BEDROOM 21 | BEDROOM 22 | BEDROOM 23 | BEDROOM 24 |

| STORAGE | BEDROOM 25 | BEDROOM 26 | BEDROOM 27 | BEDROOM 28 |

PROLOGUE
JOSIE

These bikers sure know how to throw a party.

The Stoneheart MC clubhouse is packed wall-to-wall with leather and denim. Someone's cranked up the speakers loud enough to rattle the floor-to-ceiling windows, competing with the crack of pool balls from the corner and the steady hum of voices that fills every inch of the sprawling lounge.

The place is a study in contrasts—old farmhouse bones meeting modern renovation. A massive leather sectional dominates the main room, worn and comfortable, facing a stone fireplace that's been lit despite the crowd generating more than enough heat. The kitchen gleams with dark granite counters and steel appliances, while the long wooden farmhouse table nearby is scarred from decades of use, currently covered in bottles and platters of food.

Not exactly where I normally spend my Tuesday nights. Usually, I'd be elbow-deep in case files with a glass of wine and a rerun of *Schitt's Creek* playing in the background. But standing here, surrounded by the noise and the laughter and the easy chaos of people who actually like each other? I'm surprised to realize I don't want to be anywhere else.

A year ago, walking into an MC clubhouse would've had my heart in my throat. These days, I know the leather and the tattoos are just window dressing. These guys are good people. Loud, stubborn, occasionally terrifying—but good. And somewhere along the way, I stopped feeling like the lawyer they tolerate and started feeling like someone who might actually belong.

Besides, when your highest paying client, who also happens to be President of the local Motorcycle Club, invites you to a party, you can't exactly say no.

We have plenty to celebrate, and plenty to mourn.

Somewhere in the back, Duck is holding court with a growing crowd of locals who keep encouraging him to do another shot. He's hard to miss—a barrel-chested man in his sixties with a thick white beard that would make Santa jealous and pale blue eyes. He owns the only garage in town and has been patching up bikes and bikers alike for longer than most of us have been alive. I know for a fact he's the closest thing to a father figure half these guys have ever had. His deep, smoky laugh carries over the noise as someone claps him on the shoulder.

Meanwhile Maggie, his wife, laughs at his antics. She's a compact woman with silver-streaked hair and capable hands that are equally skilled at knitting baby blankets, taping cracked ribs, and smacking sense into idiots who need it. Right now those hands are wrapped around a whiskey sour as she watches her husband with the kind of fond exasperation that only comes from forty years of marriage. She catches my eye across the room and winks.

I should be celebrating too. After all, I'm the one who woke up a judge at two in the morning to secure an emergency divorce decree, expose a dirty cop's financial ties to the cartel, outed Summit's criminal background, and freed a woman from an abusive marriage.

I watch as the woman in question, Mercy, kisses Cash, the MC's Treasurer. She's a riot of red curls and curves, a woman who takes up space and doesn't apologize for it. Her sleeve tattoos catch the bar light as her arms wrap around his neck, and when she finally pulls back, her green eyes are bright with the kind of joy I wish I could bottle. Cash—all sharp cheekbones and pale green eyes, the kind of unfairly gorgeous that makes smart women stupid—looks at her like she hung the moon and he's just grateful to be standing in its light. His hand finds the small of her back, protective and possessive all at once. He's a few years younger than her, but you'd never find a more well-matched couple.

He grins, hauling her back in again for another, longer, kiss as his biker brothers cheer.

They're free.

I'm happy for her, don't get me wrong. But watching them together, watching the way he holds her as if she's his entire world, makes something horrible twist in my chest.

I turn back to the bar, taking another swig of the beer I'm nursing. It's my third and the kind of cheap stuff that reminds me of the college frat parties I once attended back in my school days. I'm downing it as I try very hard not to stare at the man across the room.

Stone.

The President of the Stoneheart MC is talking to his Sergeant at Arms, Hawk, about something. On the surface, Hawk looks like a man built like a semi with a bad attitude. His arms are crossed over his broad chest, his dark eyes scanning the room even as he listens to Stone. But I've seen him with his partner, Andi, and their three kids, watched him melt into a puddle when one of the twins tugs on his beard or baby Adam falls asleep on his chest. The man's a softie wrapped in leather and scowls.

Stone, on the other hand...

His face is serious, his hands moving in that deliberate way he has when he's working through a problem. The party swirls around them, but Stone stands apart from it. Like a rock in the middle of a river, the jovial energy flows around him, glancing off his controlled facade.

He's only in his late forties, still young and fit, but the silver threading through his dark hair and beard gives him a distinguished edge that makes my stomach flip. His weathered face tells stories of bar fights and hard years, but it's his eyes that get me every time. Steel gray and missing nothing. The kind of eyes that make you feel seen in ways you're not sure you want to be.

God, you're pathetic, Bright. Just go talk to him.

We've been dancing around this thing between us for months. The lingering looks. The accidental touches that don't feel accidental at all. The late nights in his office when the conversation drifts from legal issues to topics far more personal.

I'm not imagining this thing between us. I *know* I'm not imagining it.

The question is whether either of us is brave enough to do something about it.

"You're staring."

I nearly jump out of my skin. Kya materializes beside me, a knowing smirk on her face.

"I'm not staring. I'm... people watching." The excuse is basically the lamest thing that's ever stumbled out of my mouth.

"Uh-huh." She slides onto the stool next to mine, taking a sip of her drink. "You've been 'people watching' the same person for the past hour."

Her blonde hair is piled in a messy bun, her mouth painted cherry red. She's gorgeous with curves that won't quit. Kya bought Devil's Bar a few months back and has been running the place ever since, turning it from a dive into a dive with standards.

Until three days ago, when Summit burned it to the ground.

"How are you holding up?" I ask, partly because I care and partly to deflect from the whole staring-at-Stone situation. "With everything?"

A series of emotions flicker across her face—anger, grief, maybe exhaustion—but she shrugs it off. "I'm okay. It's just stuff, right? Stuff can be rebuilt."

"Are you going to? Rebuild?"

"Yeah." Her smile turns genuine. "Lee's already setting up meetings with an architect. Insurance is being difficult, but the club's fronting the costs until it comes through." She glances across the room to where her boyfriend is mixing drinks, her expression softening. "He keeps saying we'll make it bigger. Better. That Summit gave us an excuse to upgrade."

I follow her gaze. Lee moves behind the makeshift bar with easy competence, all broad shoulders and dark hair cut military-short. He's got his father's steel-gray eyes and that same commanding presence—the kind that makes people pay attention without him having to say a word. A scar cuts through his left eyebrow, adding an edge of danger to features that are already sharp enough to cut glass. At thirty, he's the club's Enforcer, and he wears the role like he was born to it.

Which, I suppose, he was.

"That's a good way to look at it."

"It's the only way to look at it without falling into a heap." She takes another sip of her drink. "I refuse to let those bastards win. Devil's has been part of this town for decades. It'll take more than a match and some gasoline to kill it."

I squeeze her arm. "Let me know if you need help with the insurance company. I know a few tricks."

"I might take you up on that." Then her smirk returns, and I know the deflection is over. "Now. Back to you and your 'people watching.'"

"Kya—"

"You know, you could just go talk to him."

I don't even pretend to not know who she's referring to. "We talk all the time."

"Sure, about legal briefs and cartel shell companies. That's not what I mean, and you know it."

I do. That's the problem.

"It's complicated."

"It's really not." Kya bumps my shoulder. "He likes you. You like him. The whole club's been taking bets on when you two will finally get your shit together."

"There are *bets*?"

"Ginger's got fifty on next month. I've got twenty on tonight." She grins. "Don't let me down, Counselor."

Before I can respond, she's melted back into the crowd,

leaving me alone with my beer and my excuses and the weight of her words pressing against my chest.

Tonight.

I look at Stone again. He's moved to the back porch, visible through the window, standing alone in the darkness.

Screw it.

I set down my drink and go after him.

The night air is sharp, the kind of cold that makes your breath visible and your fingers ache. Woodsmoke drifts from somewhere nearby, mixing with the smell of coming frost. Stone stands at the porch railing, looking out at nothing, his shoulders tense beneath his cut.

"Hey," I say, because I'm apparently a master of witty conversation.

He turns and his expression shifts when he sees me—a softening, a warmth that makes my stupid heart do stupid things.

"Hey yourself." He adjusts to make room for me at the railing. "Needed some air?"

"Something like that." I move to stand beside him, close enough that our shoulders almost touch. "Big night."

"Yeah." He's quiet for a moment. "You did good work, Josie. We couldn't have pulled this off without you."

"Careful," I tease lightly. "That almost sounds like a compliment."

His hand covers mine briefly, squeezing. "It is a compliment." He lets it go, looking back at the far mountain.

I force myself not to read into it. "Then I'll treasure it always. Write it in my diary. 'Dear Diary, today Stone said something nice to me. Mark the calendar!'"

He laughs, the sound low and warm. It's so pleasant it does things to my chest that are entirely inappropriate for a professional relationship.

Is this a professional relationship anymore?

I'm not sure, haven't been for months. The lines blurred somewhere between the late-night strategy sessions and the way he always seems to find excuses to touch me— his hand on my lower back, his fingers brushing mine when he passes me a file, the weight of his gaze when he thinks I'm not looking.

"Josie."

I glance up. He's watching me with an intensity that makes my mouth go dry.

"Yeah?"

"I've been wanting to say something." He turns to face me fully, and the space between us feels very small. "About us. About... *this.*"

My heart is hammering so loud I'm sure he can hear it. "What about us?"

"I've been holding back." His hand finds my hip, warm

through the fabric of my shirt. "Trying to keep things professional. Telling myself it's the right thing to do."

"And now?"

He steps closer. His other hand comes up to cup my jaw, his thumb tracing along my cheekbone, and I forget how to breathe.

"I want you, Josie." His voice is rough, barely above a whisper. "I've wanted you for months. And I'm tired of pretending I don't."

This is it. This is finally, *finally* it.

I lean in.

His mouth is so close I can feel the warmth of his breath, can see the way his eyes darken with want—

And then he steps back.

The cold rushes in where his warmth has been, and I stand there, lips parted, heart cracking down the middle, as Boone Armstrong puts three feet of careful distance between us.

"We can't."

Two words. That's all it takes.

We can't.

Not *I don't want to.* Not *I was wrong.* Just *we can't,* which means he still wants to, which makes this whole situation so much worse.

Hot humiliation floods my chest, right on the heels of disappointment so sharp it borders on pain. Anger sparks too, bright, sudden, and quickly smothered, because how dare he pull me close like that, let me believe he was interested, say those things, and then leave me standing here like a damned fool?

I should demand an explanation. Ask him what the hell that was, why he touched me like he meant it if he was already halfway out the door.

I should do any of the things a rational adult would do when confronted with emotional whiplash of this magnitude.

Instead, I laugh.

It comes out bright and brittle, a sound with sharp edges, the kind of laugh that convinces absolutely no one, but it gives us both an out.

"Well." I step back, matching his distance, rapidly rebuilding my walls brick by brick. "That's embarrassing." I hook a thumb toward the bar, forcing a grin that feels like it might crack my face in two. *I won't cry. I won't cry. I won't fucking cry.* "Shall we blame the cheap beer?"

"Josie—"

"No, it's fine. Really." I'm already moving away, retreating before he can see the damage, before my eyes can betray me. My voice stays light even as an ugly ache settles deep in my chest. "Too much excitement, too much alcohol. We got caught up in the moment. It happens."

"That's not—"

"I should get back inside. Mingle. Celebrate." I keep that damn smile that feels like broken glass on my face, determined not to let him see how deeply this hurts. "Congratulations on the win, Stone. Really. You should be proud."

I will *not* cry over this man. Not tonight. Not freaking ever.

I don't wait for his response. I walk back inside, and rejoin the party, but the shame follows me all the same. I laugh at jokes I don't hear, dance with some of the prospects who are young and eager for attention, drink another beer, and force myself to pretend my chest doesn't feel like someone has reached in and strangled my heart.

Lesson learned, Bright. Lesson fucking learned.

Stone watches me for the rest of the night. I can feel his gaze tracking me through the crowd. It's heavy and cool.

I don't glance back. Don't meet his gaze. Not even once.

He doesn't deserve another piece of me.

By the time I leave, I've rebuilt every wall I let him knock down. Only this time, they're reinforced with steel and spite and the bone-deep certainty that I'm done hoping for a relationship that's never going to happen.

Stone wants me. I know he does.

But wanting isn't the same as having. He could have had

me. Easily. But damn if he'll get more than friendly professionalism from me from now on.

Screw you, Stone.

One of the prospects drops me home, and I let myself into my empty small house.

"Alone once more," I mutter to myself, and pour a glass of wine I don't taste.

You came here for boring, I remind myself. *Not to fall for a motorcycle club president who treats you like you're nothing.*

Tomorrow, I'll go back to being his lawyer. Professional. Distant. Polite.

Tomorrow, I'll pretend tonight never happened.

And maybe, if I'm lucky, I'll eventually stop feeling like an idiot for wanting the one person I can't have.

1

JOSIE

EIGHT MONTHS LATER

My coffee went cold three hours ago, but I drink it anyway. After all, cold coffee is still coffee and coffee is still caffeine, and caffeine is the only thing standing between me and passing out face-first on my keyboard at—I check my phone—9:47 PM on a Tuesday.

Glamorous life you've built, Bright.

My office is small, barely bigger than a closet, really, but it's mine. The office is a converted storefront at the nice end of Main Street, tucked between a boutique that sells overpriced candles and flowers, and an art gallery that caters to the country club crowd.

It's the part of town where the moneyed folks do their shopping, which means it's also where I need to be to ensure those same people will hire me. I'm not above admitting I need to eat, and rich clients have a tendency to pay their bills on time.

My name sits on the door in sensible gold lettering, *Josephine Bright, Attorney at Law*. Inside, I've made the space my own. Warm butterscotch walls lined with overstuffed bookshelves, the legal tomes' spines are cracked from use. A leather sofa sits at the front of the building, soft enough to sink into, scattered with throw pillows I picked up from a craft fair last fall. My desk is antique mahogany, scarred and beautiful, covered in papers and sticky notes and a plant I keep forgetting to water but which refuses to die. A worn Persian rug anchors the room, and the lamp on my desk casts everything in a warm amber glow.

It's a world away from the offices I used to work in back in Atlanta. All that glass and chrome and aggressive minimalism, where everything was designed to intimidate and nothing was designed for comfort. I spent far too many years in spaces that felt like surgical theaters —cold, sterile, and devoid of all personality. Years watching justice get weighed against political palatability, decisions made by people who cared more about optics than outcomes.

I don't miss it. Not even a little.

I don't have any partners or associates to deal with. There's no one to answer to except myself, the clients, and the piles of paperwork that seem to reproduce overnight like particularly litigious rabbits.

It's exactly what I wanted. Independence. Control. A practice built on my own terms.

It's also lonely as hell, but that's the tradeoff, isn't it? Freedom for company. Principles for small talk. I eat most dinners standing over my kitchen sink. I've started talking to myself just to hear a voice, but the upside is the only person whose conscience I answer to is my own.

It might be lonely, but at least I can sleep at night. Mostly.

I sigh and stare down at tonight's rabbit, a stack of documentation for the District Attorney's office regarding Summit Development and their recently-denied rezoning proposal. It's boring stuff but important. It's the kind of paperwork that could put cartel-connected real estate developers behind bars if I dot every i and cross every t correctly.

Unfortunately for the criminals, I'm good at dotting and crossing. Damn good.

My phone buzzes with a text from Kya.

KYA

Drink at the club house?

I stare at the message longer than I should. Having a drink with Kya means heading to the Stoneheart MC clubhouse. Being in the clubhouse will exponentially increase the possibly of running into Stone. And running into Stone means...

Nothing, it means nothing. Because there is nothing going on between us.

JOSIE

Rain check. Dead on my feet.

It's not a lie but not the whole truth either. Kya doesn't need to know that I'm avoiding everything MC right now because I'm a grown woman who can't handle being in the same room as the man who rejected me.

Pathetic, Bright. Truly pathetic.

I shove away from my desk and stretch, my back cracking in protest. I've been hunched over this filing for six hours straight, and my body is filing a formal complaint.

Go home. Eat something. Sleep. The cartel will still be there tomorrow.

Sound advice. I should take it.

Instead, I reach for my cold coffee and keep working.

The problem with trying not to think about something is that it requires thinking about the thing you're not supposed to think about in order to remember not to think about it.

Which is a complicated way of saying I can't get Boone "Stone" Armstrong out of my head.

Serious and deliberate, he's the kind of man who weighs every word before he speaks and never says anything he doesn't mean. He commands a room without raising his voice, leads with quiet authority instead of bluster. And he only smiles when he thinks no one's watching—these rare, unguarded moments that transform his whole face and make my stupid heart forget how to beat.

Unfortunately, I've been watching. Fuck, have I been watching.

For months, he's all I've seen. Through legal meetings and strategy sessions, through late nights poring over Summit's shell companies, through the slow, careful dance we've been performing around each other since the day Hawk brought me in to help with their cartel problem.

"I want you, Josie. I've wanted you for months."

His words from the night he rejected me surface unbidden, and I shove them back down with the ruthlessness of long practice. He said he wanted me, then stepped back like I'd burned him.

We can't.

I can still feel it—the heat of his body close to mine on the back porch, the weight of his hand on my hip, the way his eyes darkened when he leaned in. The air between us was electric, months of tension finally breaking, and for one perfect moment, I thought—

Stop. Just stop!

I thought wrong. That's all. I read the signals wrong, got swept up in the moment, made an ass of myself. It happens. People recover from worse embarrassments every day.

Right?

I rub my sternum, frowning.

Why does it still feel like there's a knife between my ribs?

Because you actually let yourself hope, you idiot. You let him past your walls, and look what happened.

The worst part is that I can't even be angry at him. He pulled back. That's his right. People are allowed to change their minds, to pump the brakes, to decide that whatever's building between them isn't what they want or need right now. .

I just wish he'd decided it *before* he touched me.

I close my laptop harder than necessary.

"This is ridiculous. I'm a successful attorney who's taken down corrupt politicians and cartel-connected businessmen. I've survived things that would have broken most people. And here I am, mooning over a motorcycle club president like a teenager with a diary full of hearts."

I stand up, needing to move.

"Time to get it together, Bright." I rub my arms, flicking off the pretend shadow of Stone that feels as if it's lingered on my skin. "Begone, Stone. I don't want you here any more."

Alas, it doesn't work, but at least I feel slightly less caged in.

I gather the files I've been working on, stacking them neatly in my briefcase. The DA documentation can wait until tomorrow. Everything can wait until tomorrow. Right now, I need to go home, pour myself a very large glass of wine, and stop thinking about Boone Armstrong's hands.

And his eyes. And his voice. And the way he says my name.

"Shut up," I mutter to myself, grabbing my coat.

The office is quiet around me with only the low hum of the ancient HVAC system and the distant sound of a car passing on Main Street. I like it here. It's peaceful and uncomplicated. There's no one to perform for, no one to answer to outside of my clients.

It wasn't always like this. Once upon a time I was a fierce prosecutor on the fast track to District Attorney.

Atlanta feels like a lifetime ago, but some nights—like tonight—the memories press close. The corner office with the skyline view. The designer suits and seven-figure cases. The endless game of political chess where justice was just another piece to be sacrificed when it suited the people in power.

I was good at that game. Too good. I learned to swallow my objections when the DA killed cases that might embarrass his donors. Learned to smile for the cameras while burying evidence that pointed to the wrong people. Learned that "justice" is often just a word politicians use when it's convenient, and discard when it isn't.

And then there was Maria Jean Santos.

Her face surfaces unbidden, and my stomach pitches sideways. She was so young and trusting the last time I saw her alive. She was my witness, my key to bringing down a trafficking ring with connections that reached all the way to the state senate. I promised her protection. I believed my own promises.

"I promise you'll be safe. We'll protect you."

The words echo in my head, sharp as the day I said them. My throat tightens, a lump forming.

Lies. Well-intentioned lies, but lies all the same. I promised protection I couldn't deliver, and Maria paid the price. She and her mother and her seven-year-old brother, all of them gone in a flash of fire and twisted metal the night before she was supposed to testify.

Even now, years later, thinking about that little boy makes my eyes sting. Seven years old. He had a dinosaur backpack. He wanted to be a firefighter.

I blink hard and stare at the ceiling until the feeling passes.

Despite the political pressure to drop the case, I got the conviction anyway. After her death, I worked around the clock until we found other evidence, built another case, and put the bastard who killed them away for forty years.

Rage and guilt and devastation—I poured all of it into that prosecution. I didn't sleep. I barely ate. I burned through every favor I'd ever earned because nothing else mattered except making sure her death was avenged.

Afterward, her family called me a hero.

I strongly suspect heroes don't lie awake at night hearing screams in the silence.

My chest aches. I press the heel of my hand against my sternum, as if I can push the feeling back down where it belongs.

I force myself to shake off Maria's ghost, and grab my keys. Stoneheart was supposed to be my fresh start. Small-town law, filled with property disputes and parking tickets. Nothing that could get anyone killed.

Then the Stoneheart MC walked through my door with a cartel problem, and suddenly I was right back in it—the danger, the stakes, the adrenaline rush of fighting for something bigger than myself.

At least the work makes sense. The work I can handle.

It's the rest of it—the way Stone's voice drops when he says my name, the heat in his eyes when he thinks I'm not looking, the goddamn *we can't* that shouldn't hurt as much as it does—that I can't seem to get a grip on.

You came here for boring, remember? Small-town law. Zoning disputes. Not falling for a motorcycle club president. Get it together, Bright.

I tuck my papers into my briefcase and lock up.

Tomorrow. I'll get over him tomorrow.

Pity I've been telling myself that for months.

The night air is warm, carrying the last breath of summer and the faint smell of cut grass. Crickets chirp somewhere nearby as I lock the office door, checking it twice out of habit, and head for my car—a sensible silver Honda that has seen better days but still gets me from point A to point B without complaint.

My phone buzzes. Not a text this time—a call. The name on the screen makes my stomach flip.

STONE

I consider letting it go to voicemail, but he's still a client. And I'm still his lawyer.

I answer. "Stone."

"Josie." His voice is rough, urgent in a way that makes my chest tighten. "Where are you?"

"Just leaving the office. Why?"

"I have a problem. One of the prospects got into a tangle over at Ole Killa. He's been arrested."

My heart rate kicks up. "What are they charging him with?"

"Aggravated assault. He was protecting a woman who was being harassed and only hit when the other guy took a swing. Pity for him, the guy went down hard and happens to be rich."

I curse softly, clicking the lock on my car door. My whole body aches with exhaustion. I was looking forward to ripping off my bra and finishing my briefs in front of the TV, but I'm already mentally reshuffling my night. The paperwork can wait, that kid can't. "Okay, I'll head over and—"

"I'm coming to get you."

I slide into the car, tossing my briefcase on the passenger seat. "That's not necessary. I can meet you at—"

"I'll be at your place in fifteen minutes."

"Stone." I pinch the bridge of my nose, irritation flaring. This is so typical—him making decisions without consulting anyone, assuming everyone will just fall in line. "I'm perfectly capable of driving myself."

"Josie." The way he says my name—low and serious—sends a shiver down my spine that I absolutely refuse to acknowledge. "It's after ten. I'm gonna assume you're running on caffeine and fumes. Let me come get you."

The man isn't wrong. My eyes are gritty, my shoulders are screaming, and I can't remember if I ate lunch or just thought about eating lunch. I'd love to ignore this, but there's a kid sitting in a cell right now, scared and alone, and I've never been able to turn my back on someone who needs help. It's a flaw, honestly. The inability to say no when someone's in trouble. It's going to kill me one of these days.

I blow out a sigh. "Anyone ever tell you, you're a bossy bastard?"

He chuckles. "You're the only one brave enough to bust my balls, honey."

I close my eyes, hating how my body reacts to his endearment.

I should say no. I should insist on meeting him at the station where I can control my exit, where I won't be trapped in a vehicle with his scent and his voice and the memory of his hands on my skin.

Instead, I hear myself say, "Fine. Fifteen minutes."

"I'm already on my way."

The line goes dead.

I stare at my phone, heart pounding.

Damn.

Main Street is quiet at this hour, most of the shops dark. I pull out of the parking lot and head toward my small home. The roads are empty, streetlights casting pools of orange light on the asphalt. My mind sifts through the charges, already trying to work up a game plan. But it drifts—to the DA filing, to tomorrow's meetings, to the way Stone's hand felt on my hip—

Stop. Just stop.

I turn onto Oak Street, passing the darkened windows of the hardware store, the closed bakery, the little park where kids play on sunny afternoons. Stoneheart is peaceful. Safe. The kind of place where nothing bad ever happens.

Which is probably why I don't see the headlights until they're already on top of me.

They come from nowhere—blazing through the Miller Road intersection. They gas through their stop sign as I'm halfway through the intersection, aiming directly at me. No braking. No attempts to slow down. Just two bright points of light getting bigger and bigger and—

MOVE—

I yank the wheel, but it's too late.

Impact.

The world explodes into glass and metal and pain—so much pain, everywhere at once. My body slams sideways, the seatbelt cutting into my chest, my head cracking against hard metal. I hear screaming—is that me?—and the shriek of tearing metal, and then everything is spinning, tumbling, wrong.

I can't breathe. Can't see. Can't feel anything except the fire in my ribs and the warm wetness running down my face.

Stone.

His name surfaces through the pain like a lifeline. Stupid. So stupid. He doesn't want me, and I'm dying in a crushed Honda thinking about his goddamn eyes.

I never told him—

Told him what? I don't even know. Don't have time to figure it out.

The darkness rushes in, hungry and absolute, and my last coherent thought is almost funny in its absurdity:

Well. This is inconvenient.

Then there is nothing at all.

2

STONE

The party's still going strong, but I can't focus on any of it.

Duck's mayoral announcement has the clubhouse buzzing—brothers slapping him on the back, old ladies already planning campaign strategies, prospects running around refilling drinks like their patches depend on it. After the planning commission victory today, everyone's riding high. Summit lost. We won. For the first time in months, the future looks bright.

I should be celebrating with them.

Instead, I'm nursing a whiskey at the edge of the room, watching the door like an idiot, when Kya drops onto the stool beside me.

"She's not coming." Kya doesn't bother to specify who. "Texted me an hour ago. Still buried in paperwork."

It's after ten. Of course she's still working.

"Wasn't waiting for anyone," I lie.

Kya snorts and steals my whiskey. "Sure, Stone. That's why you've been staring at the door for the last hour." She takes a sip and grimaces. "This is terrible, by the way."

I take it back from her. "Then stop drinking it."

She slides off the stool with a knowing look. "Just talk to her. It's been eight months. Whatever happened between you two—"

"There's nothing to talk about."

Another snort. She walks away, leaving me alone with my shitty whiskey and shittier thoughts.

Josie hasn't come to a club celebration event in eight months—not unless one of the old ladies forced her into it. And I know exactly whose fault that is.

Mine.

We can't.

Two words. That's all it took to destroy whatever was building between us. I pulled her close, told her I wanted her, then shoved her away before she could even catch her breath. And she rebuilt her walls so fast I got whiplash watching it happen.

But I'm the one who handed her the bricks.

I don't blame her. I'd have done the same thing.

But Christ, I miss her.

Not just the heat between us, though that's there too. No, I just miss *her*. Her sharp tongue and sharper mind. The way she calls me on my bullshit without flinching. The way she sees past the patch and the reputation to a man underneath that I'm not even sure exists anymore.

I've suffered through months of sitting across from her in meetings, watching her avoid my eyes, feeling the chill radiating off her like a physical force. Eight months of telling myself I did the right thing, that she deserves better, that the club has to come first.

Eight months of knowing I'm full of shit.

I take another sip of whiskey and force myself to look away from the door.

Let it go, old man. She's not coming. And even if she did, what would you say? "Sorry I broke your heart, want to try again?"

My phone buzzes. I glance at the screen, expecting club business.

It's a prospect.

> **KNOX**
>
> Got a situation. Mack got himself arrested at Ole Killa. Aggravated assault. Some rich prick started harassing a woman, Mack stepped in, guy took a swing, Ricky put him down. Now the prick's daddy is screaming for blood.

I pinch the bridge of my nose. Prospects. Every goddamn time. This is what I got for giving them the night off. A fucking migraine.

STONE

How bad?

KNOX

Bad enough. He says they're looking at AA charges. We need a lawyer, boss.

A lawyer.

The thought hits me like a bolt of lightning, and I hate myself for the relief that floods through me.

I have to call Josie. Not because I want to—not because I've been looking for an excuse to hear her voice for eight months—but because the club needs her. It's business. Professional. Completely legitimate.

You're pathetic, Armstrong.

Maybe. But I'm already pulling up her number.

She answers on the third ring. "Stone."

Just my name. Cool and professional. There's no warmth. No hint of the tension that used to simmer between us.

I deserve it. Doesn't mean I have to fucking like it.

"Josie. Where are you?"

"Just leaving the office. Why?"

I glance at the clock, frowning. It's late, far too late for her to be working. Far too late for her to still be working, but that's Josie—she doesn't know how to quit. She's probably been running on caffeine and spite for hours. She must be exhausted, and here I am adding another issue to her already full plate.

I'm not sorry for it though.

"I have a problem. One of the prospects got into a tangle over at Ole Killa. He's been arrested."

"What are they charging him with?"

"Aggravated assault. He was protecting a woman who was being harassed and only hit when the other guy took a swing. Pity for him, the guy went down hard and happens to be rich."

She curses softly. I hear the click of a car door. "Okay, I'll head over and—"

"I'm coming to get you."

"That's not necessary. I can meet you at—"

"I'll be at your place in fifteen minutes."

"Stone." Her voice sharpens with irritation. "I'm perfectly capable of driving myself."

"Josie." I let her name hang there. "It's after ten. I'm gonna assume you're running on caffeine and fumes. Let me come get you."

Silence. I hold my breath.

"Anyone ever tell you, you're a bossy bastard?"

I chuckle, tension bleeding out of my shoulders. "You're the only one brave enough to bust my balls, honey."

Honey.

The word slips out before I can catch it.

Goddamn.

The pause that follows is loaded. I can almost hear her deciding whether to call me on it.

"Fine," she says instead, letting it go. "Fifteen minutes."

"I'm already on my way."

I hang up and head for my bike, ignoring the curious looks from my brothers. Let them wonder. Right now, I don't care about anything except the fact that in fifteen minutes, I'm going to see Josie Bright.

It's just business, I tell myself as I kick the engine to life. *Nothing more.*

But the lightness in my chest says otherwise.

The ride to Josie's place takes twelve minutes. I know because I've made this drive before—late nights after strategy sessions, telling myself I was just making sure she got home safe. Never admitting the real reason I kept finding excuses to be near her.

Her house is dark when I pull up and there's no car in the driveway.

I check my phone. Fourteen minutes since we hung up. She should be here by now. Her office is only a ten-minute drive, fifteen if she hits every stop sign.

I wait.

Another five minutes pass and there's still no sign of her.

Frowning, I call her. It rings through to voicemail.

"Josie, it's me. Where are you? Call me back."

I hang up and pace beside my bike, checking my phone again.

Eighteen minutes pass and there's still nothing.

A cold sensation prickles at the back of my neck. The same instinct that's kept me alive for the twenty-plus years I've been running this club. The same gut feeling that's warned me of ambushes and betrayals and deals gone wrong.

Something's not right.

I try her again. Voicemail again.

"You've reached Josephine Bright. Please leave a message after the tone and I'll get back to you shortly."

"Where the fuck are you?" I growl. "Pick up your damn phone, Josie. Don't make me worry."

I hit end, pacing once more.

Maybe her phone died. Maybe she stopped for gas. Maybe—

But the cold feeling is spreading now, settling into my chest like ice water. Josie doesn't ignore calls. Josie doesn't run late without texting. Josie is the most punctual, organized, on-top-of-her-shit person I've ever met.

"Fuck it."

I swing my leg over the bike and head for her office.

The route is quiet this time of night. Empty streets, dark houses, streetlights casting pools of orange on the asphalt. I take the same path she would have, tracking her drive to work.

I see the lights first.

Red and blue, flashing against the buildings. An ambulance. A police cruiser. And in the middle of the Miller Road intersection, a tangle of metal that used to be two vehicles.

One of them is a silver Honda.

No.

I'm off my bike before I consciously decide to stop. Running. Shoving past a cop who tries to hold me back, ignoring his shouts, my eyes locked on that crumpled vehicle, on the paramedics working frantically on the driver—

Josie.

She's pale. Too pale. The warm olive skin that usually glows with life is ashen, almost gray under the flashing lights. There's blood on her face, matting the dark hair that's always so perfectly styled, streaking down the elegant neck I've imagined pressing my lips to more times than I can count. Her arm is bent wrong. Her eyes, those sharp hazel eyes that miss nothing, are closed.

She's not fucking moving.

This isn't her. This broken, bloodied woman isn't the Josie who strides into rooms like she owns them, who argues case law with a fire that makes me want to push her against a wall and kiss her until neither of us can breathe. This isn't the woman who wears her suits like armor and her intelligence like a weapon.

"Sir, you can't be here—"

"That's—" My voice cracks. I clear my throat, force the words out. "That's Josie Bright. I'm her—"

Technically, I'm her client and nothing more.

I'm the man who should have been with her. I'm the one who told her I was coming to get her. If I'd just driven to her office instead of her house—if I'd been faster—if I hadn't wasted eight goddamn months—

"—boyfriend." The lie comes easy.

The police officer eyes my patch, but takes me at face value. "Sir, the paramedics are stabilizing her to get her to the hospital. Are you able to follow?"

I nod. I can't speak. Can't do anything but watch as they manage to maneuver her body from the car, onto a stretcher, and load her into the ambulance. As the doors slam shut, as the sirens wail to life, I walk over to my bike, climbing on as the vehicle tears off down the road.

I sit on it for a moment, staring at the wreckage. At the shattered glass glittering on the asphalt, at the skid marks, at the other vehicle—a black SUV, empty now, its front end crumpled but its driver nowhere to be seen.

I glance at the police officer. "Where's the other driver? Did they survive?"

He hesitates, and it's then I realize he's securing the scene.

"Suspected hit and run," he says slowly. "Though it could be that the other driver is dazed and doesn't realize they're—"

Hit and run.

The cold heaviness in my chest turns to ice. Then to something hotter. Something that feels a lot like rage.

But that's for later. Right now, there's only one thing that matters.

I start my bike and follow the ambulance.

The hospital is a blur of fluorescent lights and antiseptic.

I don't remember parking. Don't remember walking through the doors. One moment I'm on my bike, the next I'm at the emergency reception desk, my hands planted on the counter.

"Josephine Bright. She just came in by ambulance. Car accident."

The woman behind the desk looks up at me—takes in the cut, the road dust, whatever expression is on my face —and has the good sense not to argue.

"Are you family?"

"Her partner." The lie slides out smooth. I'm already committed to it.

Her fingers move across the keyboard. "She's being assessed now. I'll need you to fill out some information for us while you wait." She slides a clipboard across the counter. "As much as you can."

I take it, expecting to stare at a bunch of blank lines I can't fill. We're not actually together. I'm her client, nothing more. What could I possibly know?

I look down at the form.

FULL NAME

Josephine Amy Bright. She mentioned her middle name once, months ago. I remember thinking *Amy* suited her.

DATE OF BIRTH

March 15th. Ginger had suggested we get her some flowers for her birthday.

ADDRESS

1847 Oakwood Lane. The little blue house with the overgrown rose bushes and the porch light she always leaves on. I know because I've driven past it more times than I care to admit, like some lovesick teenager who can't stay away.

EMERGENCY CONTACT

Me. Fuck if I know who else she might list, but for now I'm gonna have to do.

ALLERGIES

Penicillin. She mentioned it once when Duck had a chest infection and Maggie was pushing antibiotics on everyone in sight. "Not all of us can take those," she'd said, waving Maggie off, and I'd filed it away without thinking.

PRIMARY CARE PHYSICIAN

Dr. Sarah Cousins, Stoneheart Medical. I'd overheard her making an appointment once, months ago.

My pen hovers over the form.

I know her coffee order—black, no sugar, an extra shot when she's been working late. I know she takes her whiskey neat, her wine red, and her beer cheap. I know she stress-cleans her office when a case is going sideways, and she taps her pen against her teeth when she's thinking. I know she gets a little crease between her eyebrows when she's trying not to laugh at something I've said, and doesn't frown at all when she's annoyed in the court room.

I know she hums under her breath when she thinks no one's around—old jazz songs, the kind her grandmother used to play. I know she kicks off her heels the second she's behind closed doors, and her real laugh, the unguarded one, sounds nothing like the polished chuckle she uses in meetings with clients.

Jesus Christ.

I've been cataloging this woman for over a year. Every detail, every habit, every tiny piece of her I could collect without crossing the lines I drew between us.

What a fucking joke.

I fill out the rest of the form with a steady hand, even though I'm beginning to feel like I might have been blind sided by a fucking truck as well. When I hand it back to the receptionist, she scans it with raised eyebrows.

"This is thorough, thank you."

"No problem." I step back from the counter. "When can I see her?"

The receptionist gives me a tired, sympathetic smile. "As soon as the doctors stabilize her."

I step back, taking a seat on an uncomfortable plastic chair.

The waiting room is surprisingly quiet for an emergency department. A few scattered souls dot the rows of seats—an elderly man with a hacking cough, a young woman scrolling her phone with red-rimmed eyes, a couple huddled together in the corner speaking in hushed, urgent tones. The fluorescent lights buzz overhead, casting everything in that sickly yellow-white glow that makes everyone look half-dead.

The TV mounted in the corner plays some late-night infomercial on mute. A woman with unnaturally white teeth demonstrates a blender. Riveting stuff.

I should call the club and check in, let someone know what's happening. But I can't make myself move. Can't do anything but sit here, staring at the doors Josie's behind, replaying that fucking form in my head.

I lean forward, elbows on my knees, and scrub my hands over my face.

Twenty years of running this club. Twenty-plus years of keeping my shit locked down, of never letting anyone see weakness, of making the hard calls and living with the consequences. I've buried brothers. Held men while they bled out. Delivered news that destroyed families.

None of it—*none* of it—prepared me for the sight of Josie Bright bleeding in the wreckage of her car.

The couple in the corner gets called back. The young woman with the phone steps out for a cigarette. The old man coughs and coughs and coughs.

I sit there, surrounded by strangers and their private tragedies, and finally let myself feel the weight of my own.

I know everything about Josie. Every detail, every habit, every tiny piece of her I could collect without crossing the lines I drew between us.

I told myself I was keeping my distance. Protecting her from the mess of my life, the danger that comes with my patch, the long shadow of every mistake I've ever made.

But I wasn't protecting her.

I was protecting myself.

Wanting something—really wanting it, the way I want her—means risking losing it. And fuck knows I've lost everything before. My marriage. My wife's respect. Years with my kids I'll never get back. The version of myself that used to believe good things could last.

It felt easier to keep Josie at arm's length. Easier to want her from a distance than to reach for her and watch it fall apart.

Except now she's behind those doors, fighting for her life, and all my distance didn't protect either of us from a goddamn thing.

Eight months.

Eight months of watching her. Wanting her. Memorizing every detail like a man starving for a taste of paradise he won't let himself eat.

What a fucking waste.

The doors swing open. A doctor steps through, scanning the room.

"Mr. Armstrong?"

I'm on my feet before she finishes my name.

She's small, middle-aged, with tired eyes and the calm demeanor of someone who delivers bad news for a living. I close the distance between us in three strides, looming over her.

"How is she?"

To her credit, she doesn't flinch at the raw, rough need in my voice. "Stable."

The word hits me like a fist to the chest. My knees nearly buckle, but I force myself to stay standing.

Stable.

She consults her chart. "Ms. Bright sustained three broken ribs, a fractured left wrist, a suspected concussion, and multiple lacerations requiring stitches. She also has significant bruising to her chest and abdomen from the seatbelt, steering column and airbags."

Each injury lands like a punch. Ribs. Wrist. Concussion. Lacerations. Bruising. I catalog them, my jaw tightening with every word.

"But she's going to be okay?"

"She's very lucky." The doctor's expression is measured, professional. "The impact was primarily to the driver's side, but a few inches further forward and we'd be having a very different conversation."

A few inches.

My hands curl into fists at my sides. A few inches and she'd be gone. A few inches and I'd never get the chance to—

I shut that thought down hard.

She pauses. "Her scans look good. No internal bleeding, no spinal damage, and her brain activity is good. Though we'll need to do further testing for concussion and other complications when she wakes."

Lucky. She's lying broken in a hospital bed and they're calling her *lucky*.

She places a hand on my arm. "There is swelling on her brain though, so we've put her in a medically induced coma. It's unlikely she'll wake for a few days. She needs this time to rest, and allow the brain to heal."

I nod once.

She's alive, and that's all that matters.

"Can I see her?"

"She's being moved to a private room now. Room 114, upstairs two levels then head down the hall, it's the first on the left." The doctor hesitates. "She's still unconscious —between the concussion and the pain medication, she likely won't wake for several hours. But you can sit with her."

"Thank you."

I make my way to her room, stopping in the doorway as my chest cracks wide open.

She looks small. That's what hits me first—how small she looks in that hospital bed, surrounded by machines and wires and sterile white sheets. Josie Bright, who fills every room she walks into. Who took on Summit and a cartel and a corrupt system without flinching. Who stood toe-to-toe with me from day one and never once backed down.

She looks fragile.

Wrong.

Her face is bruised, one eye swollen, a line of stitches running along her hairline. Her left arm is in a cast, resting on a pillow. Bandages wrap around her ribs, visible through the thin fabric of the hospital gown. Monitors beep steadily, tracking her heartbeat, her breathing, her oxygen levels.

My throat closes. I have to grip the doorframe to keep myself upright.

This is my fault.

I suck in air, forcing myself to breathe.

Alive. She's alive. Focus on that.

I pull a chair close to the bed and sink into it, my hands shaking as I reach for her. I take her hand—the uninjured one—and cradle it between both of mine.

Her fingers are cold. Limp. Nothing like the warm, animated hands that gesture when she argues a point, that grip a pen like a weapon, that reached for me before I ruined everything.

"Josie." My voice comes out rough, barely recognizable. "I'm here."

No response. Just the beep of the monitors and the soft hiss of oxygen.

I bring her hand to my lips and press a kiss to her bruised knuckles. My breath hitches, and I don't bother trying to hide it. There's no one here to see.

Fuck. This happened on my watch.

"I'm here," I say quietly. "Can you hear me?"

She doesn't move.

The room is quiet. It's a shared room, with two beds but the other is vacant.

I sit here for a while, watching the steady rise and fall of her chest as I consider what's occurred.

The hot rage that's been burning inside me flares.

If this was Summit—if someone deliberately put her in this bed—there won't be enough left of when I'm done with them to bury.

I make the calls from her bedside, one hand still wrapped around hers.

First, the prospect situation. I can't leave the kid hanging in a cell all night, but I'm not leaving Josie either. I scroll through my contacts until I find the number I need.

Brick's a member of the Ridgeline Chapter, about forty minutes east. He's Ginger's baby brother—fifteen years younger and twice as stubborn. When the club expanded and needed someone to lead the new chapter, he was the obvious choice. Young, hungry, and sharp as a tack. The fact that he's practically family through Hawk and Ginger doesn't hurt either.

STONE

Got a prospect in lockup at Ole Killa. Aggravated assault, self-defense situation. Need someone to get him a decent lawyer and sit with him until morning. Can you handle it? I got another situation otherwise I'd be there.

His reply comes fast, even at this hour.

BRICK

Consider it done. Everything okay on your end?

I glance through the open door at Josie, still and pale in her hospital bed.

STONE

No. But it will be.

BRICK

You need backup, you call. Anytime.

STONE

Appreciated, brother. I might take you up on that.

One problem handled. Now for the harder call.

For this one, I step into the hallway, keeping Josie's door propped open so I can see her, and dial Tank.

He answers on the second ring. "Prez. Wondered where you disappeared to."

"Get somewhere private. I need to brief you."

A pause. Muffled voices, footsteps, a door closing. Then Tank again, more serious. "Hold on, Stone. Bones and Lee are here. I'm putting you on speaker."

I don't waste time.

"I left to pick up Josie. But she wasn't home when I got there." I keep my voice level, the voice of a president delivering a report. Not a man falling apart. "So I rode the route she takes from work. There was an accident about two miles out. T-bone collision at the intersection by Miller Road."

Silence.

"She's alive," I continue. "Ambulance got there right as I did. But she's in bad shape. I followed them to the hospital. They've got her now. I'm waiting to hear more."

"Jesus," Lee breathes.

"You sure you don't need us there?" Tank asks.

"No. I'm fine on my own." I make my voice firm. An order, not a request. "I need you three to keep this quiet. Let everyone have tonight. Keep the party going, business as usual."

"Stone—" Bones starts.

"That's an order." I cut him off. "We don't know if this was an accident or a hit yet. Could be nothing. Could be Summit sending a message. Either way, I don't want the whole club in panic mode until we know more. Keep this between us, let everyone celebrate Duck and the zoning win, and we deal with what this means in the morning."

The silence stretches. I know what they're thinking—that they should be here, that brothers don't let brothers face this alone.

But I need them there. If Summit is watching, if this was intentional, we can't show them we've been tipped off.

"Understood," Tank says finally. "You call if anything changes."

"I will. One more thing—the crash was a hit and run. Black SUV, driver fled. I want eyes on this first thing. Traffic cams, police reports, witnesses. Everything."

"I'll handle it personally," Bones says. "First thing tomorrow."

"Good." I pause, exhaustion pressing down on me like a

physical weight. "Now get back out there before people notice."

"Stone." Lee's voice is careful. "She's tough. She'll be okay."

My son, trying to comfort me. He's a good kid, he's become a better man.

"Yeah," I manage. "She will."

I hang up before they can say anything else.

The fluorescent lights buzz overhead. Somewhere down the corridor, a machine beeps. A nurse walks past, her shoes squeaking on the linoleum.

I should feel better. The club's handling things. Brick's got the prospect. Bones will dig into the crash. Everything's under control.

But nothing's under control. Not really. Not when the woman in that room almost died tonight, and I can't do a goddamn thing except sit here and wait.

I push back through the door and reclaim my seat beside her bed.

The night crawls by.

Nurses and doctors come and go, checking vitals, adjusting IVs, giving me looks that range from sympathetic to wary. I ignore them all as I sit here, holding her hand, watching her breathe.

The room is quiet except for the steady beep of the heart monitor. That sound—that rhythmic proof that she's still alive—becomes my anchor. Every beep is a promise. Every beep says *she's still here.*

Somewhere around 4 AM, my thoughts drift to places I usually keep locked down.

Rebecca.

My ex-wife is one of the reasons I've been hesitant to start anything serious up with Josie. She'd resented coming second to the club, of raising Lee and Emma mostly alone, of watching me choose my brothers over my family again and again. She tried. God knows she tried. And I just kept proving that the club would always come first.

They were my family long before she came along. She just hadn't understood they were hers too.

When she finally left, I couldn't even blame her.

"You don't know how to love anything more than that club, Boone. Maybe you never did."

Those words have rattled around my skull for years. I've worn them like armor, used them as proof that I'm not built for relationships. Not built for softness, for vulnerability, for letting someone in close.

I look at Josie and the bruises blooming across her face, the stitches along her hairline, the steady rise and fall of her chest.

Rebecca was wrong.

The realization hits me like a freight train, knocking the air from my lungs.

Rebecca was *wrong*.

I can love something more than the club. I can love *someone* more than the club. I've been doing it for months. I've been acting like a fucking pussy, finding excuses to be near her, lying awake at night thinking about the way she laughs, the way she argues, the way she looked at me on that porch before I fucked everything up.

Fisting my cock to the memory of her lips wrapped around a fucking beer bottle.

Fuck, I'm an idiot.

I didn't have the balls to call it what it was.

Love.

The word feels foreign. Dangerous. Like picking up a loaded gun after years of telling yourself you'd never touch one again.

But sitting here, watching Josie fight to stay alive, I finally understand what I've been too scared to admit.

I love her.

This feeling in my gut isn't the safe, distant wanting or carefully controlled attraction I've been pretending I could walk away from. I love her—messy and terrifying and completely fucking inconvenient.

I love her, and I almost lost her without ever telling her.

Never again.

The thought burns through me like wildfire, incinerating every excuse, every fear, every carefully constructed reason why *we can't.*

I'm done being a coward. Done hiding behind the club, behind my failed marriage, behind the weight of every mistake I've ever made. Done telling myself I don't deserve this, don't deserve *her,* because some part of me is too broken to hold onto something good.

Josie Bright is *mine.*

When she wakes up, I'm going to make damn sure she knows it.

3

JOSIE

THREE WEEKS LATER

Hospitals, I've decided, are designed by sadists.

The beds are uncomfortable, the lights are too bright, the machines beep at random intervals like they're specifically calibrated to prevent sleep. And the gown—don't even get me started on the gown. One sneeze and I'm flashing the entire nursing staff.

But the worst part? The absolute *worst* part of waking up in Stoneheart General Hospital with broken ribs and a head that feels like someone has used it for batting practice?

Boone Armstrong.

He'd moved in at some point during my coma. The coma had lasted eleven days before I'd woken up with a few new holes in my head from efforts to relieve the pressure from the swelling. The first day after waking had involved one hell of a headache.

I blink awake, searching for the giant shadow that's camping in my room.

Stone shifted from the chair beside my bed to the one by the window, a cup of coffee in his hand and his phone pressed to his ear. His voice is low, too quiet for me to make out the words, but I recognize the tone. Club business.

I watch him through half-closed eyes, not ready to announce that I'm awake.

According to the nurses—who've been far too delighted to fill me in—Stone has been here every single day since the accident. Every. Single. Day. Sitting by my bed while I lay unconscious, holding my hand, talking to me.

When the swelling got worse and they had to do emergency surgery—burr holes, they called them, which sounds far too casual for "drilling into someone's skull"— he was in the waiting room for six hours. He threatened to have the entire MC descend on the hospital if anyone tried to make him leave.

I woke up a week ago to find him asleep in that chair, his hand wrapped around mine, looking like he hadn't slept properly in days. The first word out of my mouth was his name.

I've been trying not to think about what that means.

He stayed. For three weeks, he stayed.

The thought keeps circling back, no matter how many times I try to push it away. Eight months of professional distance, of loaded silences, of pretending that night on the porch never happened—and the moment I end up in a hospital bed, he's here. Holding my hand. Looking at me like—

Stop, Josie. Don't start reading into things again.

But I've seen his face when I opened my eyes. I've seen the relief, the fear, the raw emotion he usually keeps locked down tight. Whatever else Stone is, frustrating, confusing, impossible, he hasn't been faking that.

Which makes everything so much worse.

I can imagine what I look like right now, but I'm too scared to ask. I can feel the stubble on the side of my head where they shaved it, the tight pull of stitches, the swelling that makes my face feel like it belongs to someone else. I must look like something out of a horror movie—Frankenstein's monster in a hospital gown.

Which is why when Stone walks back in and his gaze lands on me and he doesn't flinch, my chest begins to ache in ways that have nothing to do with my broken ribs.

If he doesn't care, I can hate him. Can write off the almost-kiss and the rejection and the three weeks of silence as a bullet dodged. Can tell myself I'm better off and eventually believe it.

But he does care. He's proven that by being here, by staying, by sitting vigil while doctors cut into my head and I fought my way back to consciousness.

He cares. He just doesn't want to.

I don't know what to do with that.

"You're awake."

Stone's voice cuts through my spiraling thoughts. I open my eyes fully to find him standing beside the bed, phone tucked away, coffee abandoned.

"Unfortunately." I try to push myself up and immediately regret it. Fire lances through my ribs, sharp and vicious, and I collapse back against the pillows with a hiss.

"Easy." His hand hovers near my shoulder, not quite touching. "The doctor said no sudden movements."

"The doctor can kiss my ass."

He smiles. "I'll pass that along."

Despite everything, a small laugh escapes me. Then I wince because laughing hurts. Everything hurts.

"How do you feel?" he asks.

"Like I got hit by a truck."

"It was an SUV."

"You said that already."

"You keep forgetting."

"I have a concussion. I'm allowed to forget things." I squint at him. "What time is it?"

"Almost noon."

"Shouldn't you be somewhere? Running a club? Intimidating small children? Stealing candy from seniors? Whatever it is you do all day?"

His mouth twitches. "Tank's handling things."

"For how long?"

"As long as I need."

I stare at him, waiting for the punchline. When it doesn't come, I shake my head—gently, because even that hurts.

"Stone. You can't just... camp out in my hospital room indefinitely."

"Watch me."

"That's not—" I blow out a breath, frustrated. "You don't have to do this. Whatever guilt thing you've got going on, whatever obligation you feel—you're off the hook. Go home. Get some sleep. I'm fine."

A frown flickers across his face. "Is that what you think this is? Guilt?"

"What else would it be?"

He's quiet for a long moment. Then he pulls the chair closer to the bed and sits down, leaning forward with his elbows on his knees.

"Eight months ago," he says slowly, "I made a mistake."

"Stone—"

"Let me finish." His eyes hold mine, and I find I can't look away. "I told you we couldn't. I stepped back when everything in me was screaming to step forward. And I've regretted it every single day since."

My heart is doing complicated flips in my chest. I ignore it.

"You had your reasons."

"I had excuses cause I'm a fuckhead." He scrubs a hand over his face. "I've spent years keeping everyone at arm's length. That if I don't let anyone in, I can't hurt them—or get hurt myself."

"Very healthy coping mechanism," I mutter.

"I never said I was healthy." A ghost of a smile. "But then you almost died, and I realized—" He stops. Starts again. "I realized I'd rather have you and lose you than spend the rest of my life wondering what could have been."

The words hang between us, heavy and raw.

Don't fall for this. He said he wanted you before, and then he pulled back. Words don't mean anything.

But his eyes—God, his eyes.

"Stone..." I don't know what I'm going to say, but he doesn't give me the chance to figure it out.

"I'm not asking for anything right now," he continues. "You're hurt and need to heal. You have every right to tell me to go to hell after the way I've handled this." He reaches out, letting his fingers brush my cheek. "But I meant what I said. I'm not going anywhere. And when you're ready—when you're healed and thinking clearly and not pumped full of painkillers—I want to have a real conversation. About us and what this could be."

I should say no. I need to protect myself, keep my walls up, refuse to give him another chance to break me again.

Instead, I hear myself say, "And if I'm never ready?"

"Then I'll wait."

"For how long?"

"As long as it takes."

I search his face for the lie, for the catch, for the inevitable moment when he'll pull back again. I don't find it.

"Your timing is horrible," I say finally.

"I know."

I shut my eyes then open one, glaring at him. "This doesn't mean I forgive you."

"I know that too."

I close my eyes, leaning back on the bed. "And I'm still angry."

"You should be."

"If you pull that 'we can't' bullshit again when we have that conversation, I will end you. I know people who know how to make bodies disappear."

His chuckle washes over me. "Noted."

The curtain to my left rustles.

I've almost forgotten I'm not alone in this room. The hospital has stuck me in a semi-private situation—two beds separated by a flimsy curtain that does nothing to block sound. I've heard my roommate twisting and turning in the night, muttering soft muffled curses that have worked their way into my drugged dreams. Whoever she is, she's got a mouth on her.

I haven't seen her yet. Haven't had the energy to investigate. But now the curtain shifts, and a face peers around the edge.

The woman is young, maybe early to mid-twenties. Her dark blonde hair needs washing, and her hazel eyes are sharp and assessing despite the exhaustion shadowing them. Her nose and lips are slightly too big for her drawn face, but it lends her an interesting, unique look. I can tell she's pretty, underneath the bruises.

And there are a lot of bruises.

She doesn't flinch when she sees Stone. Doesn't apologize for interrupting. She cooly assesses him with a look that says she's sized up dangerous men before and knows to keep her distance.

"Could you keep it down a little?" she asks me, her voice flat. "All the beeping and the nurses and the—" She gestures vaguely at Stone. "It's hard to sleep."

"Sorry to inconvenience you with her near-death experience," Stone mutters.

I shoot him a look. "Of course. Sorry about that. I keep forgetting someone is back there."

Her mouth twitches. Almost a smile. "At least you're not a snorer. My last roommate sounded like a chainsaw."

"I make no promises once they take me off the painkillers."

That gets a real smile, brief but genuine. It transforms her face for just a second before she locks it back down.

I study her more carefully, cataloging the injuries with the clinical eye of someone who's prosecuted too many domestic violence cases. Split lip, mostly healed. Bruising around her eye, fading from purple to yellow. Finger-shaped marks on her upper arm, visible where her hospital gown has slipped.

Someone has hurt this girl. Recently. Repeatedly.

"What landed you here?" I ask, keeping my voice casual.

Her face shutters. "I fell."

It's the oldest lie in the book. I've heard it a hundred times from women who can't admit—to themselves or anyone else—what really happened.

"That's a lot of bruises for a fall."

"It was a long staircase."

"Must have been."

We stare at each other. She knows I don't believe her. I know she knows. But I also know that pushing will only make her retreat further, so I let it go.

"How long have you been here?" I ask instead.

"Five days." She fidgets with the edge of the curtain, not meeting my gaze. "I'm supposed to leave tomorrow."

"And then what?"

"I go home." She says it flatly, like it's obvious. Like there's no other option. "My stepdad's picking me up."

The way she says stepdad lands like a stone in my stomach. I keep my expression neutral, but inside, a cold fury is waking. My hands want to curl into fists. I want to find this man and make him understand what it feels like to be small and scared and hurt.

Instead, I keep my voice gentle.

"That's good," I say carefully. "That you have someone."

"Yeah." She doesn't sound convinced. Doesn't sound much of anything, really. "He's been worried about me."

I'll bet he has.

"Hey." I wait until she meets my gaze. "If you ever need help—legal help, or just someone to talk to—I'm a lawyer. Josie Bright. I'm in the book."

Her lips twist into a thin line. It's the look of someone who knows exactly why I'm offering and hates me for it.

"I don't need a lawyer. I fell down the stairs."

"Of course you did."

She doesn't respond. Just stares at me for a long moment, then retreats behind the curtain without another word.

I lie back against my pillows, exhausted by the brief conversation.

Stone, who's stayed silent through the whole exchange, raises an eyebrow.

"Friend of yours?"

"Not yet." I close my eyes. "But give it time, I'll win her over."

~

The afternoon brings doctors, nurses, and more bad news.

The concussion has been downgraded to "moderate"—which apparently means I'll be dealing with headaches and light sensitivity for weeks.

"You're very lucky," the doctor says, flipping through my chart. "If that car had hit you dead on, your outcome could have been much worse."

Lucky. It's a word I'm really starting to hate it.

"When can I go home?"

"We'd like to keep you another few days for observation. The concussion and burr holes are our main concern—we want to make sure there's no lingering issues. If your scans stay clear, you can be discharged later this week."

"And then?"

"Rest. Lots of it. No work for at least two weeks. No driving until you're past the headache and light sensitivity phase of the concussion. Someone should stay with you for the first few days in case of complications."

I think about my empty house. My empty life. My parents are in a retirement village down in Florida. I love my parents, but they're the kind of people who had a kid cause it was expected, not because they wanted one. Their proudest moment was waiting until they'd shipped me off to college to turn my room into a man cave.

I know they love me, but asking them to come help would be a nightmare.

I rack my brain trying to think of someone who might be able to help. I guess I could ask Kya or Mercy but they're both neck deep in the reopening of Devil's. Emma is Stone's kid, so she's off the table, not to mention recovering from surgery. Poppy or Andi could be an option, but they've both got kids to focus on.

I could try Maggie or Ginger, but I don't feel like I know either of them well enough to impose upon them like that.

I glance at Stone.

The fact is the only person I want to call is currently sitting three feet away, watching me with those unreadable gray eyes.

"I'll figure something out," I say.

The doctor nods and leaves. Stone waits until the door closes before speaking.

"You're not going back to your house."

"Excuse me?"

"The crash wasn't an accident, Josie."

I've been waiting for this. Have known, on some level, since I woke up. But hearing it confirmed still hits like a punch to the chest.

"You're sure?"

"Hawk pulled the traffic cam footage. The SUV was waiting. It ran the light specifically to hit you." His jaw is tight, his eyes hard. "After impact, the driver bailed. Footage shows him staggering out, holding his ribs. He might have been moving slow, but the bastard knew exactly where he was going."

The clinical details make it worse somehow. This wasn't road rage or an accident. Someone sat in that SUV, watched me approach, and made the decision to end my life.

"Someone tried to kill you. And until we find out who, you're under club protection."

Our gazes meet, and I can see the fury banked behind his eyes.. We both know exactly who ordered the hit.

Summit.

"Club protection means what, exactly?"

"You'll stay at the clubhouse where we can keep you safe."

"Absolutely not."

"Josie—"

"I have a life, Stone. A job. A home. I can't just move into your clubhouse because someone—"

"Someone tried to *murder* you." He leans forward, intensity radiating off him. "You're the one who built the case against Summit. You're the one who connected their shell companies. Without your evidence, the DA's entire investigation falls apart." He pauses, letting that sink in. "You really think they're going to stop at one attempt?"

I open my mouth to argue—and for a split second, I'm back there. Headlights filling my windshield. The screech of metal. The world spinning, glass shattering, my own scream lost in the impact.

I blink and it's gone, but my hands are trembling in my lap.

He's right. I know he's right. Summit has cartel connections, and cartels don't believe in half-measures. If they want me dead, they'll keep trying until they succeed —unless someone stops them first.

"I don't need a babysitter," I say, but there's no heat in it.

"Then think of it as a strategic relocation until we neutralize the threat."

"And if I refuse?"

"Then I'll post guys outside your house, and you'll spend the next few weeks tripping over bikers every time you leave." He almost smiles. "The clubhouse has better coffee."

I glare at him. He gazes back, implacable.

"You're not going to let this go, are you?"

"No."

"And if I fight you on it?"

"I'll throw you over my shoulder and carry you there myself. Broken ribs and all."

"That's kidnapping."

"Sue me."

We glare at each other. His eyes are steady, unyielding. Whatever else has happened between us, whatever confusion still lingers—in this moment, he's the president of the Stoneheart MC, and he's not going to budge.

"Fine," I say through gritted teeth. "But this is temporary. And I want it on record that I'm agreeing under extreme duress."

"Duly noted."

"And I'm not going to be some damsel locked in a tower. I have work to do. Cases to manage. A DA filing to complete."

"You can work from the clubhouse. We have WiFi."

"How modern of you."

"We also have Netflix. I'll even spring for HBO, if that sweetens the deal."

I snort despite myself. "You're a jerk."

"So I've been told." He stands, stretches—I try not to notice the way his shirt pulls across his shoulders, or the strip of toned stomach that appears when his shirt rides up. He stops at my bedside, his thumb brushing across my cheekbone, feather-light.

My breath catches.

"You had fluff there," he says, removing his hand.

Somehow I don't believe him.

"Get some rest." His voice is low, rough. "I need to make some calls, set up the security rotation. I'll be back in an hour."

He's nearly out the door when I call his name. He stops, turning back toward me.

"Thank you." The words come out grudging, but genuine. "Even if you are being a high-handed asshole right now, I appreciate it."

His mouth curves into an almost smile. "You're welcome. Even if you are being a stubborn pain in the ass."

He leaves before I can throw a pillow at him.

JOSIE

Sleep, it turns out, is not on the menu.

Every time I start to drift off, discomfort pulls me back—the throb of my ribs, the ache in my wrist, the way my head pulses in time with my heartbeat like a bass drum playing inside my skull. The pain meds help, but they make everything fuzzy and strange, turning the hospital room into a funhouse of shifting shadows and too-bright lights.

It's after midnight when I finally give up.

I lie there in the darkness, staring at the ceiling tiles, counting the tiny holes in them because I've already counted sheep and that hasn't worked either. The hospital is quieter now—fewer footsteps in the hallway, fewer beeps and buzzes from the nurses' station. Just the steady rhythm of machines and the soft sound of movement from behind the curtain.

My neighbor isn't asleep either.

I can tell by the quality of her restlessness that she's also uncomfortable. It's there in the shift of sheets, the creak of the bed frame, the occasional exhale that sounds more like frustration than relaxation.

"You're not fooling anyone with the fake sleeping," I say into the darkness.

"Neither are you."

"Fair point." I shift against my pillows, wincing. "Can't shut my brain off."

"Join the club."

I wait to see if she'll offer anything else. She doesn't.

"So," I try again. "What's keeping you up? Besides the obvious."

"The obvious?"

"Hospital beds. Fluorescent lights. The existential dread of being trapped in a building that smells like antiseptic and shit-rus."

A short sound—almost a laugh, quickly suppressed. "Shit-rus?"

"Don't tell me you think the strong citrus and poop smell is nice."

She snorts.

"Want to talk about it?" I ask.

"No."

Well. That's clear enough.

I should let it go, respect her boundaries and mind my own business. But years of working with victims has given me finely tuned instincts, and every single one of them is screaming that something is very wrong with the woman behind the curtain.

"You know," I say carefully, "I spent almost a decade putting away men who hurt people. I've heard pretty much every story there is. Nothing shocks me anymore."

"Good for you." Her voice is cool. Distant.

"Wanna share your story?"

"I don't have a story."

"Everyone has a story."

"Mine's not interesting."

"I doubt that."

The curtain shifts. The woman's face appears in the gap —sharp-featured, guarded, older than I've first assumed. Mid-to-late twenties, maybe. The dark circles under her eyes speak of sleepless nights that occurred long before this hospital stay.

I wonder if she has children.

"What do you want from me?" she asks bluntly. "You don't know me. I don't know you. In a few hours, we'll both be out of here and we'll never see each other again. So why the interrogation?"

"Just trying to make conversation."

"It feels like an interrogation."

"Occupational hazard. Sorry." I hold up my hands—well, one hand; the other is in a cast. "I'll back off."

She studies me for a long moment. I let her look, keeping my expression open, non-threatening. Whatever she's running from, whoever she's protecting herself against, I'm not it.

"I'm leaving tomorrow," she finally says. "That's all that matters."

"And then what?"

"Then I go."

"Go where?"

"Away."

"That's not a destination."

She shrugs.

There's an undercurrent to her words—a thread of desperation she can't quite hide.

Who are you running from?

"If you need help—" I start.

"I don't."

"—there are resources. Shelters, legal aid, people who specialize in—"

"I said I don't need help." Her voice goes sharp, a flash of heat breaking through the ice. "I just need to leave. I've already wasted too much time laying about here when I could do the same freaking thing at home."

Wasted. Interesting word choice.

"Look." Her expression hardens. "I appreciate the concern. Really. But whatever you think is going on with me, you're wrong. I fell down some stairs. I'm fine. Tomorrow I'll be gone and this will all be a weird memory for you. So can we just... not?"

She pulls back behind the curtain before I can respond.

I lie there in the darkness, turning the conversation over in my mind. She's lying—that much is obvious.

Not your problem, Bright. You've got your own mess to deal with.

True. But everything about her nags at me.

The nurse comes in a short time later and doses me up with pain meds, silencing the rock concert in my head.

I must have dozed off eventually, because I wake to the sound of footsteps.

The pain meds have worn off enough that my senses are sharper now, and something about the room feels wrong.

I lie still, trying to work it out.

There.

Footsteps. Soft, barely audible over the hum of machines. But I've spent years learning to listen for danger, and these footsteps are wrong. Too slow. Too deliberate. Not the brisk squeak of a nurse's rubber soles or the shuffling uncertainty of a lost visitor.

These footsteps are hunting.

I keep my eyes closed, force my breathing to stay even, even though every instinct I've developed during my years in Atlanta screams at me to run. The antiseptic smell of the room sharpens, mixing with the terrifying scent of sweat, leather, the faint metallic tang of blood.

The footsteps stop beside my bed.

The air shifts. A presence looms over me, close enough that I can feel the heat radiating off a body, hear the controlled inhale and exhale of someone trying to stay quiet. A shadow falls across my closed eyelids, blocking the dim glow of the machines.

Someone is standing over me.

My heart hammers against my broken ribs, each beat sending fire through my chest. I want to move—to open my eyes, to scream, to throw myself off the bed and run. But my body won't cooperate. The lingering fog of medication has turned my limbs to concrete, my thoughts to molasses. I'm trapped inside my own skin, paralyzed by chemicals and fear.

A rustle of fabric. The whisper of an object being drawn from a pocket.

MOVE, JOSIE! MOVE!

I can't.

The presence leans closer. His breath ghosts across my face, hot and wrong.

This is it. This is how I die.

CRASH.

The presence vanishes. A grunt of pain—male, surprised—a heavy thud that shakes the floor, the clatter of something metallic skittering across linoleum.

My eyes fly open.

My roommate stands over a man in dark clothes, a dented metal bedpan gripped in both hands like a baseball bat. Her hospital gown is askew, her IV ripped out and dripping blood down her forearm, her chest heaving with exertion.

But her eyes are calm. Focused. The eyes of someone who's been in survival mode so long it has become muscle memory.

The man groans, tries to push himself up. The woman doesn't hesitate—she swings again, a clean arc that connects with his skull with a sound like a hammer hitting meat.

He goes down and stays down.

"Jesus Christ," I breathe.

She stands there for a moment, staring at the body on the floor. Then she looks at me, and I see the first crack in her composure—a tremor in her hands, a flicker of wild fury behind her eyes.

"He was going to kill you," she says. Her voice is steady, but barely. "I saw him through the curtain. He walked right past me like I wasn't even there and he went straight for you. He had a weapon in his hand—"

My heart is slamming against my ribs, and my hands won't stop shaking. I can still feel the ghost of him above me, the desperate burn in my lungs to scream but knowing the sound was choked in my throat.

I never imagined I'd be the kind of person to freeze in this situation. But I did. I'm alive, because of her.

"You saved my life," the words are raw and rough, ripping through the lump in my throat.

"I hit him with a bedpan."

Relief crashes through me—so sudden and overwhelming that for a moment I can't breathe. This woman. This brave, terrified woman who doesn't even know me, who could have stayed hidden behind that curtain grabbed a bedpan and she *fought* for me.

Gratitude doesn't begin to express the onslaught of emotions I'm feeling toward her right now.

"You *saved my life.*" I struggle to sit up, ignoring the scream of my ribs. "That man was here to kill me. And you stopped him."

She looks down at the unconscious figure, at the blood pooling beneath his head, at the weapon still clutched in her white-knuckled grip.

"I've never—" She stops. Swallows.

"Come here."

She doesn't move.

"Come here."

Something in my voice must reach her, because she drops the bedpan with a clatter and crosses to my bed on unsteady legs. I grab her hand—the one not dripping blood from the torn IV—and hold on.

"You did what you had to do," I tell her firmly. "You saw a threat and you neutralized it. Don't be ashamed. That's survival."

"Survival." She laughs, but there's no humor in it. "Yeah. I'm good at that."

Before I can respond, the door bursts open.

Stone comes through first, his face a mask of controlled fury. Hawk and Tank flank him, both armed, both scanning the room for threats.

The relief that floods through me is so intense my vision blurs. *He's here.*

Stone's eyes find me, then my roommate, then the man on the floor. His expression cracks—relief and rage warring for dominance.

"Josie." He's at my bedside in three strides. "Are you hurt? Did he—"

"I'm fine. She stopped him."

His gaze swings to the woman, who's gone very still beside me. She's watching the three men with the wariness of a wild animal.

"You did this?" Stone asks her.

A short nod. Her hand twitches like she wants to reach for the bedpan again.

"With that?" He nods toward the dented metal on the floor.

Another nod.

Stone looks at the unconscious attacker—easily twice her size—then back at her. I watch him reassess her in real-time, watch the pieces click into place behind his eyes.

I grip my blanket, pulling it around me as a bone cold chill freezes my blood.

"He knocked out the prospect we had on your door," Hawk says grimly. "Kid didn't even see him coming."

"Is he okay?"

Hawk nods. "He's alive but bleeding."

"Hawk, secure the fucker. Tank, deal with the prospect." He turns back to the woman, and when he speaks again, his voice is carefully gentle. "What's your name?"

"Isabel."

"Isabel. I'm Stone. I run the Stoneheart MC." He gestures toward me. "Josie's been working with us. Someone wants her dead, and you just stopped their latest henchman. That means you're involved now, whether you want to be or not."

Isabel's expression flickers. "I don't—I can't—I have to leave tomorrow. I can't get involved in anything."

"Unfortunately, you've been bunking with Josie so that means you're compromised. The people who sent him will be after you. If you stay here, they'll come for you."

"I don't care."

"You should."

"I *can't* care." Her voice cracks on the word, the first real emotion she's shown. "I have to—I need to go home. I can't—"

She stops herself. Clamps down on whatever she's been about to say.

A cold lump forms in my gut, the hairs raising on the back of my neck.

What are you running back to, Isabel?

Stone's expression doesn't change. He's gone still in that particular way he has—the way that means he's thinking three moves ahead, cataloging every detail, filing it away for later.

I know that look. I've seen it in interrogation rooms, across courtroom aisles, in the faces of men who've survived by assuming everyone is a threat until proven otherwise.

He doesn't trust her. Not even a little.

I bristle, my protective instincts kicking in. I narrow my gaze on him, glaring.

She just saved my life, you asshole. Go easy.

"Where do you need to be?" he asks. His voice is calm. Almost gentle. But I hear what's underneath—it's a fishing expedition.

"Nowhere. It doesn't matter."

"It obviously matters."

"It's not your problem."

"You just saved Josie's life. That makes it my problem."

The words sound grateful. They're not. They're a claim—*you're involved now, whether you like it or not*.

Isabel's jaw tightens. She looks at me, then at Stone, then at the door—measuring the distance, calculating her odds. I watch her realize what I already know: she's not getting out of this room without going through him first.

"I can't stay," she says finally. "I'll go somewhere else. Hide. Figure it out. But I can't stay here and I can't go with you and I can't—" She breaks off, frustration and fear warring in her expression. "I just can't."

Stone nods slowly.

"Okay," he says. "But here's what's going to happen right now. We're getting both of you out of this hospital before anyone else shows up. You—" he points at Isabel "—can decide what to do next once you're somewhere safe. But right now, in this moment, you're coming with us. Understood?"

It's not a question. It's not even really an offer. It's a command dressed up in reasonable words.

Isabel hears it too. Her eyes narrow.

"One night," she says flatly.

"What?"

"One night. I'll come with you, I'll answer your questions, I'll prove I'm not—" She gestures vaguely at the unconscious man on the floor. "Whatever you're thinking. But tomorrow morning, I leave. No arguments, no locked doors. One night. That's all I can give you."

Stone studies her for a long moment. His face gives nothing away—not suspicion, not trust, not anything at all. Just that calm, assessing gaze that makes people confess to things they haven't done.

I watch Isabel hold her ground under his scrutiny and my chest aches for her. She's terrified—I can see it in the white-knuckle grip she has on her hospital gown, the way she's braced like she expects to be hit. But she's not backing down.

She's used to negotiating with dangerous men, I realize. *She's had practice.*

The thought makes me want to wrap her in a blanket and hide her somewhere safe.

"Fair enough," he says finally.

Isabel blinks. She'd been braced for a fight. The easy agreement throws her.

It throws me too. Stone doesn't make deals. Stone doesn't compromise. Which means he's planning to keep her close, watching her, waiting to see what she does when she thinks no one's looking.

He thinks she's involved, I realize. *He thinks she might be part of this.*

Irritation flares hot in my chest. I want to argue. Want to tell him he's wrong, that I've looked into this woman's eyes and seen fear, desperation, and the bone-deep exhaustion of someone who's been fighting alone for too long.

For God's sake, Stone. Look at her. This isn't a woman running a con—this is a woman fighting for her life.

But I know Stone. And I know that arguing right now will only make him dig in harder. So I keep my mouth shut and let him play whatever game he's playing.

"One night," Isabel repeats, like she needs to hear it again to believe it. "And then I'm gone."

Stone turns to me. "Can you walk?"

Isabel doesn't seem to notice Stone hasn't agreed with her.

Two people who don't trust anyone, I think. *This should be interesting.*

"Probably not," I admit.

"Then I'm carrying you."

"Stone—"

He removes cords and tubes from me with surprising gentleness, then scoops me up, ignoring my hiss of pain as my ribs scream in objection. "Hold on."

"Stone, wait—I'm in a hospital gown."

"I noticed."

"My ass is literally hanging out."

"I've got you covered." He shifts me slightly, tucking the fabric underneath me with a matter-of-factness that somehow makes it worse. "No one's seeing anything."

"Except you."

"I'm not looking."

"You're a terrible fucking liar."

The ghost of a smile crosses his face. "Hold on, Josie."

He starts moving toward the door when Tank appears, blocking it.

"Kid okay?"

"In emergency. They'll patch him up." His gaze narrows on the Isabel. "We bringing her?"

"Yep, you get Isabel. Hawk, get the asshole. I don't want a shred of evidence left behind."

We're out the door and down the hall before I know it.

"Stone," I say softly. "She's not our enemy."

His eyes flick to me. Something passes between us—not

agreement, but acknowledgment. He's heard me. He just doesn't believe me yet.

He hits the elevator door, and we wait for Isabel and the guys to arrive.

The corridor is eerily empty. No nurses at the station. No orderlies pushing carts. No doctors making rounds. Just flickering fluorescent lights and the distant wail of an alarm from somewhere deeper in the building.

"Where is everyone?" I ask.

"Someone called a code brown," Tank says grimly, catching up with Isabel in tow. "Whole hospital's in emergency mode."

"Poop?" I ask, confused.

He glances at me. "No, it's the code for a hazardous material spill."

My blood goes cold. "A distraction."

"Yep. They drew the staff away. The only nurse on this floor is down the far end attending to a little old lady." Stone's jaw is tight. "It gave their guy a window to work."

They'd planned this. If Isabel hadn't been awake, if she hadn't acted...

I'd be dead. And no one would have known.

I shiver, goosebumps raising on my arms.

"They're getting desperate." Stone's arms tighten around me. "Take comfort in that. It means they're also getting sloppy."

I try to take comfort in it. I really do. But all I can think about is the sickly smell of the hitman's breath on my cheek. Twice someone has tried to kill me, and twice I've survived by sheer luck.

How many more times can I get lucky?

Hawk arrives, pushing the unconscious guy in a laundry cart. He's hog-tied him with zip ties and a pillow case around his neck.

We exit the hospital without any major issues. Isabel walks beside us, her expression shuttered, her eyes never stopping their restless surveillance.

I watch her from the safety of Stone's arms and feel a strange kinship. Two women running from men who want to hurt them. The difference is, I have an army at my back. Isabel has no one.

A black SUV idles at the curb, another man I don't recognize behind the wheel.

"Get in," Stone tells Isabel, nodding toward the back seat.

She hesitates, one foot on the pavement, one in the vehicle. "Where are we going?"

"Our clubhouse. It's secure."

"And then?"

"And then you get some sleep. We all do. Tomorrow, we'll figure out next steps."

Isabel doesn't move. Her hand is on the door frame, her knuckles white.

"I need to leave in the morning," she says. "First thing. I wasn't lying about that."

"We'll talk about it in the morning."

"I'm not asking permission."

Stone's eyes meet hers. Something unspoken passes between them—a battle of wills, brief but intense.

I should be focused on their standoff. Instead, I'm acutely aware of Stone's heartbeat against my side, the warmth of his chest, the way his thumb traces absent circles on my hip as if he doesn't even realize he's doing it.

Stop it, I tell myself. *You almost died. This is not the time.*

But my body doesn't care about timing. My body just knows he's here, he's holding me, and for the first time in hours, I feel safe.

"Get in the car, Isabel," he says finally. "We'll figure the rest out later."

For a moment, I think she'll refuse and take off running into the darkness and we'll never see her again.

Then she glances at me—still cradled against Stone's chest, broken and bruised and completely helpless.

"Fine," she mutters, and climbs into the SUV.

Stone settles me beside her, and I feel the loss of his warmth immediately. He gets in the front passenger seat. Tank slides behind the wheel, and Hawk loads the cartel henchman in the back, climbing in after him.

We pull away from the hospital into the cool night air.

Isabel stares out the window, her reflection a ghost against the glass.

I lean my head back against the seat, exhaustion crashing over me in waves. My ribs throb. My head pounds. Every part of me aches, inside and out.

Tonight, we've both survived. That's enough for now.

5

STONE

The clubhouse has never looked so much like a fortress.

I've called ahead from the hospital, and by the time we pull into the lot, every light is blazing and half the club is waiting. Hawk climbs out of the back, and is already barking orders at the prospects.

"Main room clear. Guest rooms prepped. Maggie's got the medical supplies ready."

"Good." The word comes out clipped, harsh. I don't bother softening it.

Rage is a living thing inside me right now—coiled tight, waiting to strike. Someone got past my man. Someone walked into her hospital room and tried to smother her in her bed, and if it weren't for a scared girl with a bedpan, Josie would be dead.

On my watch. Under my protection.

I want to put my fist through a wall. I want to find every single person connected to Summit and tear them apart with my bare hands. I want to burn their entire operation to the ground and salt the fucking earth.

Instead, I channel it into movement. Into purpose.

I'm out of the SUV before it fully stops, rounding to get Josie.

She's pale in the harsh overhead lights, dark circles under her eyes, her jaw tight against the pain she's trying to hide. Stubborn woman. She'd probably insist on walking if I gave her half a chance.

I don't give her so much as a whisper.

"I can—" she starts.

"No." I lift her out of the vehicle, ignoring her huff of protest. "Save your strength for arguing with me later. You'll need it."

"Promises, promises."

Despite everything—the attack, the fear still coiled in my gut, the knowledge that someone has gotten close enough to kill her in her hospital bed—I almost smile. She's bruised, broken, and still giving me shit.

That's my girl.

Isabel climbs out behind us. Her eyes sweep the lot, the building, the men gathered outside. Taking stock. Planning.

I watch her for a beat, noting how she seems to be seeking out exits and weaknesses.

Who are you, little girl?

I file the question away for later. Right now, I have more pressing concerns—but that doesn't mean I'm taking chances.

"Tank." I keep my voice low. "Stay on her. Don't crowd her, but don't let her out of your sight."

He nods once, understanding without needing an explanation.

"Inside," I tell Isabel. "Maggie will get you sorted."

She doesn't argue, but she doesn't relax either.

Maggie descends on us the moment we cross the threshold.

"Oh, honey." She's all business, her hands gentle as she checks Josie's bandages, her pupils, her pulse. "What a mess. Let's get you into a proper bed. The guest room's all set up—fresh sheets, extra pillows, the good painkillers Duck's been hoarding since his knee surgery."

"I'm fine—"

"You're not fine, you're concussed and cracked and running on fumes." Maggie shoots me a look. "Put her in the big guest room. I'll be there in five with the first aid kit."

"Yes ma'am."

Josie groans. "I hate being carried."

"Noted." I don't put her down.

The guest room is upstairs—private, quiet, with its own bathroom and a window that looks out over the back lot. I've had it set up for situations exactly like this, though I've never imagined I'd be using it for her.

I settle her on the bed as carefully as I can manage, propping pillows behind her back, pulling the blanket up over her legs. She watches me with an expression I can't quite read.

"What?" I ask.

"Nothing." A pause. "You're being very... domestic."

"Don't get used to it."

"Wouldn't dream of it."

But I like the soft look she wears as she watches me.

I want to stay. Want to sit beside her and hold her hand and make sure she keeps breathing. But I have a club to run, a man to interrogate, a threat to neutralize, and a meeting that can't wait.

"Get some rest," I tell her. "I've got business to handle, but I'll check on you later."

I move toward the door, but something stops me. The same thing that's been stopping me for months—the pull of her, the gravity she exerts without even trying.

Fuck it.

I turn back. Cross the room in three strides. I lean down and press my lips to her forehead.

She goes still beneath me. I let the kiss linger—longer than I should. Her skin is warm under my mouth, and she smells like hospital antiseptic and a hint of perfume that's all her.

When I pull back, her eyes are wide, searching my face.

"Stone—"

I brush a strand of hair from her forehead. "Rest that overworked brain of yours, Bright," I say softly. "That's all I want from you right now. Just... rest. Please."

I'm at the door before she can respond, my heart pounding like I'm twenty years younger and twice as stupid.

"Stone."

I pause, hand on the frame.

"About Isabel." Josie's brow furrows. "Something's wrong with her. I don't mean the obvious stuff—the bruises. Something else. She's got somewhere she needs to be, and it's eating her alive."

"You think she's a threat?"

"No. I think she's scared." She shakes her head slowly. "I can't put my finger on it, but I think there's something she's not telling us." She hesitates. "I know you need to protect the club, but don't spook her. Whatever's going on, she's not ready to talk about it."

"I won't."

I mean it. I won't push Isabel or corner her.

Not unless she gives me a reason.

And if she does—if she puts Josie at risk—then all bets are off.

Josie holds my gaze for a long moment, then nods and lets her eyes close. "Go do your president thing. I'll be here."

"That's what I'm counting on."

I leave before I can do something stupid, like kiss her forehead again just because I want to.

Church is already assembled when I walk in.

Hawk, Lee, Tank, Axel, Cash, Bones, Duck, and Steel. All of them grim-faced, all of them waiting. The energy in the room is coiled tight, the kind of tension that precedes violence.

Good. They should be tense. Someone tried to kill my woman in her hospital bed.

"What do we know?" I ask, taking my seat at the head of the table.

"Our guest is awake," Hawk says, a cold smile playing at his lips. "Took some convincing, but he's talking."

The hitman is in the box—a concrete bunker beneath the chapel that most people don't know exists. When the club bought this property decades ago, the previous owners had been survivalists. They'd dug out a shelter beneath the old outbuilding, reinforced the walls, installed a ventilation system. We repurposed it.

It's soundproofed, windowless, only accessible through a one way hatch in the chapel floor. Inside is a single room, now divided into two spaces by a single wall of bars. It's the kind of place where difficult conversations are made to happen—by voluntary or otherwise.

"And?"

"Ivan sent him. Confirmation that Summit's behind both hits—the car and tonight."

Ivan. The cartel's new local fixer, and the bastard who slipped through our fingers after kidnapping my daughter. The rest of them are dead for what they did to Emma.

"So it's confirmed," Lee says, jaw tight. "Summit's cleaning house."

Bones pulls up footage on his laptop. "Traffic cams caught the SUV that hit Josie. Ring cam footage from two blocks away shows the driver getting into a black Yukon —same model we've tracked to Ivan before. Tonight's guy confirms it. Same handler, same orders."

"He give up Ivan's location?" I ask.

"Claims he doesn't know. Dead drops, burner phones, the usual." Hawk shrugs. "Could be lying. Want me to ask again?"

"Later." I lean forward, palms flat on the table. "Josie's got every piece of evidence against Summit, every connection between their shell companies and the cartel. Without her testimony, the DA's case falls apart. They know it. We know it. This isn't going to stop."

Silence. The weight of it presses down on all of us.

"What about the girl?" Tank asks. "The one who took out the attacker?"

"Isabel. She's a complication."

"Complication how?"

"She saved Josie's life, which means we owe her a debt. But she's also—" I pause, choosing my words carefully. "Squirrelly. Josie thinks she's hiding something. I agree."

"Cartel plant?" Axel asks.

"I don't think so. But I'm not ruling anything out." I look around the table. "For now, she stays here. We keep eyes on her, see what she does."

"And if she runs?"

"Then we find out where she's running to."

Lee leans back in his chair, frowning. "We need more bodies. If Summit's escalating, we can't cover everything with who we've got. Surveillance, protection details, regular ops—we're stretched thin."

He's right. Between watching Summit properties, protecting Josie and Isabel, and maintaining our regular operations, we're running on fumes.

"I'll reach out to the Ridgeline chapter," I say. "See if they can spare some men."

Tank groans. "Ridgeline? Shit."

"Problem?"

"No problem. Just—" He exchanges a look with Hawk. "You know who Ridgeline's gonna send."

I do know. The Ridgeline chapter has been our closest allies for fifteen years, and whenever they send support, they send their best. Which currently means—

"Brick," Hawk says, fighting a smile. "Ginger's baby brother."

"He's good," I say. "We could use him."

"Oh, he's great. No argument there." Tank scrubs a hand over his face. "But you know what happens when Ginger's baby brother comes to town. She's gonna be insufferable for weeks. 'Bradley, are you eating enough? Tank, I think you should give Bradley some of your food. Bradley, you look tired, we'll give you our bed. Bradley Michael, I don't care if you're a grown man with a body count, you're wearing a jacket because it's cold outside. Tank, make him wear the jacket!'"

A ripple of laughter goes around the table.

"She's not that bad," Duck offers.

"She made him sit in the corner at the last cookout because he said 'damn' in front of Emma." Tank shakes his head. "The man's six-four, built like a brick shithouse, and she put him in time-out. I half expected her to force me to hold him down while she spanked his ass."

"To be fair," Hawk says, "he went."

"Because he's terrified of her! We all are!"

"Are you allowed to say that if you're married to her?" Lee asks, grinning.

Tank flicks him the bird.

"Enough." I'm fighting my own smile now. "I'll call Butters, see how many men he can spare. If Brick's one of them, Ginger will deal. We've got bigger problems than her maternal instincts."

"Easy for you to say," Tank mutters. "You're not the one she's gonna recruit to help knit him a fucking sweater."

"What's the play on Ivan?" Lee asks, steering us back on track. "We wait for them to come at us again, or we take the fight to them?"

It's the question I've been turning over since the moment I got that phone call. The instinct to hit back is overwhelming—find Ivan, find everyone connected to him, burn Summit to the ground.

But instinct isn't strategy, and strategy is what keeps people alive.

"We gather intel first," I say. "I want to know where Ivan is hiding, who he's working with, what Summit's next move is going to be. Bones, keep digging. Steel, I want surveillance on every property we've connected to their operation."

Steel nods. He spent four years as a Marine scout sniper before he left—not for lack of skill, but because he couldn't stomach the politics. His marksmanship scores were legendary; it was his attitude toward commanding officers that needed work. Their loss is our gain.

"And then?"

"We end this. Permanently." I look around the table, meeting each man's eyes in turn. "They came for Josie. They came into a hospital room and tried to kill a woman under our protection. That can't stand."

"Damn right it can't," Duck mutters.

"We'll coordinate with Josie's contacts at the FBI—she's been building a federal case alongside the local one. When we move, we move with the full weight of the law behind us. No loose ends, no comebacks." I stand, signaling the end of the meeting. "Until then, we lock down. Nobody goes anywhere alone. Prospects on the perimeter, armed guard on the clubhouse around the clock. And someone's on Josie at all times."

"What should I do with our visitor?" Hawk asks. "Not sure how long he'll want to hang in the box."

I frown. "Hold him for another few hours, see what else you can get out of him, then hand him over to the Feds. Let them deal with it."

"What about the mayoral thing?" Duck taps the campaign pin on his chest. "Maggie's been on me about campaign appearances. Got a thing at the community center next week—meet and greet with voters."

Right. The election. In the chaos of the past few weeks, I've almost forgotten we're trying to get Duck elected mayor.

"You still want to do it?"

"Hell yes, I want to do it. Best way to fight Summit is to take their puppet out of the running." Duck's jaw sets stubbornly. "Vernick's been their mouthpiece on the council for years. We put him out of office, we cut off their legitimate channels."

"It makes you a target."

"Already was a target. Might as well be a target who's doing something useful."

I can't argue with that logic. "Fine. You'll take backup. Your main focus should be on campaigning. We'll figure out details once Ridgeline gets here." I glance around once more, nodding to each of them. "Meeting adjourned. Get to work."

They file out, Tank still grumbling about Ginger and her brother. I reach for my phone.

Butters picks up on the second ring.

An hour later, I find myself back outside Josie's door.

I should have gone to bed and grabbed a few hours of sleep while I could. But the hit on Josie is still too raw for me to stay away.

I push the door open quietly, expecting to find her asleep.

She isn't.

She's propped up against the pillows, laptop balanced on her knees, frowning at the screen with the kind of intensity she usually reserves for hostile witnesses.

"Oh fuck no."

She looks up. "Hey you're back."

I point at her laptop. "Shut it off."

She bristles. "Excuse me?"

"No working. Doctor's orders. Maggie's orders. *My* orders."

She glares. "Since when do I take orders from you?"

"Since someone tried to kill you. Twice. You need to rest."

"I am resting." She gestures at the bed. "See? Bed. Pillows. Very restful."

"You're working."

"I'm reviewing documents. It's hardly working."

"The doctor said no to screen time for another week." I cross the room and gently but firmly close her laptop. "Josie. The case can wait. The DA can wait. Everything can wait until you're not running on pain meds."

She glares at me. I hold my ground.

"You're impossible," she mutters.

"So I've been told."

"I hate being useless."

"You're not useless. You're *injured.*"

"Same-same."

The frustration in her voice is real, and I understand it. Josie isn't the kind of woman who sits on the sidelines. She fights, she strategizes, she makes things happen. Being stuck in a bed while the world moves around her has to be driving her insane.

"I know this is hard," I say, sitting on the edge of the bed. "But you almost died. Your body needs time to heal."

"My body's an overachiever. It'll do what I tell it to."

I almost grin at the outlandish statement. "That's not how bodies work."

"How would you know?"

"I've broken enough of mine to have some experience." I reach out, tucking a strand of hair behind her ear. She freezes at the contact but doesn't pull away. "Please, Josie. Let yourself rest."

She stares at me for a long moment, something complicated moving behind her eyes.

"Maggie dropped by and said Ridgeline's sending people?" she asks, changing the subject.

"Tomorrow. Four men, including Ginger's brother."

"Which one? Hank, Ralph or Bradley?"

"Bradley, but he goes by Brick." I smile slightly.

"Good. We could use the help." She pauses. "You also want someone to watch Isabel, right?"

Nothing slips by her.

"That's the plan. I want to see where she goes, what she does. Figure out what she's hiding."

Josie nods slowly. "I guess that makes sense."

She holds my gaze for another moment, then sighs when I tap the top of the laptop.

"Fine," she says, handing it to me. "I'll rest. But I reserve the right to be difficult about it tomorrow."

"I'd expect nothing less."

"And I'm not doing this because you told me to. I'm doing it because I'm tired and the pain meds are making me loopy."

"Whatever you need to tell yourself."

"Shut up."

I almost laugh. Even exhausted, drugged, bruised and broken—she's still the same sharp-tongued woman I've fallen for.

I set the laptop aside and move to the bed. She's been propped up on pillows to work, but now she's listing sideways, fighting to keep her eyes open.

"Come here," I say softly, sliding an arm behind her shoulders.

She stiffens for a moment—instinct, I think—then exhales and lets me take her weight. I ease her forward, adjusting the pillows with my free hand, then lower her gently back against them.

"I can do it myself," she mumbles, but her fingers curl into the fabric of my shirt.

"I know you can."

I smooth the blanket over her, my knuckles brushing her collarbone. This close, I can see the patchy regrowth of hair where they shaved her head, soft and dark against her scalp. The bruises on her face have faded from purple to a sickly yellow-green. The stitches along her hairline are starting to dissolve.

I watch her eyes drift closed, her breathing slow and even. The tension in her shoulders softens, and she shifts a fraction of an inch closer to me, probably without even realizing it.

She's okay, I tell myself. *She's here. She's safe. That's what matters.*

But even as I think it, I know it isn't enough. Safe for now isn't the same as safe forever. As long as Summit wants her dead, she's in danger.

Which means Summit has to go.

I stay longer than I should, watching her breathe, my hand still resting on the blanket near her hip. I can't stop thinking about everything that could have gone different. About what I'd do if it had.

Finally, I force myself to leave, closing the door softly behind me.

6

JOSIE

I wake to the smell of bacon and the sound of absolute chaos.

For a disorienting moment, I have no idea where I am. The bed is wrong—too soft, too wide—and the ceiling above me is unfamiliar. Then my ribs scream in protest as I try to sit up, and everything comes flooding back.

Hospital. Attack. Stone carrying me out like some kind of leather-clad knight. The clubhouse.

Right. A murder attempt . Sorry, a second murder attempt. How well my life is going.

I lie still for a moment, taking stock. My head still throbs, but the pain is duller now—the concussion settling into a persistent ache rather than the sharp stabbing I've battled for a week. My ribs are another story. Every breath feels like someone is pressing a hot iron between my bones.

The chaos, I realize, is coming from somewhere deeper in the clubhouse. Voices—multiple, are overlapping, punctuated by bursts of laughter and what sounds like someone banging pots together.

I check my phone. 9:47 AM. I've slept almost eight hours straight, which is either a miracle or a testament to how good Duck's ill-gotten pain meds are.

Getting out of bed is a project. I move in stages—sitting up, swinging my legs over the edge, waiting for the dizziness to pass, then slowly leveraging myself upright. My left arm is still in a cast, which makes everything twice as hard.

Someone—Maggie, probably—left clothes folded on the dresser. A soft flannel shirt and leggings, along with a note that says *"These should fit."* I manage to wrestle myself into them one-handed, which takes longer than I'd like to admit.

My reflection in the mirror across the room is not encouraging. Bruised, pale, hair a disaster, wearing a borrowed t-shirt that's three sizes too big.

Gorgeous, Bright. Truly stunning.

I find a bathroom, do what I can with cold water and determination, and shuffle down the stairs toward the noise.

I reach the bottom wincing and squinting against the bright light that floods in from the floor-to-ceiling windows. My head throbs in protest, a reminder that my concussion is hanging around like a bad hangover. I raise my good hand to shield my eyes and give myself a moment to adjust.

The clubhouse kitchen is a war zone.

Ginger stands at the stove, wielding a spatula like a weapon while simultaneously directing traffic. Maggie is at the counter chopping vegetables with terrifying efficiency. Kya has commandeered the coffee maker and appears to be brewing enough caffeine to fuel a small army. Emma sits at the massive wooden table with Poppy, baby Rose balanced on her lap, both of them laughing at something on Poppy's phone.

The smell of bacon and fresh coffee hits me, and underneath it, the sweeter scent of pancakes, maybe, or cinnamon rolls. The warmth of the kitchen wraps around me, voices and laughter layering over each other in a way that should be overwhelming but somehow isn't.

I stand in the doorway for a moment, just taking it in.

This is what family looks like, I realize. Not the quiet, sterile dinners of my childhood, where conversation was polite and measured. This is noise and mess and people who want to be around each other, and enjoy each others company.

And in the middle of all the chaos, looking profoundly uncomfortable, is Isabel.

She's been cornered by Mercy near the refrigerator, clearly being subjected to some kind of interrogation disguised as friendly conversation. Her answers are monosyllabic, her body language screaming *get me out of here*, but Mercy either doesn't notice or doesn't care.

"—and then I told Cash, if you think I'm cleaning up after that dog one more time, you've got another thing coming—oh, Josie!" Mercy spots me in the doorway and her face lights up. "You're awake! How are you feeling? Do you need anything? Sit down, sit down, you shouldn't be standing—"

"I'm fine—"

"You're not fine, you're concussed. Ginger, she's concussed and she's standing."

"I can see that." Ginger abandons her post at the stove and descends on me like a sequined tornado.

She's a fiery redhead with freckles and curves. The kind of redhead who probably terrorized her teachers and charmed her way out of every detention. Silver threads liberally through her wild hair but she isn't about to apologize for it by dying them. Her lipstick is the same shade as a fire engine, and her hoop earrings are long enough they could pick up radio signals. Today she's wearing a leopard print blouse, skinny jeans, sparkles, from the glitter on her eyeshadow to the rhinestones on her belt.

She's loud, proud, and outrageously kind.

"Honey, what are you doing up? You should be in bed. Maggie, tell her she should be in bed."

"She should be in bed," Maggie says without looking up from her vegetables.

"I've been in bed for—" I try to do the math and give up. "Too long. I needed to move."

"Moving is overrated. Sitting is recommended by five out of six doctors." Ginger steers me toward the table with surprising strength for someone her size. "Park it. I'll bring you coffee and breakfast and you'll sit there and let us fuss over you."

"I don't need fussing—"

"Everyone needs fussing. Especially stubborn lawyers who get hit by cars and then try to pretend they're fine." She pushes me into a chair with a firm hand. "Sit. Stay. Good girl."

"I'm not a dog."

"You're right. Dogs are better at following instructions."

Emma snorts. Rose gurgles in what might be agreement.

I give up and sit.

Breakfast is an event.

Plates appear in front of me—bacon, eggs, toast, fruit, pancakes. More food than I can eat in a week, let alone a single morning. Coffee materializes at my elbow, hot and strong, and I wrap my good hand around the mug like it's a lifeline.

The women talk around me and over me and through me, a constant stream of chatter that's oddly comforting. They aren't treating me like an invalid or a victim. They're treating me like family.

It's been a long time since anyone has treated me like family. It's strange, being surrounded by people who care whether I've eaten, whether I've slept, whether I'm hurting. I've spent so long taking care of myself that I'd forgotten what it feels like. Being looked after. Being *wanted*.

My throat tightens unexpectedly, and I have to look down at the scarred wooden table until the feeling passes.

"So," Kya says, sliding into the seat beside me. "How's it feel to be a damsel in distress?"

"Terrible. I'm filing a complaint."

"With who?"

"I don't know yet. Whoever's in charge of clichés."

She grins. "That's the spirit. Eat your eggs."

I eat my eggs.

Across the table, Isabel picks at a piece of toast, her eyes darting between the women like she's waiting for the other shoe to drop. She's clearly been cleaned up—fresh clothes, hair brushed, bandages changed—but there's still a feralness to her. Like she'd coiled and ready to run, or strike.

I catch her eye. Try to offer a reassuring smile.

She looks away, frowning.

Le sigh. At least I tried.

The back door bangs open and the twins, Abby and Amy,

barrel through, followed by Andi carrying Adam on her hip.

"Sorry we're late—someone decided to have a meltdown about socks." She spots me and her face softens. "Oh good, you're up. How are you feeling?"

"Like I got hit by a truck."

"SUV," three people correct in unison.

I roll my eyes. "You?"

She gestures at the chaos around us. "Just another day in paradise."

"So, Isabel." Ginger's voice is carefully casual as she settles into the seat across from the younger woman. "Where are you from? Originally?"

"Stoneheart."

"Really? Born and raised?"

"Yep."

"Huh. I thought I knew everyone in this town, but I don't think I've seen you around. Do you work somewhere local?"

"Here and there."

"Here and there like odd jobs, or here and there like something specific?"

"Just... around."

Ginger's smile doesn't falter, but I see the sharpening of her gaze. She's fishing, and Isabel isn't biting.

"What about family?" Mercy jumps in. "You have people here?"

A look flickers across Isabel's face—there and gone so fast I almost miss it.

"No," she says flatly.

"Everyone's got someone—"

"I said no." Isabel's voice is hard now, a wall slamming down.

Except, I know that's not true. She said last night that her stepdad was picking her up.

Silence falls over the table. The women exchange looks—confused, concerned, a little suspicious.

"Nobody said you had to leave," Emma offers carefully. "After what you did for Josie—"

"I didn't do it for a reward." Isabel shoves back from the table. "I didn't do it for anything. It just happened, and now it's over, and I need to go."

Emma frowns. "Go where?"

"Anywhere. Away." She's already moving toward the hallway. "Thanks for the hospitality, but I can't stay. I have to—I just have to go."

"Isabel—" I start.

But she's already gone, disappearing down the hallway like the hounds of hell are at her heels.

"Well," Ginger says after a moment. "That was cryptic."

"She's hiding something," Mercy says, frowning.

"Obviously. The question is what."

"Maybe she's shy?" Poppy offers, though she doesn't sound convinced.

"That's not shyness." Emma shakes her head. "That's fear. But fear of what? We're not exactly threatening."

"Speak for yourself," Kya mutters.

I push my plate away, my appetite gone. "Well, whatever it is, it's eating her alive. She can barely sit still."

"You think she's in some kind of trouble?" Maggie asks.

"I think she's been in some kind of trouble for a long time." I touch my face, reminding them silently of her bruises "And I think she's used to handling it alone."

"Well, she's not alone anymore." Ginger's jaw sets stubbornly. "Whether she likes it or not. That girl saved your life, which means she's ours now."

"She doesn't seem to want to be ours," Emma mutters.

"Too bad. We're very persistent." Ginger stands, gathering plates. "Give her time. Whatever she's running from, she'll figure out eventually that having a safe space to land is better. And when she does, we'll be here."

The morning wears on.

I try to work. I pull out my laptop, and start reviewing files but the pain meds make it hard to focus, and my head is pounding within twenty minutes. Maggie confiscates the laptop with a look that dares me to argue.

I don't, I'm too tired.

Instead, I find myself drifting from room to room, learning the layout of the clubhouse. The main room with its battered leather couches and massive TV. The kitchen, heart of the operation. The bar in the corner, well-stocked and frequently visited. The hallway lined with doors—rooms for members who need a place to crash, offices, storage.

And everywhere, people. Club members coming and going, conducting business, shooting the shit. The women who've adopted me, constantly checking in, offering food or coffee or company.

It should feel overwhelming. Instead, it feels safe.

When is the last time I've felt safe?

I'm standing at the window in the main room, watching prospects do complicated things with motorcycles in the back lot. Ginger moves beside me, watching them work.

"Ridgeline crew's coming in," she says, her voice carefully casual.

"Stone mentioned that."

"Mmhmm." She's trying—and failing—to suppress a smile. "My brother's coming with them."

"The famous Bradley?"

"Brick, they call him now. Though he'll always be Bradley to me." She practically glows. "I haven't seen him in forever. Not since Christmas, when he came up for the week. He helped me reorganize the entire storage room."

"He sounds like a good brother."

"The best. A little rough around the edges—all these boys are—but underneath?" She presses a hand to her heart. "Biggest softie you ever met. Used to cry at dog food commercials, you know."

Something about that image that makes my chest tight.

"He sounds like a good man."

"He is. They all are, once you get past the leather and the scowls." Ginger pats my arm. "You'll see. This crew— they're family. Loud, messy, overprotective family who'll drive you crazy and love you fiercely. You just have to let them."

I think about Stone.

"Maybe I will."

Ginger smiles like she knows exactly who I'm thinking of. "Good. Now—have you seen Isabel? I want to try talking to her again. Maybe offer her a makeover. Girls love makeovers."

"I don't think Isabel's a makeover kind of girl."

"Everyone's a makeover kind of girl with the right approach."

She bustles off before I can argue, and I go back to watching the prospects.

∼

I find Isabel in the back hallway an hour later, pacing like a caged animal.

She freezes when she sees me, her body going tense, her eyes darting to the exit at the end of the hall.

"Relax," I say, holding up my hands. "I'm not here to stop you from whatever you're planning on doing."

"Then why are you here?"

"To talk." I lean against the wall, trying to look casual despite the fire in my ribs. "And to say thank you for saving my life."

"You already thanked me."

"Not properly. I was drugged and concussed, and probably not making a lot of sense."

Isabel's guard doesn't lower, but she stops looking at the exit. Progress.

"You don't owe me anything. I didn't do it for gratitude."

"I know. You did it because someone was in danger and you could help. That's rare, Isabel. Most people freeze. Or run. You grabbed a bedpan and went to war."

She frowns. "I've had practice."

"I figured." I let that sit for a moment.

Her jaw tightens. "I don't want to talk about it."

"I'm not asking you to. I'm just saying—I recognize it. The look you have. I've seen it before, in a lot of people who came through my courtroom. People who've been fighting for so long they've forgotten what peace feels like."

Isabel is very still. Watching me with those dark, wary eyes.

"You were a prosecutor," she says. "Ginger mentioned it."

"In Atlanta. I dealt with a lot of cases involving…" I choose my words carefully. "People who hurt other people. And the people who got hurt trying to survive them."

"Why'd you stop?"

Because I got someone killed. Because I made promises I couldn't keep. Because I broke myself and the lives of others in the process.

"It stopped being sustainable," I say instead. "I burned out. Came here for a quieter life."

"That seems to be working out well for you."

I laugh despite myself. "Yeah. Not exactly the peaceful slide into retirement I was hoping for."

Isabel almost smiles. Almost.

"Look," I say, "I'm not going to pry. Whatever you're dealing with, whatever you're running from—or running toward—that's your business. But I want you to know that these people aren't your enemy. They're not going to hurt you. And if you need help, they'll give it. No strings attached."

"There are always strings."

"Not here. Not with them." I push off the wall, wincing slightly. "I know it's hard to believe. I didn't believe it either, at first. But the Stoneheart MC takes care of their own. And like it or not, Isabel, you're one of their own now."

"I didn't ask for that."

"Neither did I. And yet here we are."

She stares at me for a long moment. I watch the war playing out behind her eyes—the desperate need to trust someone fighting against years of evidence that trust only leads to pain.

"I can't stay," she finally says. "There's something I have to do. I—" She cuts herself off. "I just can't stay."

She's already moving toward the back door when it opens from the outside.

Tank fills the doorway, arms crossed, expression flat.

"Going somewhere?"

Isabel freezes. For a second, I think she might try to bolt past him—but even she has to know that's suicide. Tank is built like a refrigerator with a bad attitude.

"I need air," she says tightly.

"Get it from a window." He steps aside just enough to let her back into the hallway, then positions himself in front of the door. "Stone's orders. Nobody leaves without an escort."

Isabel's jaw tightens. She shoots me a look—not angry, exactly. More like resigned. Like she's expected this.

"Fine," she mutters, and stalks back toward the guest rooms.

I watch her go, a heaviness settling in my chest.

Tank catches my eye. "Third time today she's tried to rabbit."

I wince.

"Stone's getting twitchy about her. Whole club is." He shakes his head. "Ridgeline crew can't get here fast enough. We need more bodies if we're gonna keep running a daycare for flight risks."

Something has to give, and soon.

STONE

The Ridgeline boys arrive in the early afternoon.

I've been in president mode all morning, following up on calls, logistics, security rotations, and a dozen small fires that needed stomping out. But even with all of it demanding my attention, my mind keeps drifting to Josie.

I found myself walking toward the kitchen more than once, desperately drawn to her laughter as it rang through the house.

I didn't. But God, I wanted to.

Four bikes roll into the lot in formation, engines rumbling in unison, and half the club comes out to meet them. Ginger is practically vibrating beside me, her eyes locked on the massive figure bringing up the rear.

"Bradley!" She's moving before I can stop her, launching herself at her brother like a sequined missile.

Brick catches her easily, swinging her around like she weighs nothing.

He's a beast of a man—easily six-four, built like a Viking who wandered out of a saga and onto a Harley. Wild red hair, darker and curlier than Ginger's, frames a face half-hidden by a beard that looks like it could house a family of birds. His eyes are a startling blue, bright and sharp, and when he grins at his sister, it's wide and wolfish.

He's fifteen years younger than her, just a year or two older than Lee, but you'd never guess Ginger and him were siblings if you didn't catch the matching hair color and the same mischievous glint lurking behind his eyes. They're the same fire in their coloring, but completely different energy. He looks like the kind of man who could crush a skull with his bare hands and then laugh about it over a beer.

"Hey, Ging."

"Look at you! You're too thin. Have you been eating? You look tired. When's the last time you slept properly?" She pulls back, hands on his face, examining him with the critical eye of a mother hen. "And what is this?" She tugs at his beard. "You look like a mountain man. We're trimming this later."

"It's fine, Ginger."

"You're scruffy. " She spots something on his cut and makes a distressed sound. "Is that a stain? Bradley Michael, tell me that's not a mustard stain on your cut."

"It's not a mustard stain."

"It's definitely a mustard stain."

"Then why'd you ask?"

Tank catches my eye from across the lot, his expression clearly saying *told you so*. I bite back a smile.

The other three Ridgeline boys are already being absorbed into the crowd—Reno, Dawson, and Cal.

Reno is lean and wiry, with a shaved head and a jagged scar running from his temple to his jaw that he's never explained. He's got the watchful eyes of a man who's seen too much and the quick hands of someone who learned to fight dirty long before someone taught him the concept of fairness.

Dawson is his opposite—big and broad, with a baby face that makes him look ten years younger than he is. Don't let the soft features fool you; I've seen him put three men through a wall without breaking a sweat.

Cal rounds out the trio—average height, average build, the kind of face you'd forget five minutes after meeting him. Which is exactly what makes him useful. He can blend into a crowd like smoke, be anywhere and everywhere without anyone noticing.

All solid men I've worked with before. Good in a fight, better at following orders. Exactly what we need right now.

"Let's take this inside," I say, raising my voice over the noise. "We've got work to do."

The chapel is quieter than it's been the night before—just me and the Ridgeline crew, getting them up to speed.

I lay out the situation, Summit, Ivan, the attempts on Josie's life, the ongoing threat. The Ridgeline boys listen, nodding and occasionally asking questions.

"We've got surveillance running on every property connected to Summit," I say. "But I've got another job that needs doing. Something more delicate."

"What kind of delicate?" Reno asks.

"There's a woman staying here. Isabel. She saved Josie's life during the hospital attack, which is why she's under our roof." I pause, choosing my words carefully. "But she's off. She keeps trying to run. Won't say where she's going or why. Won't answer questions about her background."

"You think she's a plant?" Brick's voice is low, thoughtful. He's extracted himself from Ginger's clutches and is leaning against the wall, arms crossed, his expression back to unreadable.

"I don't know what she is. That's the problem. Could be she's just a scared girl who stumbled into trouble. Could be Summit positioned her to get close to us." I shrug. "Either way, I need eyes on her. Someone to tail her if she runs again, see where she goes, who she talks to."

"I'll do it."

I look at Brick. "You sure? Could be boring work. Lot of sitting around, watching, waiting."

"I'm patient."

"Alright." I pull out my phone, bring up the photo we've taken when Isabel first arrived—standard procedure for anyone new in the clubhouse. "This is her."

I hand the phone to Brick.

He studies the screen for a long moment. His mouth curves into a half-smile.

"Well, shit." He zooms in slightly, tilts his head. "Not exactly a hardship, watching this one." He lets out a low whistle. "Would you look at the tits on her."

Reno snorts. "Trust you to notice that."

"What? I've got eyes, don't I?" Brick hands the phone back, still wearing that half-smile. "Alright, Prez. I'll babysit your mystery girl. She runs, I'll follow. She meets with anyone suspicious, you'll know about it."

"And if she is a plant?"

The smile fades, a cold grin takes its place.

"I'll handle it."

I nod. "Good. But Brick—don't underestimate her. She took out a full-grown man with a bedpan. Whatever else she is, she's not helpless."

"Noted." He pushes off the wall, rolling his shoulders. "Where is she now?"

"Guest room, second floor. Tried to rabbit three times. Tank and the prospects have been running interference, but we can't keep that up forever."

"I'll find a position. Keep eyes on her without spooking her." He heads for the door, then pauses. "Stone. What if she's not a plant? What if she's just... someone in trouble?"

I think about Josie's words. *She's not scared for herself. She's scared for someone else.*

"I owe her a debt for saving Josie. But we need to know which side she's on."

Brick nods once and leaves.

I turn back to the others. "Reno, Dawson—you're on rotation for Josie's protection detail. She's in the guest room upstairs. No one gets to her without going through you first."

"Got it."

"Cal, I need you on surveillance support. Bones is running point—he'll get you up to speed on what we're tracking."

"Done."

"Any questions?"

Heads shake.

"Then let's get to work."

The rest of the day is consumed with logistics—coordinating the new arrivals, updating patrol schedules, checking in with Bones about his latest intel on Summit's operations.

Around 4 PM, my phone buzzes.

> BRICK
>
> She's getting antsy. Pacing her room.
> Won't be long now.

I type back.

> STONE
>
> Stay on her. Let me know if she moves.

> BRICK
>
> Copy.

I stare at the phone for a moment, wondering what Isabel is planning—and whether we'll like the answer when we find it.

Josie finds me in the hallway an hour later, moving slowly but stubbornly under her own power.

I'm moving toward her before I realize I'm doing it, closing the distance between us like she's a magnet and I'm helpless to resist.

"You're supposed to be resting," I say, stopping just short of touching her.

"I've been resting. I'm rested. I'm sick of resting." She plants herself in front of me, attempting to cross her arms with the cast—then winces and uncrosses them, probably because the movement hurts her ribs. "What's happening? I heard the bikes earlier."

"Ridgeline's here. Four men, including Ginger's brother."

"The famous Brick?"

"In the flesh." I can't help the slight smile. "Ginger's already on his case. Something about trimming his beard and fixing a mustard stain."

Josie's mouth twitches. "Poor guy."

"He'll survive. He always does." I study her face—still too pale, still showing the strain of the past few days. "How are you feeling?"

"Not great. My ribs hurt, my head aches, the holes are fucking weird, I'm not loving the shaved patches on my head, my cast is uncomfortable, the stitches itch, and I'm grumpy. So, you know. A Tuesday."

"It's Saturday."

"Whatever." She waves a hand dismissively. "What's happening with Isabel?"

"Brick's watching her. If she runs again, he'll follow. See where she goes."

"And then?"

"And then we'll know more than we do now."

She sways slightly, and I reach out without thinking—my hand finding her hip, steadying her against me.

She goes still. Her breath catches, just for a second, and her good hand comes up to grip my forearm.

We stand like that for a beat too long. Her eyes meet mine, and I see it—the flicker of interest she's trying to hide. She's not as immune to this as she pretends to be.

Thank fucking God.

She clears her throat, letting my arm go and stepping back. "Now, if you'll excuse me, I need to go lie down before Maggie catches me out of bed and gives me another lecture about concussion protocols."

"Need help getting back to your room?"

"I think I can manage ten feet of hallway on my own, thanks."

"It includes stairs."

She shrugs. "I'll crawl if I have to."

"Offer stands."

"Noted. Declined. Good day, sir."

She turns and shuffles back toward the guest room, one hand trailing along the wall for balance. I watch her go, an ache expanding in my chest.

That woman is going to be the death of me.

My phone buzzes again.

> BRICK
>
> She's on the move. Bathroom window.

Shit.

I type back.

> STONE
>
> Don't engage unless necessary. Take a car—if she's headed somewhere specific, I want you mobile.

BRICK

Already on it.

I stare at the phone, wondering what Brick might find—
and whether we'll like the answer when we get it.

8

JOSIE

Three hours after Isabel disappears out the bathroom window, I'm going out of my mind.

Not because of Isabel—though that's part of it. Brick is tracking her, Stone has people on alert, and there's nothing I can do from here except worry.

No, the real problem is simpler and more infuriating.

I'm bored.

The clubhouse is full of people doing things—important things, urgent things—and I'm stuck on this couch like a decorative pillow, forbidden from working, forbidden from helping, forbidden from doing anything except resting.

I *hate* resting.

Maggie has confiscated my laptop. Ginger has hidden my phone charger. Emma has cheerfully threatened to sit on me if I try to get up again. The Stoneheart MC women have formed a unified front against my productivity, and they're terrifyingly effective.

So I sit. And I stew. And I watch the clock tick by, minute by agonizing minute.

I'm so bored I decide to call my parents and tell them about the crash. In unsurprising news, they send me to voicemail. About half an hour later my mother sends a text.

MOTHER

Thinking of you, sweetheart. Get well soon!

My father follows up an hour later asking if this would affect my billable hours. Neither of them offered to come. But I expected nothing different.

By 5 PM, I've memorized every crack in the ceiling. By 6 PM, I've counted the bottles behind the bar (forty-seven). By 7 PM, I'm seriously considering making a break for it, broken ribs be damned.

That's when Stone finds me.

He appears in the doorway looking like he's been running on caffeine and willpower for the past several hours. His hair is disheveled, his jaw shadowed with stubble, and there's a tension in his shoulders that wasn't there this morning.

He looks exhausted, stressed, and unfairly, devastatingly attractive.

My stupid heart does a little stutter-step in my chest, and I have to look away for a second before I can trust my face not to give me away.

Get it together, Bright.

"You look like you're plotting," he says.

"I'm plotting your murder. It's keeping me entertained."

"Should I be worried?"

"Only if you keep me trapped here much longer." I shift on the couch, wincing as my ribs protest. "Any news on Isabel?"

"Brick tracked her to a house on the east side of town. He's watching but hasn't made contact yet."

"Why not?"

"Because she went inside and hasn't come out. He's waiting to see what happens."

A house. Back to whoever—or whatever—she's been so desperate to reach.

"You should let me talk to her again. When she comes back."

"If she comes back."

"She will." I don't know why I'm so certain, but I am. "Whatever she went there for, she's not the type to run forever. She'll be back."

Stone studies me for a moment, then crosses the room and sits on the coffee table facing me. Close. Too close. I can smell him again—that distracting combination of leather and soap that makes my brain go fuzzy.

"How are you feeling?" he asks.

"Fine."

"Josie."

"I said I'm fine."

"You've been sitting in that exact position for three hours because it hurts too much to move."

Damn. He's more observant than I've given him credit for.

"It's not that bad."

"Your face says otherwise."

"My face is a liar. Don't trust it."

His mouth twitches. "When's the last time you took your pain meds?"

I don't answer, which is answer enough.

"Josie."

"They make me fuzzy. I can't think straight on them."

"That's the point. You're supposed to be resting, not thinking."

"I don't know how to not think. It's a design flaw."

He sighs, and for a moment he looks tired. Not the surface-level tired of a long day, but the deep, bone-weary exhaustion of a man carrying too much for too long.

"You're going to hurt yourself," he says quietly. "Pushing like this. Your body needs time to heal."

"I've survived worse."

"That's not the flex you think it is."

I open my mouth to argue, but his expression stops me. He isn't annoyed or frustrated. He's worried. Genuinely, deeply worried—about me.

It's been a long time since anyone has worried about me like that.

"Stone—"

"Just take the damn pills, Josie. Please. For me."

For me. Two words that shouldn't mean anything and somehow mean everything.

"Fine," I mutter. "But I reserve the right to complain about it."

"I'd expect nothing less."

He hands me the pill bottle from the side table and watches while I swallow two tablets with a grimace. The effects won't kick in for another twenty minutes, but the knot in my chest loosens. It's not the pills—just the act of giving in. Of letting someone else carry the weight for a moment.

"Happy now?" I ask.

"Getting there."

"What else do you want? A blood sacrifice? My firstborn child?"

"Just one more thing."

"What?"

He stands, and before I can process what's happening, he's scooped me up off the couch—carefully, mindful of my ribs and cast, but with a firmness that brooks no argument.

"Stone! What the hell—"

"You need to sleep."

"I've been sleeping!"

"You've been lying awake staring at the ceiling. That's not the same thing." He's already moving down the hallway, carrying me like I weigh nothing. "You need rest. In an actual bed. Away from distractions."

"I'm not tired—"

"You're exhausted. You're just too stubborn to admit it."

"Put me down—"

"No."

"This is ridiculous—"

"Probably."

"I'm a grown woman, I can walk—"

"Your ribs are broken in three places. You're not walking anywhere."

I sputter, but he ignores me, shouldering open the door to the guest room and depositing me on the bed with surprising gentleness.

"There," he says. "Was that so hard?"

"I hate you."

"No, you don't."

"I actively, passionately hate you."

"Still no." He sits on the edge of the bed, looking down at me with an expression I can't quite read. "Close your eyes."

"I'm not tired."

"Close them anyway."

"Stone—"

"Josie." His voice softens. "Please. Just try."

I want to keep arguing. Want to prove that I'm fine, that I don't need to be coddled, that I'm perfectly capable of managing my own recovery.

But the pills are starting to kick in, spreading warmth through my limbs, and the bed is soft, and Stone is looking at me with those gray eyes that see too much, and I'm so, so tired.

"Fine," I mumble. "But I'm not going to sleep. I'm just going to rest my eyes."

"Whatever you say."

I close my eyes. The darkness is immediate, welcoming, pulling me down toward the soft, quiet bliss of sleep.

I hear Stone move—the creak of leather, the thud of boots hitting the floor.

My eyes fly open. "What are you doing?"

"Making sure you stay put." He stretches out on the bed beside me, on top of the covers, one arm folded behind his head. The mattress dips under his weight, and suddenly he's *right there*—warm and solid and close enough that I can smell leather and soap.

"Stone—"

"Close your eyes, Josie."

"This is—"

"Rest."

I should argue. This is inappropriate and unnecessary. I absolutely don't need a babysitter. But the warmth of him beside me is testing my resolve, and the pills are dragging me under, and I'm so tired of fighting everything all the time.

"Fine," I whisper. "But I'm not going to sleep."

"Whatever you say."

I close my eyes again. The darkness pulls me down, soft and welcoming.

The last thing I feel before sleep claims me is his hand finding mine on the blanket, his fingers intertwining with mine.

I don't pull away.

~

I wake to the smell of leather and the sound of steady breathing.

For a moment, I'm disoriented. The light has changed—it's late evening—and my body feels heavy and loose, the pain meds still working their way through my system.

Then I register the warmth beside me.

Stone.

He's lying on top of the covers next to me, still fully dressed, one arm behind his head. His eyes are closed, his breathing even, the hard lines of his face softened by sleep.

He's stayed.

I lie there, frozen, not sure what to do. He's right there —close enough to touch, close enough that I can see the individual threads of silver in his hair, the faint stubble along his jaw, the slight part of his lips as he breathes.

He stayed.

The thought keeps circling, picking up weight with each repetition. He could have left. Should have left. He has a club to run, a crisis to manage, a dozen things more important than watching me sleep.

But he's stayed.

I let myself look at him. The strong line of his nose. The crow's feet at the corners of his eyes, earned through years of squinting into the sun and, I suspect, the occasional genuine smile. The silver threaded through his dark hair, more distinguished than aging.

You're in trouble, Bright.

As if sensing my gaze, his eyes open, catching me staring.

"Hey," he says softly, his voice rough with sleep.

"Hey."

"Sleep okay?"

"Yeah." I swallow hard. "You stayed."

"Someone had to make sure you napped." His eyes hold mine, warm and steady. "I meant it."

My chest cracks open. A wall I've been carefully maintaining for weeks, months, years—crumbling under the weight of this man and his quiet, stubborn care.

"Stone..."

"You were having nightmares."

I blink. "I was?"

"You kept making these sounds like you were scared." His jaw tightens. "I didn't want to leave you alone with that."

The dreams come back in fragments. Fire. Screaming. A little boy's hand slipping out of mine.

"Maria," I say quietly. "Daniel, her brother. And their mother, Kalisha."

"Who are they?"

The question hangs in the air between us. I could deflect. Make a joke. Change the subject. I've gotten good at that over the years—keeping the ugly parts of myself locked away where no one can see them.

But I'm so tired of carrying this alone.

I stare at the ceiling, not trusting myself to look at him. My throat tightens around the words, but I force them out anyway.

"People I promised to protect. Back in Atlanta there was a witness, Maria. We had a big case, and she was the star witness. I promised her she'd be safe if she testified. And then—" My voice cracks. "Car bomb. The night before she was supposed to take the stand."

"That wasn't your fault."

"I made promises I couldn't keep. She trusted me, and I got her killed." The words taste like ash. "Her and her mother and her seven-year-old brother. A little boy named Daniel who wanted to be a firefighter when he grew up. Who drew me a picture of a fire truck the last time I saw him."

"Josie—"

"I still have it. The picture." I laugh, but there's nothing funny about it. "It's hanging in my office. Some kind of penance, I guess. A reminder of what happens when I let people down."

Stone is quiet for a long moment. Then his hand finds mine on the blanket, his fingers intertwining with mine.

"You didn't let them down," he says. "The people who planted that bomb are evil. The system that couldn't protect them let them down. You were trying to get justice for victims. That's not something to be ashamed of."

"Tell that to Daniel."

"I would, if I could. I'd tell him his death wasn't your fault. That you did everything you could. That you carry him with you every day because you cared, not because you failed."

My eyes burn. I blink hard, refusing to cry.

"You don't know that."

"I know you." His thumb traces circles on the back of my hand. "I've watched you work for months. The way you prepare for every contingency, triple-check every detail, fight like hell for people who can't fight for themselves. You're not careless, Josie. You're not reckless. Whatever happened in Atlanta, it wasn't because you didn't try hard enough."

"Then why does it still feel like my fault?"

"Because you're human. Because you care. Because the alternative—not feeling anything, not taking responsibility—would mean becoming someone you aren't."

I turn my head to look at him. He's watching me with an expression I can't quite name. Tender. Understanding. Like he knows exactly what it feels like to carry guilt you can't put down.

"What about you?" I ask. "What keeps you up at night?"

He's quiet for a moment. "The club. Summit. Lee. Emma." He hesitates. "Rebecca, my ex-wife."

"What happened?"

"I drove her away. I put the club first. She stayed longer than she should have—for Emma, mostly, we all know Lee would have been fine—but she saw her out when Emma got accepted to that fancy New York dance school." His jaw tightens. "When she finally left, she told me I didn't know how to love anything more than this club. That maybe I never had."

The words hit me harder than I expect. I try to imagine Stone young, in love, watching his wife walk away. Tried to imagine Emma and Lee, caught in the middle.

"Do you believe that?"

I hold my breath, bracing for the answer. Part of me needs him to say no. Part of me is terrified he'll say yes— that he'll confirm what I've been afraid of all along. That he's not capable of putting anyone first, that I'd always come second.

Haven't I always?

"I used to." His eyes meet mine. "Now I'm not so sure."

My heart stumbles.

The air between us shifts. Charged. I'm suddenly very aware of how close we are, how warm his hand feels wrapped around mine, how his thumb has stilled against my skin.

"Stone—"

"I was an idiot," he says quietly. "At the party. When I pulled back. I wasn't lying when I said I wanted you—I've wanted you for months. But I was worried I'd fuck this up."

"You wouldn't."

"I have with nearly everything else. My marriage. My relationship with Emma, for years. Every woman who's tried to get close to me since Rebecca left." He laughs, but there's no humor in it. "I've got a pattern, Josie. Push people away before they can leave."

I know that pattern. I've lived it.

"And now?"

"Now you almost died, and I realized safe doesn't mean shit if it means spending the rest of my life wondering what could have been."

My breath catches. My pulse is pounding so hard I'm sure he can feel it through our joined hands.

I search his face for the lie, for the equivocation, for the inevitable moment when he'll pull back again.

I don't find it.

Fuck. I have to decide if I'm brave enough to want him too.

"I'm scared," I admit. "I've been alone for so long, I don't know how to be anything else."

"We could figure it out together."

"Could we?"

"I'd like to try." His hand comes up to cup my face, his thumb tracing along my cheekbone. "If you'll let me."

My heart is pounding so hard I'm sure he can hear it. His face is inches from mine, his breath warm on my lips, his eyes asking a question I'm not sure I know how to answer.

"Stone..."

"Tell me to stop," he murmurs. "If you don't want this. Tell me to stop and I will."

I don't want him to stop. That's the terrifying part. I want him to close the distance, to kiss me, to make good on every heated look and charged moment of the past months.

I want him. And that wanting scares me more than anything.

"I don't want you to stop," I whisper.

His eyes flare—heat, relief, hunger. His hand slides from my cheek into my hair, tilting my head back, and he leans in.

His lips brush mine. Soft. Questioning. A kiss that's barely a kiss, giving me every opportunity to pull away.

I don't pull away.

I kiss him back.

He makes a sound low in his throat—surprise, maybe, or relief—and then the gentleness evaporates. His mouth claims mine, hot and demanding, and I open for him without thinking, my good hand fisting in his shirt, pulling him closer.

He tastes like coffee and something darker, something that makes my head spin in ways that have nothing to do with the concussion. His tongue sweeps against mine, and I gasp, and he swallows the sound, one hand cradling my head while the other slides down to my hip.

"Josie," he breathes against my mouth. "God, Josie—"

I arch into him—and immediately regret it as fire lances through my ribs.

"Shit—" I hiss, pulling back.

"Your ribs. Fuck. I'm sorry—" He starts to pull away, but I grab his shirt, hold him in place.

"Don't you dare apologize." I'm breathing hard, which hurts, but I don't care. "Just... be gentle. For now."

For now. The words hang between us, heavy with promise.

Stone's eyes darken. "For now?"

"Did I stutter?"

He groans, dropping his forehead to mine. "You're going to kill me."

"That's the plan."

He laughs and the sound sends delicious shivers down my spine. He kisses me again, softer this time, careful of my injuries but no less intense.

His hand traces up my side, feather-light, and I shiver. His mouth leaves mine, trailing down my jaw, my neck, finding the spot below my ear that makes me gasp—

BANG BANG BANG.

The bedroom door shudders under someone's fist.

"Stone!" Hawk calls urgently. "Brick called in. Something's going down at that house. Sounds bad—he's requesting a clean up crew."

Stone's forehead drops to my shoulder. I feel the groan vibrate through his entire body.

"I'm going to kill him," he mutters.

"What house?" I ask, my brain still foggy. "What's going on?"

Stone pulls back, and I watch the president slide into place, locking down everything we've just shared. "Isabel. She must have slipped out. Brick followed her."

Isabel.

The fog clears instantly, replaced by a cold spike of fear. Whatever she was running back to—whoever she was so desperate to reach—it's caught up with her.

I'm already pushing myself upright, ignoring the scream of my ribs. "I'm coming with—"

"No." Stone's hand presses me back down, firm but gentle. "You can barely walk. You'd be a liability."

He's right. I hate that he's right.

"Then bring her back safe." I grip his wrist. "Whatever's happening—she's not the enemy, Stone. She's a victim. Promise me you'll remember that."

His jaw tightens, but he nods. "I promise."

"Stone—"

"I'll be back." He presses a hard, fast kiss to my mouth. "And when I am, we're finishing this conversation."

I relax. "Conversation? Is that what we're calling it?"

He's already moving toward the door, but he pauses with his hand on the knob, looking back at me with an expression that makes my stomach flip. "Next time, I'm locking the door and ignoring them. I don't care if the goddamned house is burning down around us."

"Promise?"

"Promise."

Then he's gone, and I'm left staring at the ceiling, heart racing, lips tingling, torn between the ghost of his kiss and the fear gnawing at my chest.

Be safe, Isabel.

9

BRICK

The girl is going to be a problem.

I knew it from the second Stone showed me her picture—all sharp cheekbones and wary eyes. She's the kind of pretty that comes with complications.

I'm parked three houses down from a shithole on the west side of Stoneheart, watching that same girl walk into what I'm pretty sure is going to be a disaster.

She moved fast once she hit the ground outside that bathroom window—faster than I expected. Cutting through yards, doubling back, taking routes that say she's done this before. I almost lost her twice, and I don't lose people.

Who are you, Isabel? And what the hell is in that house?

I drum my fingers on the steering wheel of the club sedan. As much as I hate being in a cage—it's far less conspicuous than the loud rumble of my bike.

The place looks abandoned. Peeling paint, sagging porch, lawn that hasn't seen a mower since the Clinton administration. The kind of house where bad things happen and nobody asks questions.

Isabel circled around to the back, checked the windows, then slipped inside like a ghost.

That was twenty minutes ago.

I text it in then wait. And wait. And wait some more.

It's growing dark when headlights sweep across the street.

A beat-up truck pulls into the driveway, engine rattling before it cuts off. The driver's door swings open, and a big man stumbles out—mid-forties, ruddy face, the swollen nose of a serious drinker. He moves around to the passenger side and yanks open the door.

"Get out," he barks. "And stop your sniveling."

A small figure climbs down from the truck. A little girl, maybe five or six, clutching a worn stuffed rabbit to her chest. Even from here, I can see she's been crying.

Jesus Christ.

The man grabs the girl's arm—too rough, way too rough —and hauls her toward the house. "Inside. Now. And if I hear one more word about your sister, I'll give you something to cry about."

Sister. Isabel's her sister.

Son of a bitch.

That's why she was so desperate to get back. Not a boyfriend. Not drugs. Not some shady deal. A kid. A little sister trapped in this hellhole.

Well, I feel like a fucking dick.

They disappear inside. Lights flicker on.

A dog starts barking somewhere nearby. Loud. Insistent.

The front door bangs open again.

"Shut that fucking mutt up!" the man bellows toward the neighbors house. He stomps down the porch steps, weaving slightly, and heads across the yard toward the source of the noise.

I'm out of the car before I consciously decide to move.

I work my way through the shadows until I find the side door and ease it open, staying quiet. The house hits me with the stench of stale beer, cigarette smoke, and neglect. It's the sour smell of a place where hope died a long time ago.

I'm far too familiar with the scent.

From somewhere upstairs, I hear voices that are soft and urgent.

"Izzy!" A child's whisper, thick with tears. "Why did you leave for so long? I was scared."

"Shh, baby. I know. I'm sorry. I'm here now. I'm going to get you out, okay? We're leaving. Right now."

"Is Daddy going to be mad?"

"Daddy's not going to know. We're going to be quiet, like mice. Like we practiced, remember? Can you do that for me?"

"Like mice," the little girl repeats.

"Good girl. Now grab Mr. Flopsy and your purple shirt. We have to be fast."

I move to the bottom of the stairs, pressing myself against the wall. Through the front window, I can see the stepfather still at the neighbors fence, gesturing angrily, his voice carrying across the yard.

Hurry up, Isabel. He's not going to be distracted forever.

Drawers open and close upstairs. Soft footsteps. The rustle of clothes being shoved into a bag.

"What about my princess cup?" the little girl asks.

"We'll get you a new one. I promise. But we have to go *now*, Lily."

"Okay."

The neighbors door slams and the dog stops barking.

Silence.

I can hear his cursing as he stomps back toward the house.

Fuck.

I duck back to the windows, hiding my massive form behind a curtain.

It's not perfect, but it'll do in a pinch.

"Izzy," the little voice trembles. "Izzy, he's coming back."

"I know, baby. I know. Come on, we'll go out the back—"

The front door crashes open.

"ISABEL!"

The roar shakes the walls. I hear the little girl scream, hear Isabel shushing her, hear footsteps pounding up the stairs.

"You think I'm fucking stupid?" His voice is closer now, climbing. "Think I don't know you've been sneaking around? The Duncans saw you creeping through their yard!"

"Lily, hide. In the closet, like we practiced. Don't come out no matter what."

"But Izzy—"

"*Do it!*"

A door creaks, and I hear Isabel's voice, steady despite the looming threat. "Leave her alone. I'm the one you want. Let me take her and we'll go. You'll never see either of us again."

A bark of ugly laughter. "Let you take her? She's *mine*. My blood. You think I'm gonna let some ungrateful little bitch steal what belongs to me?"

"She doesn't belong to anyone. She's a *child*—"

The crack of flesh on flesh. A cry of pain.

White-hot fury floods my veins.

I'm moving, pounding across the room toward the stairs.

"You always thought you were better than me," he snarls. Another blow lands. "Too good for this family. Running off to that hospital, making me look like a fool—"

"I fell down the stairs." Isabel's voice is thick, wet. "That's what you told everyone, isn't it? That's what you *always* tell everyone—"

Another crack. She cries out.

My jaw locks so tight I feel my teeth creak. My vision narrows to a single red point. Every muscle in my body is screaming for violence—the kind of violence I've spent years burying, years pretending I outgrew.

I'm going to kill the fucker.

I hit the top of the stairs.

He's standing over her, massive and mean, fist raised for another blow. Isabel is on the floor, arms protecting her head, blood streaming from her nose. The closet door is cracked open an inch—a small, terrified eye peering through.

My chest cracks open, bleeding from a wound that's decades deep.

I know what it's like to be small and helpless, watching violence unfold and praying you stay invisible. Know what it feels like to hold your breath so long your lungs burn, to make yourself as small as possible, to pray that this time—*this time*—it won't be your turn.

And I know Isabel too. Know what it costs to put yourself between a monster and someone you love. Know the particular kind of courage it takes to stand up when you know you're going to lose.

The rage that floods through me is cold. Controlled. The kind of anger that doesn't burn hot and fast—it freezes everything down to a single, crystal-clear purpose.

He's never going to touch either of them again.

"Hey, fuck head."

He spins. His eyes go wide when he sees me—all six-four of me filling the hallway.

"Who the fuck—"

I don't let him finish.

~

ISABEL

The blows stop.

There's a crash. A grunt. Something heavy hits the wall.

I lift my head, vision blurry, and see—

A man. He's huge. Bigger than my stepfather, Jared. Bigger than anyone I've ever seen. He has wild red hair and a beard like some kind of Game of Thrones character, with shoulders broad enough to block out the hallway light.

He pins Jared against the wall by his throat, lifting him until his feet kick uselessly.

Jared's face is turning purple. His eyes bulge. His hands claw uselessly at the stranger's grip.

Good.

The thought should horrify me. It doesn't. I watch him struggle and I feel nothing but cold, vicious satisfaction. After everything he's done—to me, to Lily, to our mother before she died—he deserves every second of this.

I've never seen our hero before in my life. But I think I might marry him.

"Get your sister." The man tells me, his voice calm. Terrifyingly so. "I own the black sedan down the street. Keys are in it. Go and take her there."

I can't move.

"Now."

The command cuts through my shock. I scramble up, everything screaming in protest, and stumble to the closet.

"Lily. Baby. We have to go."

She launches into my arms. I hold her despite the fire in my shoulder, the blood on my face.

"Don't look," I tell her, pressing her face to my neck. "Eyes closed. Hold on."

I carry her past the stranger and my stepfather —past the

choking sounds I can't bring myself to care about. Down the stairs. Through the living room. Out the front door.

The night air hits me like salvation.

The sedan is where he's said. I get Lily into the backseat, climb in beside her, holding her while she sobs.

"It's okay," I whisper. "We're safe now."

I don't know if it's true. I don't know who that man is or why he's saved us or what comes next.

But Lily is in my arms, and we're out of that house, and for now, that's enough.

BRICK

I wait until I hear the front door close.

Then I give this fucker my full attention.

I let go of his throat. He drops to the floor, gasping, scrambling backward until he hits the wall.

"Please—" he starts.

I don't let him finish.

My fist connects with his face—once, twice, three times. His nose breaks on the second hit, blood spraying across my knuckles. He tries to curl up, protect himself, but I grab him by the shirt and haul him up, slam him against the wall again.

"That's for her face," I say.

I drive my knee into his gut. He doubles over, retching.

"That's for every hit you just landed."

I let him fall. Then I kick him—hard—in the side. Once. Twice. Again. Every bruise I saw on Isabel's face, I give back double.

He's sobbing now. Begging. Curled on the floor in a puddle of his own blood and piss, hands raised like they can stop me.

They can't.

I crouch down, grab a fistful of his hair, and force him to look at me.

"That little girl was hiding in a fucking closet." My voice is cold as ice. "Shaking. Terrified. Because of *you*."

I slam his head against the floor. Not hard enough to kill. Just hard enough to ring his bell for a week. Or three.

"They're mine now." I let that sink in. "They belong to me and the Stoneheart MC. You don't touch them. You don't look for them. You don't even think about them."

"They're my family—" he slurs through broken teeth.

"No." I stand up. "They're not. Not anymore."

I kick him one more time in the groin. I want him to feel it every time he pisses for the next month.

He curls in on himself, screaming. I glare down at the pathetic, broken mess on the floor and spit in his face.

"If you come looking for them, I'll finish what I started."

I walk out without looking back.

ISABEL

The driver's door opens and the stranger slides in—giving me my first real look at him. My initial impression was correct, he's massive. Six-four at least, with shoulders that barely fit behind the wheel.

His knuckles are split and bleeding.

He starts the engine and pulls away without a word.

I don't know his name. Don't know why he's been there. Don't know anything except that he's walked into that house and done what I've tried to do for six years.

We drive in silence. Lily has cried herself out, her face pressed against my chest.

Then she stirs.

"Izzy?" Her voice is tiny. "Where's Mr. Flopsy?"

My heart cracks.

The go-bag. I've had it—upstairs, before everything went wrong. Lily's clothes, the money I've saved, her toy rabbit. I must have dropped it when he—

"Baby, I'm so sorry. I lost—"

Something lands on the seat beside me.

It's Lily's backpack, the worn purple canvas bulging—filled far fuller than I originally packed it.

"Dig in, kid," the stranger says.

Lily sits up and unzips the bag, gasping.

"Mr. Flopsy!" She pulls out the worn rabbit, clutching it like a lifeline. "Izzy, he got Mr. Flopsy! And my purple shirt! And my crayons! Look! My princess cup!"

I stare at the bag. The slowly lift my gaze to the rearview mirror, where dark eyes meet mine.

He'd not only rescued us, he'd been thoughtful enough to grab a six-year-old's stuffed rabbit.

My eyes burn.

I can't speak. Can't find words for what I'm feeling.

So I just look at him in the mirror and mouth two words.

"Thank you."

He jerks his chin up. Once in acknowledgment. Then he turns his eyes back to the road.

We don't speak for the rest of the drive. Don't need to.

Lily falls asleep against my shoulder, Mr. Flopsy clutched in her arms. I watch the streetlights pass, one after another, carrying us away from everything I've known.

I don't know where we're going. Don't know what comes next.

I touch Mr. Flopsy's ear, my mind going blank as he drives through the streets of Stoneheart.

The Stoneheart MC clubhouse appears in the distance. Lights blazing, people spilling out the front door.

The stranger pulls into the lot and kills the engine.

Fuck, he's a biker.

I don't know what to do with this information.

"Ready?" he asks.

First word he's spoken since *dig in, kid.*

I look at the crowd—strangers, all of them, waiting for us. Look at Lily, still sleeping. Look at my own reflection in the window—bruised, bloody, broken.

These are the people who came for us when no one else did.

"No," I admit.

"But you'll do it anyway?"

I gesture at Lily. "I have to. For her, right?"

He nods like that's the right answer. I stay put as he gets out and opens my door, offers his hand.

I take it.

His grip is warm and steady, and when he helps me out of the car, he doesn't let go until I find my footing.

Then a woman is rushing toward us—small, blonde, wearing enough sequins to blind someone.

Ginger.

She's already tried to mother me since I've been here, so I

brace, expecting her to run to me. Instead, she throws herself at the stranger.

"Bradley! Oh my god, your hands! Is that blood? Whose blood is that?"

Bradley.

So that's his name.

"I'm fine, Ging," he says, but his eyes flick to me. Making sure I'm still standing.

I am. Barely.

Another woman appears—older, with kind eyes and capable hands. "Let's get you inside, honey."

I pull back, turning to bend down and gather my sleeping sister into my arms.

Lily stirs as I pick her up "Izzy? Where are we?"

I look at the clubhouse. At the people gathering around us. At the stranger named Bradley, who's packed a rabbit for a little girl he's never met, but who he knew would need it.

"Somewhere safe."

10

JOSIE

I hear them before I see them.

The rumble of an engine, voices in the parking lot, then the front door opening and a rush of activity that pulls me off the bed and downstairs before I can think better of it.

My ribs scream. I ignore them.

Ginger's voice is high and worried. "Oh my god. Oh my god, Bradley, what happened? Is that blood? Whose blood is that?"

"Seriously, I'm fine, Ging. It's not mine."

"It's on your hands! It's all over your hands!"

"I said I'm fine."

I reach the main room just as they come through the door.

Brick is first—massive, impassive, his knuckles split and bloody. Behind him, supported by Maggie's arm around her waist, is Isabel.

I barely recognize her.

Her face is a mess of fresh bruises, one eye already swelling shut. Blood mats her hair on one side, and she moves like every step costs her. But her arms are locked tight around a small figure pressed against her chest.

A child. A little girl with dark hair and huge eyes, clutching a stuffed rabbit like her life depends on it.

My stomach drops. My hand flies to my mouth before I can stop it.

Oh God. Oh, Isabel.

This is what she was running back to. This is why she was so desperate, why she couldn't stay, why she fought Stone so hard on that one-night deal. Not stubbornness. Not secrets. A little sister trapped in a house with a monster.

And I let her go alone.

Guilt twists in my chest, sharp and ugly. I should have pushed harder. Should have seen past my own pain and exhaustion to what she was hiding. I'm a goddamn lawyer—I'm supposed to read people. I'm supposed to help.

Instead, I was tangled up in Stone while she walked back into hell.

"Oh my god," I breathe.

Isabel's gaze finds mine across the room. Something passes between us—recognition, understanding.

This is what I was protecting. This is why I couldn't stay, she seems to say.

"Josie." Stone appears beside me, his hand on my arm. "You should be in bed."

"Later." I shake him off, already moving forward. "What do you need? What can I do?"

"She needs a doctor," Brick says. His voice is flat, but his eyes track Isabel's every movement. "The kid needs food and a bed."

"We can do that." Maggie is already in motion. "Ginger, get my kit. Emma, see if we have anything a child would eat. If not, run across the street and grab something from Andi. Kya—towels and blankets."

The clubhouse erupts into organized chaos. Women moving with purpose, men clearing space, everyone falling into roles like they've done this a hundred times before.

I find a spot against the wall, out of the way but close enough to watch.

Isabel has been deposited on the couch, Maggie working on her injuries with quick, efficient hands. She hasn't let go of Lily—the little girl is curled in her lap, face buried against her chest, the rabbit clutched between them.

"This is going to sting," Maggie warns, dabbing at a cut on Isabel's forehead.

Isabel doesn't flinch. Just holds Lily tighter.

"The ribs?" Maggie asks.

"I've had worse."

"That's not comforting, honey."

Emma appears with a plate—peanut butter sandwich, apple slices, a glass of milk. She crouches down next to the couch, her voice soft.

"Hey there, sweetheart. Are you hungry?"

Lily peeks out from Isabel's chest. Her eyes are red, her cheeks tear-stained, but she looks at the sandwich with obvious longing.

"It's okay, baby," Isabel murmurs. "You can eat."

Lily hesitates. Then she reaches out and takes an apple slice, nibbling it like a little mouse.

Emma smiles. "There's more where that came from. As much as you want."

"Really?"

"Really. And chocolate chip cookies, if you're good."

Lily's eyes go wide. She looks up at Isabel for confirmation.

"She's telling the truth," Isabel says. "These people— they're nice. They're going to help us."

It's the first time I've heard her say anything positive about... well, anything. It makes my throat tighten.

Whatever Brick has done—whatever happened in that house—Isabel isn't fighting anymore.

She's letting people in.

I watch her smooth Lily's hair back, watch the way she leans into Maggie's steady presence instead of pulling away. This is what it looks like when someone finally feels safe. When the weight they've been carrying alone gets shared.

I hate that it took this much to get her there. Hate that she had to be beaten bloody before she could accept that not everyone is a threat. Hate that somewhere out there, a man is still breathing after doing this to her.

But she's here now. She and her sister are safe.

Thank God.

STONE

I find Brick in the garage, running water over his hands.

The blood swirls down the drain—his and someone else's, mixed together. His knuckles are raw, split in several places. He's done some damage tonight.

Good.

"How bad?" I ask.

"She'll live. Ribs might be cracked, lot of bruising. Head wound looks worse than it is." He doesn't look up from his hands. His voice is flat, clinical, like he's giving a report, not talking about a girl who was nearly beaten to death.

But I can see it's affected him. Water runs red over his hands, then pink, then clear, but his fingers stay curled, knuckles rigid. His jaw is set hard enough to ache, his eyes dark and shuttered.

"She's been through worse," he mutters, his frown deepening. "You can tell by the way she takes a hit."

My jaw tightens. "What was the situation?

"Stepfather wailing on the both of them, I suspect."

"Is the kid hers?"

He shakes his head. "Her sister, I think."

I nod, filing that away. "And the dad?"

"Alive." Brick turns off the water, grabs a rag. "Not happy about it. But alive."

"Blow back?"

He glances up, his gaze ice cold. "If he comes sniffing around, he knows the consequences."

The way he says it tells me everything I need to know.

"She's ours now. Both of them. You understand?"

"I told him the same thing." Brick's eyes meet mine. "Right before I broke his ribs."

"Good."

He goes back to drying his hands, methodical, thorough. But there's a tremor in his fingers that wasn't there before. A tightness around his eyes that has nothing to do with the fight.

I've known Brick for years. Watched him walk into firefights without flinching, take bullets without complaint, put down threats with cold efficiency. I've never seen him rattled.

He's rattled now.

Whatever he saw in that house—whatever memories it dragged up—it got under his skin.

I don't ask. He wouldn't answer if I did. Best I can do now is wait for him to decide what filth is sitting under his skin that he wants to share.

Unfortunately, this isn't my first rodeo waiting out men who would prefer to punch out their feelings than talk about them.

Though, if he asked, I'd let him go a few rounds with the new prospects.

Silence stretches between us.

"I thought she was a plant," Brick says quietly. "Followed her expecting to find a traitor. Instead I found—" He stops. Shakes his head.

"I get it."

He looks down at his ruined hands. "There was something about that house. The way it smelled. I knew before I knew, if that makes sense."

It does. I've had moments like that—where your gut understands something before your brain catches up.

"You did good tonight," I say. "Whatever else happens, you did good."

Brick nods once. "She doesn't know if I'm real."

"What?"

"Isabel." He almost smiles. "She's been looking at me like she's trying to figure out if I'm real."

"Give her time. She's had a rough night."

"Yeah." He wraps the rag around his knuckles, makeshift bandage. "She's had a rough life."

I can't argue with that.

~

JOSIE

The chaos settles as the night wears on.

Lily has fallen asleep on the couch, the sandwich mostly eaten, the rabbit clutched under her chin. Someone has found a blanket—soft and pink, probably Emma's contribution—and tucked it around her small body.

Isabel sits beside her, refusing to move despite Maggie's protests. She's been bandaged and dosed with painkillers, but she won't leave her sister's side. Won't even close her eyes.

"She needs to rest," Maggie murmurs to me. "They both do. But she won't go anywhere without the kid."

"Then we make sure they stay together."

"We will. Ginger's already setting up the big guest room—the one with two beds." Maggie shakes her head. "That poor girl. Both of them. What they must have been through..."

I don't want to imagine it. The bruises tell enough of the story.

"She's safe now," I say. "That's what matters."

"Is she? Safe doesn't just mean walls and locks. Safe means feeling like you can breathe. Feeling like the worst is over and you can trust those around you." Maggie looks at Isabel, still rigid on that couch. "That kind of safety takes time."

"Then we give her time."

"We will." Maggie pats my arm. "You should rest too. Your ribs aren't going to heal if you keep running around."

"I'm fine."

"You're a terrible liar." But she smiles. "Just like the rest of them."

I find Stone on the back porch.

He's standing at the railing, looking out at nothing, a beer dangling from his fingers. The tension in his shoulders says he's been carrying the weight of the world again—and probably will keep carrying it, because that's who he is.

"Hey," I say.

He turns, his face relaxing when he sees me.

"Hey yourself." He shifts to make room. "You should be—"

"If you say 'in bed,' I'm going to throw a prospect at you."

"I was going to say 'off your feet.' But the sentiment stands."

I move to stand beside him, close enough that our arms brush. The night is cool, the stars bright, the sounds of the clubhouse muffled behind us.

"Hell of a night," I say.

"Hell of a week."

"That too."

We stand in silence for a moment.

"She was protecting a six-year-old," I say quietly. "This whole time. That's what she was hiding."

"I know."

"And we thought she was a spy."

"We had to be sure." His voice is tired. Resigned. "It's my job to be suspicious."

"I'm not blaming you. I'm just—" I stop, searching for words. "She gave up everything. Her whole life. To keep that little girl safe. And she never asked anyone for help. Not once."

"Some people don't know how to ask."

"Maybe." I turn to look at him. "Or maybe no one ever gave her a reason to think asking would help."

Stone is quiet for a long moment. Then his hand finds mine in the darkness.

"She has a reason now," he says. "They both do."

I lace my fingers through his. Let myself lean into his warmth.

"We got interrupted earlier," I say.

"We did."

"That keeps happening."

"It does."

"It's very frustrating."

His mouth curves. "Is it?"

"Extremely." I turn to face him fully. "I was promised a conversation. And a locked door."

"The door can be arranged." His free hand comes up to cup my face. "The conversation might have to wait."

"Why?"

"Because right now, all I want to do is kiss you. And I'm not sure I can talk and do that at the same time."

My heart stutters. "That's a problem?"

"Could be. I'm very focused when I set my mind to it."

"Is that so?"

"Mmm." His thumb traces my lower lip. "Very focused."

I lean into his touch, let my eyes drift closed. "Stone—"

"STONE!" Tank's voice bellows from inside. "Bones found something. Says it can't wait."

Stone's hand freezes on my face. His forehead drops to mine.

"I'm going to have them all killed," he mutters. "I'm thinking poison in the pancakes. The fuckers won't know what hit them."

"It does seem like the only solution."

"Mass murder. Very efficient."

"I support this plan."

He laughs despite himself—a rough, exhausted sound—and presses a kiss to my forehead.

"Tomorrow," he says. "Tomorrow, we're finishing this."

"Promise?"

"On my fucking life."

He pulls away, and I immediately miss his warmth. But

he pauses in the doorway, looking back at me with an expression that makes my stomach flip.

"Josie?"

"Yeah?"

"Don't go anywhere."

"Where would I go?"

"Doesn't matter. Just—stay." His eyes hold mine. "Please."

"Okay," I say softly. "I'll stay."

He nods once, then disappears inside.

I stay on the porch for a while longer, watching the stars, thinking about everything that's happened and everything that's still to come.

Isabel and Lily, finally safe after god knows how many years of hell.

Stone and me, dancing around something that feels bigger than either of us.

A cartel that wants me dead. A campaign that needs winning. A club full of people who've somehow become family.

It's a lot. Maybe too much.

But standing there, with Stone's promise still warm in my ears and the sounds of the clubhouse behind me, I don't feel overwhelmed.

I feel hopeful.

"How surprising."

I'm heading back inside when I see her.

Isabel is standing in the hallway outside the room where they've put Lily. Her arms are wrapped around herself, her face pale in the dim light. She looks lost. Adrift. Like she's been running for so long she's forgotten how to stand still.

"You okay?" I ask softly.

She startles. Then relaxes when she sees it's me.

"Hey."

"Can't sleep?"

"Don't want to." She glances toward the door. "Lily's finally out. It's the first time in—" She stops. "A long time."

"That's good."

"Yeah."

I lean against the wall beside her, ignoring the protest from my ribs. "You know, you don't have to stand guard. The club's got people on the doors. No one's getting in."

"I know."

"But you're going to stand here anyway."

"Probably."

I almost smile. "I get it."

"Do you?"

"I spent years prosecuting monsters. I know what it's like to feel responsible for someone's safety. To lie awake wondering if you've done enough."

Isabel is quiet for a moment. "Did you? Do enough?"

Maria's face flashes through my mind. Daniel's drawings.

"Not always," I admit. "Sometimes no matter what you do, it's not enough. People still get hurt."

"That's not very comforting."

"No. But it's honest." I turn to face her. "The difference is, you got her out. Lily's safe because of you. Whatever happened before tonight—that's over. You won."

Isabel's jaw trembles. Just for a second, before she locks it down.

"Doesn't feel like winning."

"It never does. Not at first." I reach out, touch her arm. "But give it time. Tomorrow, when you wake up and she's still here—that's when you'll feel it. That's when it gets real."

She stares at me with those dark, wary eyes. I can see her fighting it—the urge to believe, the fear of hoping.

"Why are you being so nice to me?" she asks.

"Because you saved my life."

"I hit a guy with a bedpan. It wasn't exactly medal worthy."

"You saw someone in danger and you acted. Without hesitation. Without thinking about yourself." I hold her gaze. "That's not nothing, Isabel. That's everything."

Her eyes glisten.

"The man," she says quietly. "The one who came for us. Bradley?"

"He prefers Brick. That's his road name."

"Brick." She repeats. "He packed Lily's things. Her rabbit, her clothes. Before any of it happened. He didn't even know us, and he—" She stops, shakes her head. "Why?"

I think about Brick's face when he's walked through that door. The blood on his knuckles. The way his eyes have tracked Isabel's every movement.

"Because that's what this club does," I say. "They protect people. Even when it doesn't make sense. Even when they don't know the full story." I smile. "Especially then."

Isabel is quiet for a long moment. Then she exhales, some of the tension bleeding out of her shoulders.

"I don't know how to do this," she admits. "How to trust people. How to let someone else carry the weight."

"Neither do I." I shrug. "But I'm learning. Maybe we can figure it out together."

"Maybe."

"Get some rest. Lily's going to need you tomorrow."

Isabel nods slowly. Then, surprising us both, she reaches out and squeezes my hand.

"Thank you," she says. "For everything."

"Thank me by getting some sleep."

"Yes ma'am."

She slips into the room, closing the door softly behind her.

I stand in the hallway for a moment, listening to the quiet of the clubhouse settling around me. Somewhere, voices murmur. Somewhere, boots cross a floor. The sounds of people keeping watch, keeping safe, keeping each other.

This club is a family. It's nice to be a part of it.

I turn to leave but stop when movement at the far end of the corridor catches my eye.

Brick.

He's leaning against the wall in the shadows, arms crossed, those sharp blue eyes tracking Isabel until she disappears inside. Standing watch. Whether it's to keep her safe or keep her from running, I can't tell—maybe both.

His gaze flicks to me. A brief nod of acknowledgment.

I nod back, then head to my room, smiling.

11

JOSIE

I'm ready to commit murder.

Not literal murder—I'm a lawyer, I know how that ends—but the kind of murder you fantasize about when you've been stuck in a guest room with nothing but pain meds, daytime television, and the constant parade of well-meaning bikers checking to make sure I'm still breathing.

You're fine, Josie. You're healing. You're definitely not going slowly insane.

I push myself up from the bed, ignoring the twinge in my ribs. The burr holes in my head have scabbed over nicely —Maggie changed the dressings this morning and declared me "on the mend"—but my head still throbs if I move too fast, and my wrist itches constantly under the cast.

The worst part isn't the physical pain. It's the waiting.

Waiting for my body to cooperate. Waiting for news about Summit. Waiting for Stone to get his act together and come kiss me again.

Seriously? Way to give a girl blue bean.

That kiss—or kisses, plural, because we lost ourselves for a good ten minutes before Hawk interrupted—has been replaying in my mind on a constant loop. The heat of his mouth. The way his hands felt cradling my face. The rough sound he made when I bit his lower lip.

And then... nothing.

Oh, he's been attentive, checking on me every few hours, bringing me meals, sitting with me while I pretend to watch TV and he pretends to review club paperwork. But he hasn't kissed me again. Hasn't even tried.

It's driving me absolutely insane.

Maybe he's having second thoughts. Maybe the kissing was a one-time thing. Maybe—

"What's got you frowning?"

I jolt, nearly dropping the water glass I've been clutching. Stone stands in the doorway, one shoulder propped against the frame, watching me with those unreadable gray eyes.

"I'm not."

"Oh, so your forehead always gets this little crease when you think?" He pushes off the frame and crosses toward me. "It's been there for the past ten minutes."

"You've been standing there for ten minutes?"

"Five." His mouth curves. "I was enjoying the view."

Heat floods my cheeks. Dammit. I'm a forty-year-old woman with a law degree and a four-figure body count of corporate executives I've destroyed in courtrooms. I should not be blushing like a teenager because a man says he enjoys looking at me.

"Shouldn't you be doing president things?" I manage.

"Took a break." He stops at the edge of the bed, close enough that I can smell leather and soap and that indefinable scent that's just him. "Thought I'd check on my favorite patient."

The way he's looking at me does things to my chest that I refuse to examine too closely.

"Stone." I set down the water glass, meeting his gaze. "We should talk."

"About?"

"About the kissing." I force myself to be direct. It's the only way I know how to be. "And the not-kissing. And the —" I wave a hand vaguely. "Purgatory of passion that we've created."

He snorts. "That's certainly one way to put it."

I wave a hand breezily. "I nearly died. I reserve the right to be as dramatic as I want." I point at him. "Now, let's talk about the kissing."

"You want to talk?" He moves closer, and suddenly the room feels very small. "Or do you want me to?"

My breath catches. "Stone—"

"I've been trying to be a gentleman, Josie." His voice drops, rough and low. "Trying not to be the asshole who takes advantage of a woman recovering from serious injuries." He stops right in front of me, close enough to touch. "But if you're telling me you want more…"

"I—yes. Obviously yes."

His expression shifts, the careful control cracking to reveal the heat underneath.

"Okay." He sits on the edge of the bed, the mattress dipping under his weight. "But first, we talk. Cards on the table. Because I'm not interested in a one-time thing with you, and I need to know you understand what you're getting into."

"And just what exactly am I'm getting into?"

"Me. The club. All of it." His gray eyes hold mine. "I want you, Josie. I've always wanted you. But if we do this, it's not casual. Not for me."

Oh.

It's such a Stone answer—turning my inside out once more.

His words land deep in my chest, expanding as I absorb his meaning. They take up space I didn't know was empty.

Part of me wants to run. To make a joke, deflect, protect myself. His admission is terrifying, but it's also everything I've wanted to hear someone say to me.

If I say yes—if I let myself have this—there's no going back to safe. No more hiding behind professional distance and pretending I don't feel what I feel.

Courage, dear heart.

"And if I say it's not casual for me either?"

His eyes darken. "Josie…"

"I'm serious." I shift closer to him, ignoring the twinge in my ribs. "I've been around the club, I get how this works. You're the go-to guy. You're the one they come to and rely on." I place a hand on his thigh. "Maybe I want to be the one *you* need."

He curses. "You're pushing my buttons, sweetheart."

I chuckle. "Good. Does that mean you're giving into my feminine wiles?"

He leans over me, hesitating. "You're still recovering. This can't go far."

I fist his shirt in my hands. "I'm not made of glass, Stone. I'm a little banged up, sure. But I know what I want. And what I want is you."

"Your ribs—"

"Are healing nicely." I hold his gaze, letting him see the truth of what I'm saying. "I'm not asking you to throw me against a wall. I'm asking you to stop treating me like I'll shatter if you touch me."

I watch as raw, hungry need washes over his face.

"Josie." His voice is rough, strained. "I need you to be sure. Because once I have you, I'm not letting go."

"I'm sure."

The words are barely out of my mouth before he's kissing me.

It's not like before—not gentle or questioning. This kiss is a claiming. His hand fists in my hair, tilting my head back so he can take my mouth at exactly the angle he wants. He tastes like sin, and I want to fucking drown in him.

His lips are firm, demanding, coaxing mine open so his tongue can sweep inside. The scrape of his stubble against my chin sends shivers down my spine. He kisses like he does everything else—thorough, intense, completely focused on the task at hand. Like I'm the only thing in the world that matters.

I moan into his mouth, my hands clutching at his shoulders, feeling the heat of him through his shirt, the bunch and flex of muscle beneath my fingers. He swallows the sound and makes one of his own—a low growl that vibrates through me and settles somewhere deep in my belly.

"God, the sounds you make." He breaks away just long enough to speak, his lips brushing mine with every word. Then he nips at my lower lip, a sharp sting that makes me gasp, before soothing it with a slow drag of his tongue. "I've been imagining them for months."

"Is the reality better?" I manage, breathless.

"Infinitely." He trails kisses down my jaw, my neck, finding the sensitive spot below my ear that makes me gasp. "Tell me if anything hurts."

"Nothing hurts. Don't stop."

He eases me back against the pillows, careful of my injuries even as his mouth does sinful things to my collarbone. His hand slides under my shirt—his shirt, actually, since I've yet to head home—and I arch into his touch.

"You're wearing my clothes," he murmurs against my skin. "Do you know what that does to me?"

"Tell me."

"Makes me want to see what's underneath." His fingers trace up my side, leaving trails of heat in their wake. "Makes me want to mark you. Claim you. Make sure everyone knows you're mine."

I should probably object to the possessiveness. Instead, I find myself saying, "Then do it."

He lifts his head, those gray eyes burning into mine. "You don't know what you're asking for."

"Maybe not." I pull him back down, kissing him with everything I have. "But I want to find out."

He takes his time with my shirt—each button freed with deliberate slowness, his mouth following to press kisses to every inch of newly revealed skin. When he reaches my cast, he pauses, easing the sleeve over it with a gentleness that makes my chest ache. By the time he pushes the fabric aside, I'm trembling.

"Beautiful." He traces the edge of my bra with one finger. "So fucking beautiful."

"It's just a plain cotton bra—"

"I don't care about the bra." He meets my eyes. "I care about what's underneath it. About you."

He reaches behind me, unclasping it with practiced ease, and I have a moment of self-consciousness—I'm forty, my body bears the marks of time and gravity—but the way he looks at me erases every doubt.

"Perfect," he breathes. "Absolutely perfect."

"Boone—"

The use of his real name makes him groan. "Say it again."

"Boone." I arch into his touch as his hands cup my breasts. "Please."

"Please what?" He brushes his thumbs across my nipples, and I whimper. "Tell me what you want."

I tug at his shirt, desperate suddenly. "Off. Take this off."

He pulls back just long enough to yank it over his head, and then he's back, and oh God, the feel of his skin against mine. Warm and solid and real.

I run my free hand over his chest, his shoulders, the hard planes of his stomach. Memorizing him. Grounding myself in the fact that this is actually happening—that he's here, that he wants me, that I'm allowed to touch him like this.

"Josie." His voice is strained, his muscles twitching under my fingertips.

"I needed to make sure this was real," I whisper. "That you're real."

A soft, fierce look flickers across his face. He catches my hand, presses a kiss to my palm.

"I'm real," he says. "I'm right here. And I'm not going anywhere."

My throat tightens. I pull him back down to me.

"I want your mouth on me."

He obliges immediately, drawing one nipple into his mouth while his hand works the other. The sensation shoots straight to my core, and I cry out, my good hand tangling in his hair.

"So responsive." He switches sides, lavishing the same attention on my other breast. "I could do this for hours. Just watch you come apart."

"I need more." I'm beyond pride now, beyond pretense. "Please, Boone. I need—"

"I know what you need."

His mouth moves lower—across my stomach, my hipbones, the sensitive skin just above the waistband of my borrowed sweatpants. He hooks his fingers in the elastic and looks up at me.

"Yes?"

"Yes. God, yes."

He slides the sweatpants down my legs, taking my underwear with them, and I'm bare before him. Completely vulnerable.

For a long moment, he just looks. His gaze travels over me like a physical touch—my breasts, the soft curve of my stomach, the flare of my hips, the place between my thighs where I'm already aching for him.

I'm suddenly, painfully aware of what he's seeing. Not just the body of a forty-year-old woman with all its imperfections—but the patches of stubble where they shaved my head for surgery. The angry red line of stitches near my temple. The ugly purple bruising that still runs along my ribs. The bulky cast encasing my wrist like a plaster prison. Not to mention that I haven't exactly been personally grooming lately.

I'm a mess. A disaster. The furthest thing from sexy I've ever been.

But the way he's looking at me—like I'm a feast and he's been starving for years—makes none of that matter.

"I'm not exactly at my best," I manage, gesturing vaguely at the stitches, the cast, the general wreckage of my body.

"You're alive." He presses a kiss to the bruise on my ribs—so gentle it makes my chest ache. "You're here." Another kiss, to the inside of my arm, just above the cast. "You're mine." His eyes meet mine, blazing with heat. "That makes you the most beautiful thing I've ever seen."

Jesus Christ. I've never felt more powerful.

"Look at you." His voice is lower now, rougher. Reverent. He settles between my thighs, broad shoulders forcing my legs wider, and the position feels obscene in the best way—me spread open, him still fully clothed, all that coiled power focused entirely on me. "So wet already. Is this all for me?"

I make a noise of affirmation.

"Yeah." He presses a kiss to my inner thigh. "Good girl."

Oh god.

And then his mouth is on me, and I stop thinking entirely.

He licks me with long, slow strokes—learning my body, discovering what makes me gasp and moan and writhe. The flat of his tongue drags through my folds, hot and wet, and I hear myself make a sound I don't recognize. Something between a whimper and a plea.

"That's it," he murmurs against me. "Let me hear you."

He explores me like he has all the time in the world. Traces the seam of me with the tip of his tongue. Dips inside, just barely, then retreats. Finds my clit and circles it lazily—once, twice—before moving away to press open-mouthed kisses to my inner thighs.

"Boone—" My hips buck, chasing his mouth. "Stop teasing."

"Not teasing." He holds my hips down with one broad hand, pinning me in place. "Savoring."

He returns to my center, and this time his tongue moves with more purpose. Long strokes from my entrance to my clit, over and over, each one building the pressure coiling low in my belly. He finds a rhythm that has me keening, my good hand fisting in the sheets, my head thrown back against the pillows.

But every time I get close—every time I feel myself climbing toward the edge—he pulls back. Changes the pressure. Slows down.

"Boone—" I'm panting now, my skin flushed and damp, desperation clawing at my throat. "Please—"

He lifts his head just enough to meet my eyes. His lips are swollen, his chin wet with me, and the sight of this powerful man between my thighs—wrecked and hungry and completely in control—makes my core clench deep.

"Please what?" His voice is rough, raw. "Tell me."

"Make me come. I need to come."

"Since you asked so nicely."

This time, he doesn't tease.

He seals his mouth over my clit and sucks—hard, relentless—at the same moment he slides two fingers inside me. The stretch burns in the best way, and he crooks his fingers, dragging against my front wall, finding a spot that makes my vision blur.

His mouth works me in time with his hand. Tongue flicking, lips pulling, fingers thrusting in a rhythm that tightens the coil inside me until I can barely breathe. The pleasure builds and builds, layer upon layer, climbing higher than I thought possible.

"That's it," he growls against me, the vibration shooting through my nerve endings. "Come for me, Josie. Let me feel it."

I shatter.

The orgasm tears through me like a wave—cresting, crashing, dragging me under. I come with a scream that I'm sure the entire clubhouse can hear, my body arching off the bed, thighs clamping around his head, pleasure pulsing through me in endless, devastating waves.

He doesn't stop.

His fingers keep moving, gentler now but relentless, wringing every last tremor from my body. His tongue laps at me softly, easing me down even as he stokes the embers for a new peak.

"One more," he murmurs against my sensitive flesh. "Give me one more, Josie."

"I can't—"

"You can." His fingers curl inside me, finding a spot that makes me see stars. "You will. Come on, baby. Be a good girl for me."

He works me relentlessly—tongue and fingers in perfect concert—and I feel the second orgasm building even as aftershocks from the first still ripple through me. It's too much. It's not enough. It's everything.

"That's it," he coaxes. "Let go. I've got you."

The second orgasm blindsides me—sharper, deeper, ripping a sob from my throat. I clench around his fingers, crying his name, my whole body shaking with the force of it.

He eases me through the aftershocks, his touch gentling until I'm boneless and trembling. Then he withdraws this fingers slowly—so slowly—and crawls up my body, pressing kisses to my hip, my stomach, the curve of my breast, my collarbone. When he settles beside me, he pulls me into his arms.

I can feel him against my thigh—hard, straining against his jeans—and I reach down, my fingers finding his belt.

"Your turn."

He catches my hand, bringing it to his lips instead. Kisses my knuckles. My palm. The sensitive skin of my inner wrist, just above the cast.

"Later."

"Boone—"

"Later," he repeats, softer this time. He threads his fingers through mine, pinning our joined hands against his chest. "When you're healed and I don't have to worry about hurting you."

"You won't hurt me."

His smile is crooked, almost boyish. "But I want to take my time with you, Josie. Hours. And I can't do that while you're still recovering." He presses a kiss to my forehead, careful to avoid the stitches. "Tonight was about you. Let me have that."

The tenderness in his voice undoes me more than the orgasms did.

"Okay," I whisper. "But I'm collecting on that debt. With interest."

"I'm counting on it."

I lie curled against Stone's chest, his fingers tracing lazy patterns on my hip.

He makes a rumbled sound of contentment. I shift so I can look at him, propping my chin on his chest. In the dim light of the guest room, he looks softer than he does during the day. Less invincible MC president, more man who just spent two hours learning exactly how to make me fall apart.

"That was a supremely satisfied sound for someone who has yet to get off."

He grins. "I have the taste of you on my lips, and the promise of more to come. I'd say I'm doing okay." His hand comes up to cup my face, thumb tracing my cheekbone as he sobers. "I was an idiot, Josie. I'm sorry."

My heart clenches. "You're forgiven. I'm just glad you finally gave in."

His mouth curves once more. "You're very persuasive, Counselor."

"I've been told that before." I lean up to press a kiss to his jaw. "Usually right before I win a case."

"I bet." He pulls me closer, tucking me against his side. "I'm not going to push you away again, Josie."

"Good." I settle against him, feeling the steady beat of his heart beneath my ear. "Because I'm not going anywhere."

We lie in comfortable silence, the sounds of the clubhouse muffled through the walls. Somewhere, I can hear music playing. Voices. The normal chaos of MC life carrying on around us.

"We should probably make an appearance at some point," I murmur. "People will talk."

"Let them talk." Stone's arm tightens around me. "I'm not ready to share you yet."

"Possessive beast." I love it.

"You have no idea." He tilts my chin up, brushing a kiss across my lips. "But we do need to eat. I'll have someone bring up food."

"Such service."

"Only the best for my woman."

My woman.

Damn if I don't like that.

12

STONE

I wake with Josie in my arms and fuck if she doesn't feel incredible pressed against me.

She's still asleep, her face soft in the early morning light, one hand curled against my chest. The borrowed t-shirt has ridden up during the night, exposing a strip of skin at her hip that I ache to touch. But I don't want to wake her. Not yet. Not when I can just lie here and watch her breathe.

This is dangerous.

I know it is. This woman—with her sharp tongue and soft heart and absolute refusal to be intimidated—has knocked down every wall without even trying.

She stirs, her eyes fluttering open, and when she sees me watching her, she smiles.

"Stop being creepy," she murmurs.

"I prefer 'devoted.'"

"Tomato, tomahto." She stretches, wincing slightly when the movement pulls at her ribs. "What time is it?"

"Early. Go back to sleep."

"Can't." She's more awake now, her lawyer brain clearly coming online. "Things to do. Cases to review. Cartels to take down."

"The cartel can wait."

"Can it, though?" She pushes herself up on her good elbow, meeting my eyes. "Stone. We've been in a holding pattern for three weeks. Summit's still out there. The attack on me proved they're willing to escalate. We need to move."

She's right. I hate that she's right.

"Steel's been working on cracking their warehouse security."

She glares. "And you were going to tell me this when?"

"When you weren't recovering from a brain injury."

"My brain is fine." She taps her temple with her casted hand. "A little rattled, maybe, but fully operational. I want to help. Let me help, Boone."

The use of my real name still hits me somewhere deep. She only uses it in intimate moments—and apparently when she's trying to get her way.

"Fine." I press a kiss to her forehead. "Church is at ten. I'll fill you in after."

"Why not during?"

"Because you're not a member."

"I'm your lawyer."

"Who's currently on medical leave."

She glares at me, but there's no real heat in it. "You're lucky you're pretty."

I snort. "You mean I'm lucky I gave you orgasms."

She spreads her legs. "You'd be luckier if you did it again."

"Well, who could refuse such a tempting offer?"

An hour later I finally roll out of bed, leaving a sweaty, smiling Josie behind.

~

Church is tense.

Steel stands at the head of the table, laptop open, walking us through what he's found. The kid's come a long way from the nervous prospect who could barely make eye contact. He's a big guy—the kind of big that makes drunk idiots think twice, though the beard and glasses soften the effect. I've seen him let Hawk's twins braid tinsel into his hair without complaint, but I've also seen him on the range. Kid shoots like he was born with a rifle in his hands.

Now he holds the room's attention like he was born to that, too.

"I managed to crack their security feeds," he explains, turning the laptop so everyone can see. "They're running a drug processing operation out of the old textile warehouse on Route 9. But that's not the interesting part."

He pulls up another image—grainy surveillance footage of two men talking in what looks like an office.

"The guy on the left is Ivan. We already knew he was their muscle. But the guy on the right?" Steel zooms in on a face I recognize far too well. Every muscle in my body locks.

Fuck.

"Vincent Caruso," Steel confirms. The man we handed to the FBI on a silver platter months ago.

"How the hell is he still walking around?" Hawk's voice is tight with disbelief.

"Good question." Steel shakes his head. "Either the feds fumbled the case, or Caruso's got friends in higher places than we thought."

The room goes silent.

"Fuck," Tank mutters.

"This changes things," Lee says. "We're dealing with people who have the resources to make us all disappear."

"Which is why we need to be smart about this." I lean forward, studying the footage. "Steel, how solid is this evidence?"

"Solid enough for a federal case. I've got timestamps, facial recognition matches, even some audio. They're not exactly careful when they think no one's watching."

My hands curl into fists against my thighs. We'd already given the local feds everything—the footage, evidence of Vincent paying off cops, the whole goddamn conspiracy. And this bastard is still walking on my turf.

Fuck that.

"We need to get this to the *right* hands ASAP." I think of Josie, still upstairs, probably already reviewing case files despite my orders to rest.

"You want Josie to add it to her file?" Lee asks, reading my mind.

I hesitate.

"We'll need to be careful if Caruso has guys on the inside of the bureau," Hawk warns.

That's what I'm afraid of. But letting this guy slip through our fingers isn't an option.

"Josie's still got contacts from her Atlanta days. People she trusts. If we can get this to the right people—"

"We end Summit and Caruso in one move," Hawk finishes.

"I still think it's a risky move, bringing in even more feds," Tank points out. "They're not exactly our biggest fans."

"Neither is the cartel." I stand, signaling the end of the meeting. "I'd rather deal with federal scrutiny than a bullet in the back of my head. Steel, get me everything you have. I'll brief Josie this afternoon."

The brothers file out, but Lee hangs back.

"You okay?" he asks.

"Why wouldn't I be?"

"Because you've got that look." He crosses his arms. "The one you get when something's eating at you."

My son knows me too well.

"Just thinking about next steps."

"Uh huh." Lee doesn't buy it for a second. "This about the club? Or about the woman upstairs?"

I should have known he'd call me on it. The whole damn club probably has bets going on how long I'd hold out. Fuckers.

"Both," I admit.

"You love her."

It's not a question.

"Yeah. I do. How you feel about that?"

Lee studies me for a long moment. Then, slowly, he smiles.

"Good. It's about time you let yourself have some good."

"Lee—"

"I mean it, Dad." He grips my shoulder. "You've been a ghost since Mom left. Going through the motions.

Running the club. Raising us. But not really living. Mom moved on, it's about time you did as well."

I reach out, scuffing his hair. "Get out of here before I get sappy and hug you."

He grins, clapping me on the shoulder as he goes.

He's right, it is about time I move on. I just need to dismantle the cartel first.

JOSIE

Stone briefs me after Church, spreading Steel's evidence across the desk in his office like a war map.

It's damning. Timestamps, facial recognition, audio clips of Caruso discussing shipments. Steel's done incredible work—the kind of work that would make federal prosecutors weep with joy.

"This is solid," I say, flipping through the printouts. "Steel's wasted as a prospect. You should kick him out so he can become a CIA operative."

"Don't tell him that. His head's big enough." Stone leans against the desk, watching me work. "Can your contact use it?"

"If she's still the same Alex I remember? Then yeah. She'll build a cathedral out of this evidence and burn Caruso at the altar." I pull out my phone. "Give me twenty minutes."

"You want me to stay?"

"I want you to watch." I meet his eyes. "You should see what you're getting with me."

His expression flickers—curiosity, maybe. Or heat. Hard to tell with him sometimes.

He settles into the chair across from me, arms crossed, and nods.

I dial.

Agent Alexandra Pilkin picks up on the third ring.

"Josie Bright." Her voice is friendly but there's a question in it. "It's been a while."

"Two years." I lean back in Stone's chair, letting the leather creak. "How's the husband?"

"Divorced. How's the small-town lawyer gig? I heard you got pulled into some white collar crime with a touch of local cartel. Sounds like it hasn't been the restful change you were searching for."

"That's actually why I'm calling."

"I'm listening."

I let the pause stretch just long enough to build anticipation. "How badly does the Bureau want Vincent Caruso?"

The silence on the other end is deafening. I can practically hear her sitting up straighter.

"What do you know?" Alex's question is sharp. The voice of an agent who's suddenly very, very interested.

"What if I told you I have evidence sitting on my desk that you and your team might want." I examine my nails casually, even though she can't see me. "Enough to build a case that'll stick."

"You're telling me you have actionable intelligence on one of the most wanted men in the country, and you're just... calling me up to chat about it?"

"I trust you. But, I also need a guarantee in return."

"Of course you do." I can almost hear her rolling her eyes. "What's the ask, Josie?"

"Full immunity for my clients. The people who obtained this footage are civilians caught up in his operation. They've been threatened, targeted, nearly killed." I glance at Stone, who's watching me with an unreadable expression. "I want protection for them. Complete insulation from any blowback."

"That's a big ask."

"It's a big case." I let steel enter my voice—the same steel that made defense attorneys flinch when I was prosecuting in Atlanta. "Alex, I know exactly what Caruso means to the Bureau. I know how long you've been chasing him, and I know how many careers have stalled because no one can pin him down." I pause. "I'm offering you the chance to be the agent who finally takes him down. The one whose name goes in the history books."

"And all you want is immunity for some civilians?"

"That's all I want."

"The footage would need to be verified—"

"It will be. Public-facing security systems with inadequate encryption. Chain of custody is clean. Nothing that won't hold up in court." I've already run through the legal angles in my head—twice. "This is gift-wrapped, Alex. All you have to do is take it."

Another pause. Longer this time. I can hear her breathing, can almost hear the gears turning in her head.

"I'll need to talk to my superiors," she finally says. "And the lawyers."

"You have twelve hours."

"Josie—"

"Twelve hours. After that, I start making other calls." I let a hint of steel creep into my tone. "The ATF has been sniffing around for a win for months. I'm sure they'd love a shot at Caruso. Or maybe the DEA—I heard whispers they've been feeling left out lately."

"You wouldn't—"

"Try me." I smile, even though she can't see it. "Twelve hours. I'll look forward to hearing from you."

I end the call and let out a breath.

Stone is staring at me.

"What?" I ask.

"That was…" He shakes his head slowly. "Impressive doesn't cover it."

"I used to do this for a living."

"Yeah, but watching you do it…" He uncrosses his arms, pushing out of the chair, moving toward me with intent in his eyes. "Watching you take control like that. Bend a federal agent to your will with nothing but words."

"Are you turned on right now?"

"Incredibly so."

Heat floods through me. "The door—"

"Is locked." His mouth brushes my ear. "I locked it when the call started. Just in case."

"Just in case of what?"

"Just in case I needed to do this."

He drops to his knees, pulls down my sweats, and ravishes me.

Apparently assertive women are his kink. Good to know.

He gets me off quickly and surges back up, kissing me until the taste of my orgasm decorates my tongue. I'm trembling, nerve endings sparking, but instead of sating me, the orgasm made me hungrier.

I want more. I want to feel the weight of him in my hand, want to know what sounds I can drag out of that controlled mouth. I need Stone.

Now.

"Boone." I push against his chest until he straightens. "I believe I mentioned collecting on a debt."

His eyes darken. "Josie—"

"Sit down."

For a moment, I think he's going to argue. Then, slowly, he backs up until his legs hit the leather couch against the wall. He sits.

I stand, crossing to him with deliberate slowness, watching his eyes track my every movement. My pulse pounds between my thighs, still swollen and sensitive from his mouth. But this isn't about me anymore.

I've been imagining this for weeks. What he looks like underneath all that leather and control. How he'll feel against my tongue. Whether I can make the president of the Stoneheart MC lose that iron composure.

I'm soaked, already aching for him once more. I move, and we both hear the soft slick of my thighs. His gaze darkens, his mouth twisting into a feral grin.

Oh, this is going to be fun.

"You've been taking care of me," I say, stopping between his spread knees. "Now it's my turn."

I sink to my knees between his thighs, and his breath catches.

"You don't have to—"

"I want to." I hold his gaze as my good hand goes to his belt. "I've been thinking about this constantly. About what you'd look like. What you'd feel like. What sounds you'd make."

"Josie..."

"Let me take care of you." I work his belt open one-handed, then his zipper. "The way you've been taking care of me."

He lifts his hips to help me free him, and then he's there—hard and thick and already straining toward me. I wrap my good hand around him, feeling him pulse against my palm.

"God," he breathes.

"You're beautiful." I stroke him slowly, learning his shape. "Has anyone ever told you that?"

"No."

"They should have." I lean forward and press a kiss to the tip—just a whisper of contact.

He groans like I've wounded him.

"Patience," I murmur. "I'm not rushing this."

I explore him slowly, tracing the veins with my tongue, learning what makes him gasp. When I finally take him into my mouth, his hand flies to my hair.

"Fuck—" The word is torn from him. "Your mouth—Josie—"

I set a deliberate rhythm, taking him deeper with each stroke. His hips twitch beneath me, fighting the urge to thrust, his hand trembling where it's gently tangled in my hair. Even this close to losing it, he's still taking care of me, mindful of the still healing scars.

"Look at me," I say, pulling back just enough to speak. "I want you to watch."

His eyes meet mine—dark, desperate, burning with need—as I take him deep again. I hollow my cheeks, suck hard, and his head falls back with a moan.

"Josie—close—you should—"

I don't pull back. Instead, I take him deeper, swallowing around him, working him with everything I have. He comes with a shout, his release flooding my mouth. I take everything he gives me, gentling my touch as he comes down.

When I finally let him slip from my lips, he looks wrecked. Absolutely destroyed.

"Get up here." His voice is hoarse. He hauls me into his lap, crushing his mouth to mine. "That was—you're—Christ."

I smile against his lips. "Good?"

"Good doesn't begin to cover it." He cups my face in his hands, his expression suddenly serious. "I love you."

The words hit me like a physical force. Everything stops. My breath. My heart. The spinning of the earth on its axis. I search his face for the tell—the flicker of regret, the backpedal already forming. But there's nothing. Just

Boone, looking at me like I'm the answer to a question he's been asking his whole life.

My throat tightens. No one has ever said those words to me. God they sound incredible.

"I know it's fast," he continues. "And you'll probably think it's just the dopamine talking."

"Well I did just give you a superior blow job," I force myself to joke around the lump in my throat.

"But I've been falling for you since the day you walked into my clubhouse and told me my legal strategy was shit."

"It was shit." But my voice is shaking. "You were planning to threaten a judge."

"And you showed me a better way." He brushes his thumb across my cheek. "You've been showing me a better way ever since."

"Boone..."

"You don't have to say it back. I just needed you to know."

I pull him down and kiss him with everything I have.

"I love you too," I whisper against his lips. "I think I've loved you for months. I was just too stubborn to admit it."

His smile is like sunrise—warm and bright and full of promise.

"Two more weeks," he says. "Two more weeks until that cast comes off. And then, Josie, I'm going to show you exactly what loving you means."

"I'll hold you to that."

"I'm counting on it."

14

JOSIE

"Well, Ms. Bright, the good news is your wrist has healed beautifully."

Dr. Patterson positions the cast saw, and I try not to hover. But watching that plaster prison split apart feels like watching the last barrier between us crumble.

The cast falls away in two pieces, revealing pale, slightly atrophied skin beneath. Josie flexes her fingers experimentally, wincing at the stiffness.

"You'll need some physical therapy to rebuild strength and mobility," the doctor continues. "But considering your concussion has cleared and your ribs look good, I'd say you're cleared for normal activity."

Normal activity.

Josie catches my eye, and I see the same thought reflected

there. Her cheeks flush pink, and a hot and possessive need coils in my chest.

"Thank you, Doctor," she manages, her voice admirably steady.

We make it all the way to the parking lot before I pin her against the side of my truck.

"Stone—" She's laughing, her newly freed hand coming up to grip my shoulder. "We're in public."

"Don't care." I kiss her neck, her jaw, the corner of her mouth. "Do you know how long I've been waiting for this? Counting down the days until I could touch you without worrying?"

"I have some idea." She arches into me. "But maybe we should continue this somewhere more private?"

"The clubhouse is twenty minutes away."

"Then you better drive fast."

My phone buzzes before I can respond. I consider ignoring it—really, really consider it—but Josie's already pulling back, her lawyer brain engaging.

"That could be Alex."

She's right. It could be.

I check the screen. Unknown number.

"Shit, it might be Alex." Josie takes it from me, "Josephine Bright speaking."

"Ms Bright," Agent Pilkin's voice is brisk, professional. "I'm calling about your offer. I've spoken to my people, and we'd like to arrange a meet to discuss the terms."

Josie puts the phone on speaker so I can hear.

"Define discuss."

Josie's switch to badass professional is so quick I'm worried I'll get whiplash. Her expression shutters, her shoulders rolling back as her professional mode kicks in.

Christ. I told her I love her, and now I'm watching her prove exactly why. She's magnificent—beautiful, confident, calm.

Mine.

"We're interested enough to coordinate a joint operation. We've been building a case against Caruso for years. Your evidence could be the final piece we need."

"And our conditions?"

"Full immunity for your people. Protection if needed. The Bureau takes down Caruso and his leadership; your people stay out of the official records."

Josie and I exchange looks. It's more than we expected.

"What's the timeline?" Josie asks.

"We can have teams in position within seventy-two hours. We'll need your surveillance footage, your intel on the warehouse layout, and complete cooperation during the operation."

"You'll have it," I say. "But my people stay clear of the raid itself. This is your show, Agent. We're just providing the opening."

"Understood. I'll be in touch with coordinates for the evidence handoff."

The line goes dead.

Josie lets out a breath. "That was faster than I expected."

"They want Caruso badly." I pull her back against me. "And thanks to you, they're going to get him."

"Thanks to Steel. He's the one who cracked their security."

"Steel got the footage. You got the FBI to actually use it." I kiss her forehead. "We make a good team."

"We do." She tilts her face up, inviting a real kiss. "Now take me home. We have seventy-two hours before everything goes sideways, and I intend to spend at least some of that time in bed with you."

"Yes ma'am."

The ride back to the clubhouse is torture.

Josie's hand rests on my thigh—her newly freed hand, pale and slightly weak but functional—and she keeps tracing patterns that inch higher and higher with every mile.

"You're playing with fire," I warn her.

"Maybe I want to get burned."

"Josie—"

"Eyes on the road, Mr. President." Her fingers brush dangerously close to where I'm already hard for her. "Safety first."

"You're going to pay for this."

"God, I hope so."

We barely make it through the clubhouse doors.

I'm vaguely aware of brothers calling out greetings, of Ginger saying mentioning dinner, but all I can focus on is getting Josie upstairs. Getting her alone. Getting my hands on her without any barriers between us.

"Stone." Hawk steps into our path, and I nearly growl at him. "Do you have any updates on the FBI situation?"

Fuck.

I stop. "Organize Church for an hour."

"Two," Josie squeaks from behind me.

"Two," I agree.

"Also, Duck wants to talk about the rally tomorrow—"

"SAVE IT FOR CHURCH!"

Hawk takes one look at my face, then at Josie's flushed cheeks, and wisely steps aside.

"Got it, Prez. Two hours."

I practically drag Josie up the stairs.

The moment my bedroom door closes behind us, she's on me—pulling at my shirt, kissing my neck, making those little sounds that drive me absolutely insane.

"Eager," I manage.

"I've been waiting weeks." She yanks my shirt over my head. "Months if you include—"

I shut her up with a kiss.

"Tonight," I promise against her mouth. "After Church, after the briefing, after everything is handled—tonight, Josie. I'm going to take my time with you. Do everything I've been dreaming about. Make you scream my name so loud the whole clubhouse hears."

She shivers in my arms. "Is that a threat or a promise?"

"Both. But right now?" I walk her backward until her knees hit the bed. "Right now I'm going to make you come because I fucking can. Because you're mine and I've got two hours to kill."

Her eyes darken. "Are you sure that's enough time?"

"Sweetheart, I can do a lot of damage in an hour. Two is practically a luxury."

"Prove it."

I don't give her time to say anything else.

My mouth crashes into hers, swallowing her gasp as I bear her down onto the mattress. She tastes like the coffee she stole from my mug this morning, like the mint toothpaste we now share, like mine. Her fingers dig into my shoulders, pulling me closer, and when I lick into her mouth she makes a sound that goes straight to my cock.

"Fuck you," she pants between kisses. "I can't believe you made me wait for this."

"I know." I drag my mouth down her jaw, her neck, finding that spot below her ear that makes her shiver. "I know, baby."

She hooks a leg around my hip, grinding up against me, and the friction through our clothes is torture—the sweetest kind. Her nails rake down my bare back, hard enough to sting, and I hiss against her throat.

"Fuck—those claws."

"You love it."

I do. God help me, I do.

I pull back just enough to look at her—flushed cheeks, swollen lips, her hair spread across my pillow like she belongs there. Because she does. She belongs here, in my bed, in my life, in every part of me I'd locked away for fifteen years.

"Stop looking at me like that," she breathes.

"Like what?"

"Like you're about to devour me."

"That's exactly what I'm about to do."

Her eyes darken, pupils blown wide. "Then stop talking about it and do it."

I take her mouth again, rougher this time, one hand fisting in her hair while the other slides under her shirt. Her skin is so soft—warm silk under my calloused palm—and she arches into my touch like she's been starving for it.

"Off." I tug at her shirt. "I need this off."

She sits up just enough for me to pull it over her head, and then my hands are on her bra—plain white cotton, practical, the sexiest thing I've ever seen because it's covering her—and I'm fumbling with the clasp like a teenager.

"Having trouble?" She's laughing at me, the brat.

"Shut up." The clasp finally gives and I toss the bra somewhere over my shoulder. "I was distracted."

"By what?"

"By you." I cup her breasts in my hands, feeling their weight, watching her nipples pebble under my palms. "By these. By the fact that I finally get to touch you without worrying about breaking you."

"I told you I wouldn't break."

"And I didn't believe you." I lower my head, pressing a kiss to the swell of her breast. "But the cast is off. The stitches are out. And I have exactly—" I glance at the clock. "— an hour and fifty-three minutes to make you come as many times as humanly possible."

"That sounds like a challenge."

"It's a promise."

I draw her nipple into my mouth, sucking hard, and she cries out—her hands flying to my head, fingers tangling in my hair. I lavish attention on one breast while my hand works the other, rolling her nipple between my fingers, pinching just hard enough to make her gasp.

"Boone—" Her hips are moving restlessly beneath me, seeking friction. "More. I need more."

"Patience."

"Fuck patience. I've been patient for months."

She's yanking at my belt before I can respond, her newly freed hands—no more cast, thank Christ—working the buckle with desperate efficiency. I let her, groaning when her fingers brush against my cock through my jeans.

"Someone's eager," she murmurs.

"You have no idea."

She gets my belt open, then my button, then my zipper, and when she shoves her hand inside my boxers and wraps her fingers around me, I have to squeeze my eyes shut and think about engine parts to keep from losing it right there.

"Jesus—" I thrust into her grip involuntarily. "Your hand—"

"You like that?" She strokes me slowly, root to tip, her thumb swirling through the moisture already leaking from the head. "Like feeling me touch you?"

"Josie—"

"I used to lie awake imagining this." Her voice is low, throaty, doing things to me that should be illegal. "About what you'd feel like in my hand. How thick you'd be. How hard." She squeezes, and I groan. "Reality's even better than the fantasy."

"Keep talking like that and this is going to be over embarrassingly fast."

"We can't have that." She releases me with a wicked smile. "Not when you promised to make me scream."

I take back control, pinning her wrists above her head with one hand. She tests my grip, her eyes flashing with equal parts challenge and desire.

"Stay," I command.

"Make me."

I kiss her hard enough to bruise, keeping her wrists pinned while my free hand works at her jeans. The button gives, then the zipper, and I shove the denim down her hips along with her underwear—plain cotton to match the bra, practical, perfect.

"Lift up."

She does, and I strip her bare, tossing her jeans somewhere across the room. Then I sit back on my heels and just look.

She's gorgeous. Spread out on my bed, wrists still held above her head even though I've released them, her thighs parted just enough to give me a glimpse of glistening pink. The bruises have faded. The stitches are gone. All that's left is smooth skin and soft curves and the woman who's turned my entire life upside down.

"You're staring again," she says, but her voice is breathless.

"I'm savoring."

"Savor later. We're on a deadline."

"Right." I hook my hands under her thighs and drag her to the edge of the bed. "Better be efficient about this, then."

I drop to my knees.

"Boone—" She props herself up on her elbows, watching me. "You don't have to every time we—"

"I want to." I press a kiss to her inner thigh, feeling the muscle quiver under my lips. "Need to."

I don't tease this time. We don't have the luxury. I spread her open with my thumbs and lick a long stripe through her center, groaning at the first hit of her arousal on my tongue.

"Fuck—" Her head falls back, her hips lifting toward my mouth. "Yes—"

She's so wet already, slick and swollen and ready for me. I lap at her hungrily, learning her all over again—the spots that make her gasp, the pressure that makes her moan, the rhythm that makes her thighs clamp around my head.

"More," she demands, her hand finding my hair. "I need —Boone, please—"

I slide two fingers inside her, crooking them forward, and she shouts. Her inner walls clench around me like a vice, hot and tight and perfect.

"That's it." I pump my fingers in and out, matching the rhythm of my tongue on her clit. "Let me feel you. Let me hear you."

She's not quiet. Never has been. The sounds she makes—the moans and whimpers and breathless curses—fill the room, and I drink them down like water in a desert. I've been waiting so long for this. So long to have her like this, spread out and desperate and mine.

"I'm close—" Her hand tightens in my hair. "God, Boone, I'm so close—"

I seal my mouth over her clit and suck hard, curling my fingers against that spot inside her, and she shatters. Her whole body goes rigid, her back arching off the bed, a scream tearing from her throat that I'm sure the whole clubhouse can hear.

I work her through it, gentling my touch as the waves subside, pressing soft kisses to her inner thighs as she comes down.

"Holy—" She's panting, boneless, her hand still tangled in my hair. "That was—"

"One." I climb up her body, trailing kisses over her stomach, her ribs, her breasts. "That's one."

"You're keeping count?"

"Promised to make the most of our hour." I capture her mouth, letting her taste herself on my lips. "I take my promises seriously."

She reaches for my jeans, shoving them down my hips along with my boxers. My cock springs free, hard and aching, and when she wraps her hand around me again I have to grit my teeth against the pleasure.

"Inside me." Her voice is urgent, demanding. "Now. I need you inside me."

"Condom—"

"I'm on birth control. I'm clean." Her eyes meet mine, dark with need. "I want to feel you. All of you. Nothing between us."

The trust in those words undoes the knot in my chest. "Josie—"

"Now, Boone. Please."

I kick off my jeans and settle over her, notching myself at her entrance. She's so wet, so ready, but I make myself pause. Make myself look at her.

"This changes things," I say quietly.

"I know."

"Once I'm inside you—"

"I know." She cups my face in her hands, pulling me down for a kiss. "I'm yours. I've been yours. Now prove it."

I push inside in one long stroke.

We both groan—her at the stretch, me at the tight, wet heat that's gripping me like a fist. I hold myself still, buried to the hilt, giving her time to adjust. She feels incredible. Better than anything I've ever experienced. Like coming home to a place I didn't know existed.

"Move." Her legs wrap around my waist, heels digging into my ass. "Boone, move, or I swear to God—"

I move.

There's nothing slow about it. Nothing gentle. This is weeks of want, months of denial, years of loneliness—all of it pouring out in every thrust. The headboard slams against the wall. The bed creaks beneath us. And Josie—beautiful, fierce, perfect Josie—meets me stroke for stroke, her nails scoring lines down my back, her voice rising with each snap of my hips.

"Harder," she demands.

I give her harder. Hitch her leg up over my shoulder, change the angle, drive into her until the only word she can say is my name.

"Boone—God—right there—don't stop—"

I couldn't stop if the clubhouse burned down around us. Not when she's clenching around me like that. Not when her face is twisted in pleasure. Not when I can feel her climbing toward another peak.

"Touch yourself." I'm barely holding on, pressure

building at the base of my spine. "I want to feel you come on my cock."

She slides a hand between us, fingers finding her clit, and the sight of her pleasuring herself while I fuck her is almost enough to finish me. I grit my teeth, forcing myself to hold back, to wait for her.

"That's it," I groan. "So fucking beautiful. Come for me, Josie. Let me feel it."

Her orgasm hits like a wave—her whole body going taut, her walls clamping down on me so hard I see stars. She screams my name, and the sound breaks what's left of my control. I bury myself deep and follow her over, spilling inside her with a groan that tears from somewhere deep in my chest.

For a long moment, neither of us moves. We just breathe together, foreheads pressed close, our bodies still connected.

"Two," she murmurs.

I laugh—a breathless, wrecked sound. "You're counting now?"

"Learning from the best." She shifts beneath me, and we both hiss at the sensation. "How much time do we have left?"

I glance at the clock. "Not nearly long enough."

"Enough for three?"

"Woman." I pull out slowly, groaning at the loss, then flip

her onto her stomach before she can protest. "I like the way you think."

I pull her hips up, positioning her on her hands and knees, and she looks back at me over her shoulder with a smile that's pure sin.

"Well?" she challenges. "Clock's ticking."

I thrust back inside her, and we both moan. This angle is deeper, tighter, and she drops to her elbows with a cry, her back arching like a cat.

"Fuck—you feel even better like this—"

"So do you." I grip her hips hard enough to bruise, setting a relentless pace. "God, Josie. The way you take me—"

She's pushing back against every thrust, meeting my rhythm, her moans muffled by the pillow. I reach around, finding her clit, and she jerks beneath me.

"Yes—right there—don't stop—"

I work her clit in tight circles while I pound into her, chasing our mutual release. Sweat drips down my spine. My thighs are burning. But I don't slow down. Can't slow down. Not when she's making those sounds. Not when I can feel her tightening around me again.

"One more," I grit out. "Give me one more, baby."

"I can't—"

"You can." I lean over her, pressing my chest to her back, my mouth at her ear. "You will. Come for me, Josie. Scream for me."

She does.

The third orgasm rips through her like a wildfire, and she screams into the pillow—my name, maybe, or maybe just a wordless cry of pleasure. Her walls flutter around me, milking me, and I follow her with a roar, emptying myself inside her for the second time.

We collapse onto the mattress in a tangle of sweaty limbs.

"Three," I manage, between ragged breaths.

"Three," she agrees, laughing weakly. "You're a man of your word."

"Always." I press a kiss to her shoulder, her neck, the back of her ear. "How do you feel?"

"Like I've been thoroughly fucked." She turns her head, smiling at me. "In the best possible way."

"Good." I check the clock and groan. "I have to go. Church."

"I know." She stretches languidly, looking satisfied as a cat in cream. "Go do your president thing. I'll be here when you get back."

"You'd better be." I force myself out of bed, wincing at the protests from my muscles. "Because tonight, we're doing that again. Slower."

"Promise?"

I lean down, kissing her deep and thorough. "Promise."

By the time I finally make it to Church, I'm ten minutes

late and Josie's walking funny. Hawk takes one look at my face and wisely doesn't comment.

Tonight, I'll take my time. But right now? Right now was just the appetizer.

15

JOSIE

Church runs long.

Of course it does. Because the universe apparently has a sick sense of humor when it comes to my love life.

I pace in Stone's room—our room, I've started thinking of it as ours—and try not to check the clock every thirty seconds. The FBI briefing needed to happen. The logistics needed to be discussed. The brothers needed to know what was coming.

But that doesn't mean I have to like it.

I can still feel him. That's the thing. Hours later, freshly showered, wearing one of his t-shirts and nothing else, and I can still feel the ghost of his hands on my hips. The stretch of him inside me. The way he made me scream three times in under two hours like it was nothing.

Every time I move, my muscles remind me of what we did. The good kind of sore. The kind that makes me want to do it all over again.

That was the appetizer, he'd said.

God help me when we get to the main course.

I've tried to distract myself. Reviewed case files, checked my email, attempted to read the novel I'd been working through for the past month. But the words kept blurring, replaced by images of Boone's face as he came. The sound of his groan, the way he'd looked at me after, like I was precious to him....

When the door finally opens, I practically jump out of my skin.

Stone looks as frustrated as I feel. His hair is mussed—he's been running his hands through it, a tell I've come to recognize—and there's tension in his shoulders that wasn't there this afternoon.

"Sorry." He closes the door behind him, flipping the lock with deliberate emphasis. The click of the deadbolt sounds impossibly loud in the quiet room. "Hawk had questions. Tank had concerns. Duck wanted to talk about his goddamn speech for tomorrow."

"Is everything handled?"

"Everything is handled." He crosses to me, pulling me into his arms like it's the most natural thing in the world. Like he's been doing it for years instead of days. "For the next twelve hours at least, there are no emergencies. No crises. No interruptions."

I melt into him, breathing in the scent of leather and soap and spice that's just *him*. "You told them not to disturb you?"

"I told them I'd shoot anyone who knocked on that door before sunrise."

I laugh, but it dies in my throat when I see the intensity in his eyes. This is different from earlier. This afternoon was urgent, desperate, two people who'd been holding back for too long finally snapping. This is... something else.

Something that makes my heart beat faster for reasons that have nothing to do with lust.

"Boone..."

"I made you a promise." He backs me toward the bed with slow, deliberate steps, but there's no urgency in it. Just intent. Purpose. The kind of focus he usually reserves for club business, now directed entirely at me. "This afternoon was fast. Hard. Everything we needed it to be."

The backs of my knees hit the mattress.

"But tonight?" His hands come up to cup my face, tilting it toward his. His thumbs stroke my cheekbones with devastating gentleness. "Tonight I'm going to take my time. Learn every inch of you. Make you feel things you've never felt before."

"That's a bold claim," I manage, my voice already breathless. "Considering what you did to me earlier."

"Earlier was just the warm-up." He brushes his thumb

across my lower lip, and I have to resist the urge to draw it into my mouth. "This is the real thing."

He kisses me—slow and deep and thorough. Not rushed, not frantic. Like he really does have all the time in the world and intends to use every second of it. His tongue slides against mine in a lazy rhythm, tasting, savoring. I melt into him, my hands fisting in his shirt, pulling him closer even though there's no space left between us.

He kisses like he's memorizing me. Like every press of his lips is a promise he intends to keep.

When he finally pulls back, we're both breathing harder.

"Arms up," he murmurs.

I comply, and he draws the borrowed t-shirt over my head with reverent care. I'm not wearing anything underneath —hadn't seen the point after my shower—and his breath catches at the sight of me.

"Beautiful." His eyes trace over me like a physical touch, leaving heat in their wake. "Every time I see you, I can't believe you're real."

"You saw me naked three hours ago."

"And I plan to see you naked every day for the rest of my life." He meets my eyes, and the intensity there steals my breath. "If you'll let me."

The words hit me somewhere deep. This isn't just sex. This is a declaration. A vow.

"I'll let you," I whisper.

He smiles—soft, private, just for me—and then his mouth is on my neck, trailing kisses down to my collarbone. Slow. Deliberate. Each press of his lips sending sparks across my skin.

"Lie back," he says against my throat. "Let me worship you."

"That's very biblical of you."

"I'm feeling reverent." He nips at my pulse point, making me gasp. "You bring out my spiritual side."

"Is that what we're calling it?"

"Lie back, Josie."

I sink onto the bed, and he follows me down, settling beside me rather than over me. The mattress dips under his weight, and I find myself rolling toward him instinctively, seeking his warmth.

"Patience," he murmurs, pressing me gently onto my back. "I've got plans."

"You keep talking about these plans."

"Because I'm very committed to them."

His hand traces patterns on my stomach—light, teasing, his calluses rasping against my soft skin—while his mouth explores my shoulder, my collarbone, the swell of my breast. He takes his time, mapping me like uncharted territory.

"Earlier," he murmurs between kisses, "I didn't get to do this properly. Didn't get to taste every inch of you."

"You tasted plenty."

"Not enough." He circles my nipple with one finger, not quite touching where I want him. "Never enough with you."

I arch into his touch, seeking more, but he pulls back with a low chuckle.

"Patience."

"You keep saying that."

"Because you keep needing the reminder." He finally—*finally*—closes his mouth over my nipple, and I gasp at the wet heat. "We have all night, Josie. I intend to use every minute."

He lavishes attention on my breasts with excruciating slowness. Licking, sucking, nipping—alternating between them until I'm writhing beneath him, my hands fisted in the sheets. He draws one nipple into his mouth and sucks hard while his fingers pinch and roll the other, and the dual sensation makes me cry out.

"Sensitive," he observes, releasing me with a wet pop.

"You know I am."

"I know." He blows cool air across my damp nipple, and I shudder. "I just like hearing you admit it."

"Smug bastard."

"Your smug bastard." He switches sides, giving my other breast the same treatment. "Forever, if you'll have me."

"Forever is a long time."

"Not long enough." He moves to sucks my nipple into his mouth, but stops, pulling back. He's frowning, a serious expression that seems at odds with the teasing of the moment.

"I need to ask you something."

I tense. "That's ominous."

"It's not." He props himself up, one hand still warm on my hip. "Kids. Do you want them?"

The question doesn't catch me off guard—I've been asked it enough times by well-meaning relatives and nosy colleagues. But from him, it's different. This is the man I want to spend the rest of my life with. There's a risk this is a make-or-break conversation.

"No." I hold his gaze, waiting for the flicker of disappointment. "I love Poppy's baby, and Andi's kids, and every other rugrat running around the clubhouse. But I love giving them back more." I shrug. "I don't have the maternal instinct. Never have. I'm happy with my life, Boone. My career, my freedom, and now us—that's enough for me. More than enough."

He nods slowly, and I'm relieved I don't see any disappointment.

"What about you?" I ask. "Do you want more?"

"I love being a dad." A soft smile crosses his face. "Emma and Lee are the best things in my life. Present company excluded, of course."

"Of course," I agree, grinning.

"I'd do it again, if you asked. But given the choice, I'm getting older. The thought of diapers and school runs and teenage drama gives me hives." He huffs a laugh.

"So we're on the same page?"

"Almost." He traces a lazy circle on my hip. "Emma and Lee might have kids someday. Maybe not soon, but eventually. I'm going to want to be there for that. Grandpa duties. Spoiling them rotten, getting them hyped up on sugar, then sending them home." His gaze searches mine. "You okay with that? Being part of our family, down the road?"

I picture it—holidays at the clubhouse, a new generation of chaos, Stone with a grandbaby in his arms while I pour wine and offer unsolicited parenting advice.

"Sounds perfect, actually." I smile. "I'm excellent at spoiling children and returning them."

"Then we're set." He leans down, pressing a kiss to my sternum. "You and me. Cool grandparents who ride motorcycles and corrupt the next generation."

"I do look good on the back of a bike."

"You look good everywhere." His voice drops, and the wicked gleam returns to his eyes. "Now. Where was I?"

He lowers his mouth to my breast, sucking my nipple between his lips. He swirls his tongue and I lose the ability to form coherent thoughts.

"Boone—" I'm panting already, my skin flushed and tingling. "More. I need more."

"You'll get more." He presses a kiss between my breasts, then continues his downward path. "When I'm ready to give it to you."

His mouth traces over my ribs—kissing each one individually, because apparently he really does intend to worship every inch—then down to my stomach. He pauses at my navel, dipping his tongue inside, and I squirm at the ticklish sensation.

"Ticklish?" He grins against my skin.

"A little."

"Good to know." He files the information away, I can tell, for future torment. Then he moves lower, pressing an open-mouthed kiss to the jut of my hipbone.

I feel his smile against my flesh when I whimper.

"So responsive," he murmurs. "I love how your body reacts to me. Like you were made for my touch."

"My body is very enthusiastic about you."

"Good." He shifts lower, his shoulders spreading my thighs as he settles between them. "Because I'm very enthusiastic about it."

But he doesn't go where I expect. Instead, he presses kisses to the inside of my knee. My inner thigh. The crease where my leg meets my hip. Everywhere except where I'm aching for him.

"You're a tease," I accuse, propping myself up on my elbows to glare at him.

"I'm thorough." He nips at my thigh, making me jump. "There's a difference."

"The difference is I'm going to die if you don't touch me."

"Dramatic." But he relents, spreading me open with his thumbs, and I feel his breath hot against my center. The anticipation is almost worse than the waiting. "Look at you. Still wet from earlier. Still swollen. Still ready for me."

"I've been ready for hours. I've been lying here thinking about you, about this, about how good you felt inside me—"

He licks me—one long, slow stroke from entrance to clit—and the words die in my throat. My head falls back, my elbows giving out, and I collapse against the pillows with a moan.

"Keep talking," he says, his voice muffled against my flesh. "Tell me what you were thinking about."

"I can't—not when you're—*oh*—"

He's eating me like I'm a delicacy to be savored. Long, lazy strokes of his tongue. Gentle suction on my clit. Nothing like the urgent devouring of this afternoon—this is slow, deliberate, designed to build me up gradually rather than push me over the edge.

"You were thinking about me," he prompts, pausing just long enough to speak. His lips are wet, glistening with my arousal, and the sight makes my thighs clench. "About this. What specifically?"

"About—" I gasp as his tongue circles my clit. "About how you felt inside me. How big you are. How full. How I could barely walk after."

He groans against me, the vibration making my hips buck. "What else?"

"About how you—*fuck*—how you pinned my wrists down. How you took control. How you made me beg for it." I'm babbling now, saying anything to keep him going. "About how you made me come three times like it was nothing, like you could have kept going all day—"

"I could have." He slides a finger inside me, so slowly I feel every inch, every ridge of his knuckle. "Would have. If we'd had time."

"We have time now."

"We do." He adds a second finger, stretching me, filling me, curling them forward to find the spot that makes me see stars. "All the time in the world."

He works me with his fingers while his tongue continues its maddening rhythm—slow circles around my clit, punctuated by long licks and gentle suction. The pleasure builds like a tide—slow and inevitable—and I feel myself climbing toward the edge.

"That's it," he murmurs, the words vibrating against my most sensitive flesh. "I can feel you getting close. Feel you tightening around my fingers. Feel how much you want this."

"Boone—"

"Don't hold back." He curls his fingers, stroking that spot inside me in time with his tongue on my clit. "Give it to me. Let me feel you come."

The orgasm rolls through me like a wave—not the sharp, explosive peak of earlier, but deeper. Longer. I cry out his name as it crests, my whole body trembling with the force of it, my walls clenching around his fingers in rhythmic pulses.

He works me through it, gentling his touch as the aftershocks fade, pressing soft kisses to my inner thighs. His fingers slip free slowly, and I whimper at the loss.

"Beautiful," he breathes, crawling up my body to hover over me. His chin is wet with my arousal, and he doesn't seem to care. "So fucking beautiful when you come."

I reach for him, pulling him down for a kiss. I taste myself on his lips—tangy, musky—and the intimacy makes me even hotter.

"Inside me," I murmur against his mouth. "Now. I need to feel you."

"Not yet." He kisses me deeper, his tongue sliding against mine. "I'm not done worshipping you."

"Boone—"

"Turn over."

I blink at him. "What?"

"Turn over." His voice is soft but commanding. The voice of a man who's used to being obeyed. "On your stomach."

I comply, and he settles over me, his weight pressing me into the mattress. He's still mostly dressed—jeans and an unbuttoned shirt—and the contrast of his rough clothing against my bare skin makes me shiver.

His mouth finds the back of my neck, kissing down my spine one vertebra at a time.

"I didn't get to do this earlier," he says against my skin. "Didn't get to explore all of you. I was too busy trying not to come in the first five minutes."

I laugh into the pillow. "You did remarkably well, for the record."

"I'm a man of discipline." He presses a kiss between my shoulder blades. "When properly motivated."

His hands knead my shoulders, my back, working out tension I didn't know I was carrying. It's half massage, half seduction—his fingers digging into my muscles while his mouth traces patterns across my shoulder blades.

"You're so tense," he observes.

"I wonder why. Couldn't be the multiple orgasms or the impending FBI raid or the fact I'm in bed with the most infuriating man I've ever met."

"Infuriating?" He nips at my shoulder blade. "That's harsh."

"Infuriatingly sexy," I amend. "Better?"

"Much."

His hands move lower, thumbs pressing into the muscles along my spine, and I groan into the pillow. It feels incredible—like he's unwinding every knot in my body, every bit of stress I've been carrying.

"Where did you learn to do this?" I ask.

"Twenty years of riding will wreck your back if you're not careful." He works a particularly stubborn knot near my lower spine. "Learned to take care of myself."

"Lucky me."

"Lucky both of us."

His hands reach the curve of my ass, and the massage takes on a decidedly less therapeutic tone. He cups my cheeks, squeezing gently, kneading the flesh with his strong fingers.

"Perfect," he murmurs. "Every inch of you is perfect."

"Boone, if you don't fuck me soon, I'm going to—"

"You're going to what?" He spreads my legs, settling between them. I feel the rough denim of his jeans against my inner thighs, and I realize with a start he's still dressed while I'm completely naked. The power imbalance shouldn't be as hot as it is. "Tell me."

"I don't know. Combust. Die. Something dramatic."

"We can't have that." I hear his zipper, the rustle of fabric, and then the hot press of his cock against my ass. "I have plans for you. Can't have you dying before I execute them."

"Then execute them already."

He laughs softly, positioning himself at my entrance. The head of his cock presses against me—teasing, threatening, not quite pushing inside.

"Say please."

"Are you serious?"

"Say please, Josie."

I grind my hips back against him, trying to take what I want, but he holds himself just out of reach. The bastard.

"Please," I grit out.

"Please what?"

"Please fuck me before I murder you."

"Good enough."

He pushes inside—slowly, so slowly—and I feel every inch of him stretching me, filling me. This angle is different from earlier. Deeper. More intense. The weight of him presses me into the mattress, and I feel claimed in a way that makes me purr with primitive satisfaction.

"Fuck," he groans when he's fully seated, his hips flush against my ass. "You feel incredible. Every time. How is it better every time?"

"Because you keep making me wait for it."

He laughs, the sound strained with pleasure, and pulls out almost completely before sliding back in with the same torturous slowness. "Patience is a virtue."

"Patience is overrated."

But even as I say it, I understand what he's doing. This afternoon was about release—about finally giving in to months of tension. This is about connection. About learning each other. About proving that this isn't just physical.

He sets a rhythm that's almost meditative. Long, deep strokes that drag against every nerve ending. His body covers mine completely, his weight a comforting pressure, his mouth at my ear.

"I love you," he murmurs, and the words send a different kind of pleasure through me. "I love you so fucking much, Josie."

"I love you too." My voice catches. "Boone—I love you too."

"I know." He reaches beneath me, finding my clit, rubbing in slow circles that match his thrusts. "I've got you. I'll always have you."

The pleasure builds slowly, inexorably. Layer upon layer of sensation—his cock stroking deep inside me, his fingers working my clit, his weight pressing me into the mattress, his mouth hot against my ear. I'm moaning into the pillow, my hands fisting in the sheets, my whole body tightening around him.

"That's it." His voice is strained now, his control starting to fray. "Come for me, Josie. Come with me inside you."

I shatter with a sob, the pleasure crashing through me in endless waves. He follows seconds later, groaning my name, his hips stuttering as he spills inside me.

We lie there for a long moment, both of us breathing hard, still connected. He's heavy on top of me, but I don't want him to move. I want to stay like this forever—pinned beneath him, filled with him, completely his.

Eventually, he softens enough to slip free, and he rolls onto his back with a groan, pulling me against his chest.

"That was..." I trail off, unable to find the words.

"Worth taking our time." He presses a kiss to my hair. "How do you feel?"

"Like I never want to move again."

"Good." His hand traces lazy patterns on my hip, his touch now gentle rather than demanding. "Because I'm not done with you yet."

"There's more?"

"I told you." He tilts my chin up, brushing a soft kiss across my lips. "All night. And I'm a man of my word."

True to his word, he's insatiable.

After a brief rest—during which I doze against his chest while he plays with my hair—he wakes me with kisses down my spine and coaxes me onto my side. We make love face-to-face, legs intertwined, moving together in a slow rhythm that feels more like dancing than fucking.

"I can see you," he murmurs, his forehead pressed to mine. "I can watch you fall apart."

"Is that what you want? To watch me?"

"I want everything." He hitches my leg higher over his hip, changing the angle. "Every expression. Every sound. Every shudder and moan."

"Possessive."

"Absolutely."

He draws it out until I'm begging, then brings me over the edge with a twist of his hips and a thumb on my clit that makes me see stars.

Afterward, we raid the mini-fridge—bottles of water and leftover pizza eaten naked in bed, laughing at nothing, talking about everything. The sheets are a disaster, tangled at the foot of the bed, but neither of us cares.

"Tell me something I don't know about you," he says, licking pizza sauce off his thumb.

"Like what?"

"Anything. Everything." He reaches over to tuck a strand of hair behind my ear. "I want to know all of it."

So I tell him. About Atlanta—the high-profile cases that made my career, and the one that broke it. About the defendant who walked despite overwhelming evidence, and how I'd found out later that the judge had been bought. About the death threats that followed when I tried to expose it, and the quiet resignation that came after.

"I came to Stoneheart looking for boring," I admit. "Small town. Simple cases. Nothing that could follow me home."

"Bet you didn't expect this." He gestures vaguely at the room. At us. At the MC paraphernalia visible through the open closet door.

"No." I curl closer to him, pressing my face against his chest. "But I'm not complaining."

"Good." He wraps his arms around me, pulling me tighter. "Because you're stuck with me now."

He tells me about his ex, then. About Rebecca—how they'd been high school sweethearts, how he'd gotten her pregnant with Lee at seventeen and married her because it was the right thing to do. How she'd stuck around for thirteen years before finally admitting she couldn't compete with the club for his attention.

"She wasn't wrong," he admits, his voice rough. "I was a shitty husband. Put the club first, every time. She deserved better."

"Do you regret it?"

"I regret hurting her. I regret what it did to the kids, growing up with parents who couldn't make it work." He's quiet for a moment. "But I can't regret the club. It's who I am. And I'd rather be honest about that than pretend to be something I'm not."

"You're not the same man you were then," I point out. "People change."

"Some things don't change. The club will always be part of my life. Part of any life with me." He meets my eyes, and there's a vulnerability in his gaze—what he'd likely call weakness, but I call trust.

I take my time thinking about it rather than offering platitudes. The 2am calls, the secrets I'll never be told, the danger that comes with loving a man like him.

But here's the thing—my life isn't so different.

I've taken calls at midnight from clients in crisis. I've kept secrets that would destroy families if they ever came to light. I've spent my entire career balancing a hundred spinning plates while pretending I have it all under control. Confidentiality isn't new to me. Neither is operating in the spaces between what's legal and what's right.

And if I'm being honest with myself? I like this. The thrill of being with a man who's dangerous and unpredictable, but fiercely protective of the people he loves. The club operates in ways I can't—where the law fails, where the system grinds people up and spits them out, they step in. They protect their own. They get things done.

Not everything is black and white. I learned that my first year practicing law. Sometimes justice lives in the gray areas.

"I can live with that," I say finally. "As long as you don't shut me out. As long as I'm your partner, not just your woman."

"You're both." He kisses my forehead. "You're everything."

We fall silent after that, tangled together in the darkness, but sleep doesn't come. There's too much energy still buzzing between us. Too much want.

"I believe," I say eventually, tracing a finger down his chest, "that you promised me all night."

"Did I?" His cock twitches against my thigh, already starting to harden again. "I suppose I did."

"A man of your word, you said."

"I did say that."

"Then I think—" I wrap my hand around him, stroking slowly. "—you have more work to do."

He groans, his hips thrusting into my grip. "Woman, you're going to kill me."

"But what a way to go."

The last time is just before dawn, when the sky outside is starting to lighten and we're both exhausted in the best possible way. He pulls me on top of him—"Want to watch you ride me," he says, his voice rough with want—and I sink down onto him with a moan.

This is different from the others. Lazier. Half-asleep. More about connection than climax. I rock against him slowly, my hands braced on his chest, while he watches me with an expression that's equal parts lust and love.

"Beautiful," he murmurs, his hands on my hips, guiding me. "So fucking beautiful like this."

"You're not so bad yourself."

He laughs, and I feel it everywhere—the vibration of his chest, the way it makes his cock twitch inside me. I clench around him in response, and his laugh turns into a groan.

"Close," he warns.

"Me too."

When we finally come together, it's quiet. Soft. A whispered promise rather than a shout. I collapse against his chest, and he wraps his arms around me, holding me there while we both come down.

I fall asleep with his heartbeat beneath my ear and his arms wrapped around me like he's never letting go.

He isn't. I know that now.

And neither am I.

16

JOSIE

I'm curled up in the window seat, watching the sun sink behind Stoneheart mountain.

The sky's putting on a show tonight—streaks of orange and pink bleeding into purple, the kind of sunset that makes you understand why people write poetry about this place.

Across the road I can see Andi and Hawk sitting on their porch, sipping beers and laughing. Trees cast long shadows across the street, and somewhere in the distance I can hear the faint rumble of bikes cruising through town.

It's peaceful.

Down the hall, I'm hoping Isabel has managed to settle Lily for the night. She had a nightmare yesterday—I heard Isabel's soft voice through the wall, soothing her back to sleep—and the circles under Isabel's eyes this morning told me everything she wouldn't say out loud.

They're safe here. I know that. Stone's made sure of it, and the club has eyes on the property around the clock. Isabel's holding it together for Lily, but I see the cracks.

I should do more. I just don't know what yet.

The last sliver of sun disappears behind the ridge, and the sky deepens to violet.

"Close your eyes."

I raise an eyebrow at Stone, who's standing in the doorway of our bedroom with an expression that's trying very hard to be casual and failing miserably.

"Why?"

We've already spent the day in bed, so I have to assume that this is something sexual.

"Because I'm asking you to."

"That's not a reason."

His mouth twitches. "Josie. Please close your eyes."

"And if I don't?"

"Then the surprise is ruined, and I'll have to find some other way to make you happy tonight." He crosses his arms, leaning against the doorframe. "Your choice."

I study him—this man who runs an entire motorcycle club, who's faced down cartels and corrupt developers, who can intimidate grown men with a single look. And here he is, practically fidgeting because he's planned something and wants me to play along.

God, I love him.

"Fine." I close my eyes dramatically. "But if you walk me into a wall, I'm billing you for the medical expenses."

"Noted."

His hand finds mine, warm and calloused, and he guides me out of the room. I hear the creak of the hallway floorboards, feel the slight change in air temperature as we move through the clubhouse. Somewhere in the distance, I can hear music playing—a soft and jazzy tune, not the usual rock that pounds through these walls.

"Where is everyone?" The clubhouse is never this quiet.

"Elsewhere."

"That's not an answer."

"It's the only one you're getting." He squeezes my hand. "Watch the step."

I feel the threshold under my feet as we move from carpet to the wood of the deck. The air smells different here—candles, I think, and something savory that makes my stomach growl.

"Okay." Stone's voice is close to my ear, his breath warm against my neck. "Open."

I open my eyes.

And promptly forget how to breathe.

The clubhouse's back patio has been transformed. String lights crisscross overhead, casting everything in a warm golden glow. A table for two sits in the center, draped in an actual tablecloth—white linen, for God's sake—with candles flickering in mason jars. Beyond the railing, the sun is just starting to set, painting the sky in shades of orange and pink.

"Boone..." I turn to look at him, and the vulnerability in his expression nearly undoes me. "What is this?"

"A date." He shrugs, but there's nothing casual about the way he's watching my reaction. "We've never actually had one. Seemed like an oversight."

"We've been a little busy. What with the cartel trying to kill me and all."

"Which is why I figured we were overdue." He pulls out my chair with an old-fashioned gallantry that sets off a flutter in my chest. "Sit. Eat. Let me take care of you for once."

I sit, still taking in the details. There are actual cloth napkins. Wine glasses that don't look like they came from a gas station. A small vase with wildflowers that I suspect came from Ginger's garden.

"Did you do all this yourself?"

"Maggie helped with the food. Ginger handled the flowers. The rest..." He settles into the chair across from me. "The rest was me."

"The string lights?"

"YouTube tutorial. Only electrocuted myself twice."

I laugh, and he grins—that rare, unguarded smile that transforms his whole face.

"I'm impressed," I admit. "I didn't know you had a romantic bone in your body."

"I have several. They've just been dormant for a while." He reaches across the table, taking my hand. "You woke them up."

"That's either the sweetest thing anyone's ever said to me, or a really weird medical condition."

"Can't it be both?"

Maggie appears from inside, carrying two plates with the efficiency of someone who's done this a thousand times. She sets them down with a wink in my direction.

"Herb-crusted salmon, roasted vegetables, and garlic mashed potatoes," she announces. "Don't tell Duck I used the good butter."

"Your secret's safe with us," Stone says.

"It better be. That man would put good butter on everything if I let him." She pats Stone's shoulder as she passes. "You kids have fun. I'll bring dessert in an hour."

She disappears back inside, and we're alone.

The salmon is incredible—flaky and perfectly seasoned, the kind of meal I'd expect from a high-end restaurant, not a biker clubhouse. I tell Stone as much, and he shrugs.

"Maggie's been cooking for the club for twenty years. She could have her own show if she wanted."

"Why doesn't she?"

"Because she likes cooking for family, not strangers." He takes a sip of wine. "That's what the club is to her. Family."

"And what is it to you?"

The question comes out more serious than I intended. Stone sets down his glass, considering.

"Everything," he says finally. "For a long time, it was the only family I had. The only place I belonged." His eyes meet mine. "But now..."

"Now?"

"Now I'm starting to realize family can be more than just the club." He reaches across the table again, his thumb tracing circles on my palm. "It can be this. Us. Whatever we're building."

My throat tightens. "Boone..."

"I know I'm not good at this." His voice is rough. "The romance, the feelings, the... talking about things. I spent fifteen years shutting all of that down. But with you..." He shakes his head. "With you, I want to try. I want to be the man you deserve."

"You already are."

"I'm working on it." He lifts my hand to his lips, pressing a kiss to my knuckles. "Every day, I'm working on it."

We eat in comfortable silence after that, the kind of quiet that doesn't need filling. The sun sinks lower, the string lights growing brighter against the darkening sky. Somewhere in the distance, an owl calls.

"It's your turn to tell me something I don't know about you." I push my empty plate aside. Resting my hands on my fist.

"Like what?"

"Anything. Something from before the club. Before you became the Stone everyone knows."

He's quiet for a moment, and I wonder if I've pushed too far. But then he leans back in his chair, a distant look in his eyes.

"I wanted to be a teacher."

Of all the things I expected him to say, that wasn't it. "A teacher?"

"History. I was obsessed with it as a kid—the Civil War, World War II, ancient Rome. I used to check out stacks of books from the library and read them under my covers with a flashlight." A small smile plays at his lips. "My mom caught me once at 2am reading about the Battle of Gettysburg. She was so mad she grounded me from the library for a week."

"That's adorable."

"It was nerdy as hell." He shrugs. "But I had this idea that I'd go to college, get a degree, come back here and teach at the high school. Make a difference, you know? Help kids see that history isn't just dates and dead people—it's stories. Human stories."

"What happened?"

"Rebecca got pregnant. I was seventeen, she was sixteen, and suddenly college wasn't in the cards anymore." He meets my eyes. "I don't regret it—my kids are the best thing I ever did. But sometimes I wonder what that other life would have looked like."

"You could still do it," I say. "Go back to school. It's not too late."

"Maybe." But he doesn't sound convinced. "Right now, I've got other priorities."

"Like running a motorcycle club and taking down cartels?"

"Like making sure the woman I love knows how much she means to me." He stands, extending his hand. "Dance with me."

"There's no music."

"There's music." He pulls out his phone, taps a few buttons, and suddenly soft jazz is floating through the air —Coltrane, if I'm not mistaken. "I came prepared."

I take his hand and let him pull me to my feet. His arms wrap around me, one hand at the small of my back, the other holding mine against his chest. We sway together, not really dancing, just moving.

"I never took you for a jazz man," I murmur against his shoulder.

"There's a lot you don't know about me yet." His lips brush my temple. "I'm looking forward to showing you all of it."

"Even the embarrassing stuff?"

"Especially the embarrassing stuff." He pulls back just enough to meet my eyes. "I want you to know all of me, Josie. The good, the bad, the history-nerd kid who never got to chase his dreams. All of it."

"I want that too." I rise on my toes to kiss him—soft, sweet, full of promise. "Every piece of you, Boone Armstrong. I want it all."

We finish our kiss and he pulls me back into him, holding me close as we slowly sway.

I close my eyes and let myself sink into him.

This is the part that still catches me off guard. Not the danger—I knew what I was getting into the day I walked into that clubhouse. The late-night calls, the violence that hums beneath the surface, the weight of command that never fully leaves his shoulders. I've seen him stare down threats that would make lesser men crumble. I've watched him make decisions that live in moral gray areas I once thought I'd never accept.

But this? The jazz. The candlelight. The way he holds me, swaying in our bedroom like we're the only two people in the world.

This is the part no one else sees.

The MC gets the president—granite jaw, iron will, a man who'd burn the world down to protect his people. But I get *this*. The man who remembers that I mentioned Coltrane once, weeks ago. Who plans romantic gestures.

Two halves of the same man. Dangerous and tender.

I used to think those things couldn't coexist. That men like Stone were one thing all the way through—that the darkness would eventually swallow everything else. But I was wrong. He's not dark pretending to be light, or light pretending to be dark. He's both, fully and unapologetically, and somehow that makes him the safest place I've ever known.

We dance until the candles burn low and Maggie brings out chocolate cake that's so rich I moan with the first bite. We talk about everything and nothing—his favorite books (historical fiction, naturally), my guilty pleasure TV shows (trashy reality dating competitions), the places we've always wanted to visit (he says Ireland; I say Greece).

By the time we make our way back inside, I'm full and warm and so stupidly happy I could cry.

"Thank you," I tell him at the door to our room. "For tonight. For all of it."

"Thank you for letting me try." He cups my face in his hands. "I know I'm not perfect at this. But I'm going to keep trying. Every day."

"That's all I ask."

He kisses me then—slow and deep and full of everything we've said and everything we haven't. And when he finally pulls back, his eyes are dark with want.

"I believe I promised you dessert," he murmurs.

"I already had cake."

"I wasn't talking about cake."

He pulls me into the room and closes the door behind us.

STONE

I wake to the smell of bacon.

For a moment, I just lie there, trying to remember the last time someone cooked breakfast for me. Maggie makes food for the club, sure, but that's different. That's communal, impersonal. This smells like someone is specifically making breakfast for *me*.

The bed beside me is empty but still warm. Josie hasn't been gone long.

I pull on a pair of sweatpants and follow the smell downstairs to the kitchen.

And stop dead in the doorway.

Josie is standing at the stove in one of my t-shirts, her hair piled in a messy bun, singing along to a song playing softly from her phone. She's swaying slightly as she flips pancakes, completely absorbed in the moment, clearly unaware that she has an audience.

She's the most beautiful thing I've ever seen.

"You're staring."

I jolt. She hasn't turned around.

"How did you know?"

"I can feel you." She glances over her shoulder with a smile. "Also, you're not exactly subtle. I could hear you breathing from across the room."

"Sorry."

"Don't be. I like it." She gestures to the table with her spatula. "Sit. Coffee's ready."

I pour myself a cup and settle into a chair, watching her move around the kitchen with easy confidence. She's clearly done this before—there's a rhythm to it, a practiced efficiency that speaks to years of early mornings and solo breakfasts.

"I didn't know you could cook," I say.

"I'm a woman of many talents." She slides a plate in front of me—pancakes, bacon, eggs over easy. "My grandmother taught me. She believed everyone should know how to feed themselves and the people they love."

"Smart woman."

"The smartest." Josie settles into the chair across from me with her own plate. "She raised me, mostly. My parents were... not great at the whole parenting thing."

"You don't talk about them much."

"Not much to talk about." She shrugs, but I can see the old hurt beneath the casual gesture. "They had me because it was expected, but it wasn't what they wanted. Some people just aren't meant to have kids. By the time I was twelve, I was basically living with my grandmother full-time."

"I'm sorry."

"Don't be. Grandma was the best thing that ever happened to me." Her expression softens. "She's the one who encouraged me to go to law school. Told me I had a mouth made for arguing and I might as well get paid for it."

I laugh. "She sounds like a firecracker."

"She was. Died my second year of law school." Josie's smile turns sad. "Stroke. Quick, at least. She would have hated a long, drawn-out decline."

"Is that why you became a prosecutor? To make her proud?"

"Partly." She takes a bite of pancake, chewing thoughtfully. "But also because I believe in justice. Or I used to, anyway. Before Atlanta."

"And now?"

"Now I believe in a different kind of justice." Her eyes meet mine. "The kind that protects people who can't protect themselves. The kind that takes down the bad guys when the system fails."

"That's why you work with us."

"Yeah," she agrees. "The club does what the courts can't. Or won't." She reaches across the table, taking my hand. "I know it's not always pretty. I know there are things you do that would make a judge blanch. But I've seen enough of the system to know that sometimes, pretty doesn't get the job done."

"And you're okay with that? Really?"

"I'm okay with you." She squeezes my hand. "All of you. The president, the protector, the man who wanted to be a history teacher." A small smile. "Even the part that snores."

"I do not snore."

"You absolutely snore. Like a chainsaw with a sinus infection."

"That's slander."

"It's truth. I have recordings."

"You recorded me sleeping?"

"For evidence." Her eyes sparkle with mischief. "I'm a lawyer. We document everything."

I stand, rounding the table, and she squeals as I haul her out of her chair.

"What are you doing?"

"Getting revenge." I toss her over my shoulder, ignoring her laughing protests. "No one slanders me in my own clubhouse and gets away with it."

"Put me down! I'll burn the pancakes!"

"The pancakes are already done." I carry her toward the stairs. "And I can think of better uses for the next hour than breakfast."

"Boone! The eggs—"

"Will keep."

"You're impossible!"

"And you're beautiful, and you cooked me breakfast, and now I'm going to show you exactly how much I appreciate that."

I kick the bedroom door closed behind us.

The eggs, as it turns out, do keep.

17

JOSIE

Picnic tables line the clubhouse backyard, loaded with more food than a small army could eat. The smell of grilling meat fills the air, mixing with laughter and the steady thump of classic rock from someone's speakers.

It's the kind of gathering that would have terrified me a year ago. A biker barbecue, complete with leather cuts and tattoos and men who look like they could kill you with their bare hands.

Now it just feels like a family gathering.

Stone presses a kiss to my temple. "Try to relax. No one here is going to mug you."

"I know." And I do. Doesn't mean it's not awkward now that people know we're banging.

Stone gets pulled away by Tank to deal with an issue—there's always something—and I find myself drifting toward the drinks table. I'm reaching for a beer when a voice stops me.

"He's out of your league, you know."

I turn to find Lee leaning against the fence, arms crossed, watching me with an expression I can't quite read.

"Excuse me?"

"Not you." He nods toward where Stone is conferring with Hawk. "Him. You could do better."

I blink. "That's... a pretty shitty thing to say about your father."

He grins. "What did you expect me to say?"

"Threats, maybe. 'Hurt my dad and I'll bury you in the woods.' That sort of thing."

Lee's mouth twitches. "Emma already called dibs on the threatening speech. I'm supposed to be the reasonable one."

"And is this reasonable?"

He pushes off the fence, coming to stand beside me. "After Mom left, he shut down. Went through the motions. Ran the club, raised us, but he wasn't really there. You know?"

I nod slowly. I've seen hints of it—the walls Stone keeps up, the way he deflects anything too personal.

"He's different with you," Lee continues. "He laughs. He smiles. He talks about things other than club business." He meets my eyes. "When you were in the hospital, I thought he was going to burn down the entire county looking for who hurt you."

"Lee—"

"I'm not warning you off." His expression softens. "I'm saying thank you. I know you could do better, but..." He takes a breath. "I'm really fucking glad you're not interested in anyone but him."

"I mean, if Paul Rudd offered, I might be tempted to run away to Hollywood."

He grins.

I hip bump him gently. "Your dad is a good man. And he's raised two awesome kids. You think I'm out of his league, but I don't see him as anything but the man he is. Protective, smart, funny, and a guy who looks out for those he loves."

Not to mention exceptional in bed. I don't say that part aloud, I suspect Lee wouldn't appreciate the info.

"I guess there's only one thing left to say." He gives me an awkward half-hug. "Welcome to the family."

A warmth spreads through my chest. "Yeah?"

"Yeah." He drops his arm and goes back to watching the party. "Emma's going to be pissed when I tell her I beat her to the blessing thing. She had a whole speech prepared."

"I won't tell her you did it first."

"Please do. It's more fun that way."

He wanders off to join Tank by the grill, and I'm left standing there with a beer I haven't opened and an unexpected lump in my throat.

Emma finds me twenty minutes later.

"Lee already did it, didn't he?" She plops down on the picnic bench beside me. "He had that smug look he only gets when he thinks he's been emotionally mature."

"I have no idea what you're talking about."

"Liar." But she's smiling. "Fine. I'll give you the speech anyway. Ahem." She clears her throat dramatically. "Josie Bright. You're the first woman my father has looked at with any kind of interest beyond sexual since Mom left. I was so angry at him for so long—for not being present, for putting the club first, for missing my ballet recitals and forgetting my birthday that one year—"

"Emma—"

"Let me finish." She holds up a hand. "But you make him show up. You make him be present. He texts me back now within the same day. He asked about my audition last week. He's trying, and I think... I think it's because of you."

"Can I say something now?"

She waves her hand. "Go ahead."

"I didn't make your dad anything." I turn to face her fully. "Emma, that man has loved you fiercely since the day you were born. I've seen how he talks about you—his whole face changes. You and Lee are the center of his world."

"Then why—"

"Because he gets lost sometimes." I keep my voice gentle. "The cut, the president role, the weight of keeping everyone safe—it swallows him whole if he's not careful. It's not that he forgets you. It's that he forgets himself. Forgets the man underneath all the responsibility."

Emma's quiet, her jaw tight.

"I don't make him better," I continue. "I just... remind him who he already is. The guy who coached your peewee soccer team and cried at your first recital—yeah, he told me about that—he's always been in there. He just needed someone to pull him out of president mode once in a while."

"He cried at my recital?" Her voice is smaller now.

"Apparently he was very proud. Said it was rather undignified for an MC president."

She laughs, but it's watery. "He never told me that."

"He's not great at the emotional stuff. But love was never the problem, Emma. The showing it was." I reach over and squeeze her hand. "He's trying, but it's not because of me—it's because of you. Because he doesn't want to miss any more of your life."

Emma swipes at her eyes. "Okay. Fine. That was... annoyingly insightful." She draws in a breath, shaking off her melancholy. "And now for the big bad step-kid warning," she adds, recovering her composure, "I will make your life a living hell if you hurt him. I have a lot of dancer friends, and we're surprisingly vicious."

I hide a smile. "Noted."

She hugs me—quick and fierce—and then she's gone, disappearing into the crowd before I can respond.

Stone catches my eye across the yard. He raises an eyebrow. *You okay?*

I smile at him. *More than okay.* His kids just gave me their blessings. That's huge.

Ginger finds me next. Of course she does. The woman has a sixth sense for emotional moments.

She settles beside me on the picnic bench, two fresh beers in hand, passing one over without asking.

"Honey, I've been an old lady for twenty years. I know the look." She takes a sip. "You're wondering if you can do this."

I cock an eyebrow. "Is that what I'm thinking? I thought I was tossing up between a burger or dog for dinner."

The smell of the barbecue is making my mouth water.

She shakes her head. "No, you're wondering if you can deal with the late nights, the unexplained disappearances, the blood stains that you'll have to somehow get out of their clothes."

I wince. "Well I wasn't but I am now."

"Look, I've been there. I get it. Tank's been gone three days without a word more times than I can count. I've held dinner, canceled plans, lied to my mother about why

I couldn't make Christmas." She shrugs. "And I'd do it all again."

"Why?"

"Because the club isn't competition, Josie. It's part of who he is. I didn't fall in love with some watered-down version of Tank who punches a clock and comes home at five. I fell in love with the whole man—the one who'd ride through hell for his brothers, who'd take a bullet for this family without thinking twice." She looks at me. "Stone's the same. You either want the whole package, or you don't."

I watch Stone across the yard. He's laughing at something Hawk said, his whole face transformed by it. This fierce, protective, complicated man who's let me see the soft parts he hides from everyone else.

"I want the whole man," I say quietly.

"I know." Ginger smiles. "That's why I'm talking to you instead of warning you off."

"Does it get easier? The worry?"

"Never." She's honest about it. "But you learn to live with it. And the good parts—the family, the loyalty, knowing you're loved by someone who'd burn the world down for you—that makes the worry worth it."

I think about what she's saying. About the choice I'm making, and the life I'm stepping into.

"I might get annoyed sometimes," I admit. "When he disappears at 2am or Church runs three hours long."

"Of course you will. That's normal."

"But it's not like my life is so different, especially when I'm working a case." I shrug. "So yeah, I'm sure I'll get annoyed sometimes. But I get it. And this—him, all of you—it's worth the occasional inconvenience."

Ginger's smile is warm and approving. "That's my girl. Now, tell me about the sex. Was it good?"

The evening moves on, the bikers getting rowdier as the night deepens. I'm getting another drink when I notice them.

Isabel is sitting on the back porch steps, Lily drowsing against her shoulder. The little girl's arms are wrapped around that ratty stuffed rabbit—Mr. Flopsy, she calls him—and her eyes are at half-mast, fighting sleep.

Steel is leaning against the porch post nearby, telling Isabel something that makes her almost-smile. Which for Isabel is practically hysterical laughter. He's relaxed in a way I haven't seen before, his usual guardedness softened.

And Brick...

Brick is watching from across the yard.

He's not obvious about it. He's in conversation with Tank, nodding at whatever's being said, his massive frame somehow managing to look casual. But his eyes keep drifting back to that porch.

Steel notices. His jaw tightens, just slightly.

Oh. That's going to be interesting.

Isabel, oblivious to both of them, adjusts Lily's weight and says something that makes Steel laugh.

Brick's beer bottle creaks in his grip.

Well, damn.

Stone appears at my elbow. "What are you looking at?"

"Nothing." I turn to face him.

"Is it the Isabel situation?"

"You noticed too?"

"Hard not to." He glances toward the porch. "Steel's been hovering since the day he met her. And Brick hasn't stopped watching her since he brought her home."

"Does that concern you?"

"Not yet." He pulls me against him. "Right now, I'm more concerned with making sure my woman knows she's the only one I'm watching."

"Smooth."

"I try."

He kisses me—soft and sweet in front of everyone—and I let myself sink into it. Into him. Into this life I never expected to want.

I fit here.

The realization settles over me like a warm blanket.

I truly fit here.

18

STONE

I can't stop watching her.

The party's been going for a couple of hours now, and somewhere along the way Josie slipped out of my orbit and into everyone else's. Josie's a natural hostess—chatting with Kya by the drinks table, laughing with Maggie, letting Ginger rope her into a conversation that involves a lot of hand gestures and knowing looks.

Mine.

"You're staring, Prez."

I don't bother turning. "Mind your business, Hawk."

"Your business is my business. That's literally my job." He comes to stand beside me, following my gaze. "She fits."

"Yeah."

"Took you long enough to figure it out."

"Hawk—"

"Just saying." He holds up his hands. "We've all been waiting for you to pull your head out of your ass. Glad it finally happened."

Before I can respond, my phone buzzes. Club business that needs handling—something about the security rotation for tomorrow's rally. I sigh.

"Go," Hawk says. "I'll keep an eye on things here."

I find Josie first, pulling her aside.

"I need to handle some shit. Twenty minutes, maybe thirty."

I wait for the disappointment. The frustration. The argument about priorities that I got every time the club pulled me away from family time.

Instead, Josie just rises on her toes and kisses my cheek.

"Go. I'll be here when you get back."

"You're not upset?"

"Stone." She cups my face in her hands. "This is who you are. The club needs you. Go handle it."

She says it so simply, like it's obvious. Like she's not asking me to choose, because there's no choice to be made—just a life to be lived, together, with all its complications.

God, I love this woman.

I kiss her properly—deep enough to earn a few whistles from nearby brothers—and force myself to walk away.

The security issue takes longer than expected.

By the time I get back to the party, the moon has risen and the string lights have taken over, casting everything in a warm gold. I scan the crowd for Josie, expecting to find her waiting for me, maybe looking a little bored.

She's not waiting.

She's in the middle of a poker game with Ginger, Andi, and Maggie, and from the pile of chips in front of her, she's winning. She throws her head back laughing at Ginger, completely at ease, completely happy.

She didn't need me to have a good time.

The realization hits me like a punch to the chest—but not in a bad way. She's built her own place here, made her own connections, found her own joy.

And she's still going to be in my bed tonight.

She's the one.

I've known it for a while, but watching her now—laughing with my family, fitting seamlessly into my world—the certainty crystallizes into something unshakeable.

I'm going to marry this woman.

I tuck the thought away for later and head toward the back porch, giving her space to finish her game. That's when I find Lily.

She's sitting alone on the back steps, clutching Mr. Flopsy, her little face pinched with worry.

"Hey, kid." I lower myself to sit beside her, joints protesting. "Aren't you meant to be in bed?"

She shrugs, cuddling Mr. Flopsy close.

"Party too loud?"

She frowns, her mouth turning into a cute little pout. "Mr. Flopsy doesn't like crowds. Too many people make him nervous."

Sure, Mr. Flopsy doesn't like it.

"Yeah? What helps him feel better?"

She thinks about it, her brow furrowing with the seriousness of the question. "Knowing where Bel is. And quiet. And..." She looks up at me with those big eyes. "Knowing the loud people aren't mad-loud. Just happy-loud."

Fuck, that hurts to hear.

"They're happy-loud," I tell her gently. "Everyone here is happy. And safe. No one's going to hurt you or Mr. Flopsy. Not ever again."

She stares at me, her little face pinched.

"I promise."

She studies me for a long moment, weighing my words with a gravity no six-year-old should possess. Then, slowly, she leans against my arm—just slightly, just testing.

I don't move away.

She settles in a little more.

We sit there together in silence, watching the party from our quiet corner. I think about what it means to make promises to a child like this. What it means to be the kind of man who can keep them.

"Is this our home now?" Lily asks quietly.

I look at her—this tiny, fierce survivor who's been through more than any child should—and I know there's only one answer.

"Yeah, Lily. For as long as you and Isabel need."

She nods, satisfied, and goes back to watching the party. A few minutes later, Isabel skids out the door, looking frantic until she spots her sister.

"Lily! There you are!" She stalks over to us. "You're meant to be in bed. You scared me."

"Mr. Flopsy wanted to watch the party."

Isabel meets my eyes over her sister's head. An understanding passes between us. A shared recognition of what it means to protect the people you love.

"Thank you," she says quietly.

"Anytime."

She scoops up Lily and heads inside, and I'm left alone on the steps, thinking about family. About the ones you're born into and the ones you build.

Josie finds me a few minutes later, dropping onto the step beside me.

"Andi cheats at poker," she announces. "I'm almost certain of it."

"Oh, she definitely cheats at poker. Hawk taught her."

"And you didn't warn me?"

"Thought you could handle it." I pull her against my side. "Looks like I was right."

She hums contentedly, leaning into me. "How was the club business?"

"Handled."

"And the mysterious conversation with Lily?"

"Also handled." I press a kiss to her hair. "You fit, you know. With all of us."

"I know." She sounds almost surprised by her own certainty.

"Good." I tighten my arm around her.

We sit there as the party winds down around us—watching, listening, being part of something bigger than ourselves.

Tomorrow, everything changes. The rally. The FBI raid. The end of Summit.

But tonight, there's just this, her warmth against my side, and the sound of my family laughing.

19

JOSIE

Duck's rally draws the biggest crowd Stoneheart has seen in years.

The town square is packed—families with children, elderly couples holding homemade signs, young professionals who've never attended a political event in their lives. The energy is electric, hopeful in a way I haven't felt since I first moved here.

Stone insisted I stay close. After everything with Summit, he's not taking chances. But I don't mind the protective detail. It's actually kind of sweet, watching Hawk and Axel pretend to casually position themselves between me and any potential threats.

"You'd think I was the one running for office," I mutter to Kya.

"You're the president's old lady." She grins. "That makes you a target and a VIP. Get used to it."

Duck takes the stage to thunderous applause. He looks good up there—confident, commanding, nothing like the nervous man who asked me to review his speech three times this morning.

"Friends, neighbors, family," he begins. "I'm not going to stand up here and make a bunch of promises I can't keep. You know me. You know I'm not a politician—I'm a guy who runs a garage and happens to care a whole lot about this town."

The crowd cheers. Someone yells, "That's why we love you, Duck!"

"And I love you too." Duck grins. "But listen—we've been through a lot this past year. Outside interests trying to buy up our land, drive out our businesses, turn Stoneheart into something it was never meant to be. And we said no."

More cheers. I find myself clapping along.

"We said no because this town—our town—is worth fighting for. Not because of the buildings or the land values or whatever the hell Summit Properties thought they could profit from. But because of you. The people. The community. My neighbors, the people who make Stoneheart home."

He's hitting his stride now, and the crowd is eating it up.

"So here's my promise—the only one I'm going to make. If you elect me mayor, I will fight for this town every single day. I will fight for our businesses, our families, our right to exist without some corporate vulture trying to pick our bones. I will—"

He pauses for dramatic effect, reaching for a cord at the side of the stage.

"—be your PUBLIC SERVANT!"

He yanks the cord.

The banner unfurls behind him in all its fifty-foot glory.

VOTE DUCK WHEELER: YOUR PUBIC SERVANT

For a split second, nobody reacts. Duck is still facing the crowd, arms spread wide, basking in what he thinks is his big moment.

Then the laughter starts.

It begins at the back—a snort, a giggle—and spreads forward like a wave. People are pointing, pulling out their phones, absolutely losing it. Duck's triumphant expression falters.

"What? What's so funny?"

Someone in the front row turns their phone around to show him. Duck squints at the screen, then slowly turns to look at the banner behind him.

The crowd absolutely loses it.

Duck stares at the typo for a long, silent moment. Then he turns back to the crowd with an expression of pure, deadpan acceptance.

"Well, shit."

The laughter doubles.

Someone in the back yells, "You've got my vote!"

"That's what I like to hear!" Duck is fully rolling with it now, leaning into the disaster. "Listen, I may not be able to spell, but I can damn sure lead. And unlike my banner, my commitment to this town is one hundred percent accurate."

The crowd roars its approval. Phones are recording. This is going to go viral.

Stone appears at my elbow, his eyes scanning the crowd even as he's fighting back a smile.

"He's going to win because of this," I say.

"Probably. Nothing like a good typo to humanize a candidate." His hand finds mine. "You doing okay?"

"I'm great." And I am. Surrounded by people I've come to care about, watching democracy in action, feeling like part of something bigger. "This is fun."

"Good." He squeezes my hand. "Stay close. FBI raid is set for midnight. I want us back at the clubhouse well before then."

"Yes sir, Mr. President."

"Brat." He slaps my ass.

I laugh, leaning into him, feeling safer than I have in weeks. The rally is winding down now, Duck still working the crowd, shaking hands and posing for selfies with the typo banner. It's the kind of wholesome chaos that makes Stoneheart feel like home.

"I need to use the restroom," I tell Stone. "Too much lemonade."

He doesn't hesitate. "I'll come with you."

"To the bathroom?" I raise an eyebrow.

"To the café." He nods toward Rosie's, the newly opened cafe sits on the corner of the square. "I could use a coffee."

I don't argue. After everything we've been through, I understand his need to stay close.

Rosie's is quiet compared to the bustling square—most people are outside for the festivities. The bell chimes as we enter, and Stone guides me toward the counter with a hand on my lower back.

"A black coffee," he tells the barista—a college-aged girl I don't recognize. He glances at me. "You want a drink?"

"A bottled water would be great. Do you have a bathroom?"

"Restroom's down the hall on the left," the girl offers.

I squeeze Stone's arm. "Two minutes."

"I'm timing you."

I roll my eyes. "Of course you are."

The hallway is narrow, dimly lit compared to the bright café. There's a small three stall bathroom on the left, storage closet on the right, and at the far end, a door marked EMPLOYEES ONLY which I assume leads to their locker room.

The bathroom is empty except for one occupied stall. I take the one furthest from the door, do my business, and I'm washing my hands when the other woman emerges.

She's young—mid-twenties maybe, wearing a sundress and a Stoneheart Farmers Market tote bag. She gives me a polite smile as she moves to the sink beside me.

"Hell of a rally, huh?" she says. "I've never seen the square this packed."

"Duck's got a lot of supporters."

She flashes me a smile. "Well, have a nice day."

"You too."

She pushes through the bathroom door ahead of me, and the lights go out.

I hear a scuffle. A muffled cry, cut short.

My blood goes cold.

Through the crack of the still-closing door, I can see shapes moving in the darkened hallway. The woman's tote bag hits the floor. Someone's dragging her toward the EMPLOYEES ONLY door at the end of the hall.

Get out. Get to Stone. Now.

I shove through the bathroom door—

And walk straight into a wall of muscle.

"Ms. Bright." The voice is calm. Professional. "We've been waiting for you."

A hard object presses into my ribs before I can scream.

"Don't," he says quietly. "The woman we just took? We'll let her go if you come with me. But if you make a sound, if you try to run, she dies. Understand?"

I nod, my throat too tight for words.

"Good. Walk."

The EMPLOYEES ONLY door opens onto a back alley where a black SUV idles at the mouth of it, engine running. Two men have propped the unconscious woman against the wall of the alley—I see her chest rise and fall, *alive, thank God*—before they turn their attention to me.

The alley swallows me whole. Two men in front, one behind, the gun never leaving my side. All I can hear is the pounding of my heart.

Stone must have heard the commotion. He'll save me. He'll come get me.

The door behind us remains firmly shut.

"She's secure." One of the men speaks into a phone. "Moving to secondary location. Dump the bait."

She crumples to the ground, as they push me into the vehicle.

"Get in. *Now*."

I get in.

The door slams behind me, and the SUV pulls away.

20

STONE

Two minutes, she said. I'm counting.

There's a roar from the rally outside, loud enough to draw the attention of those outside and temporarily drown out the chatter around me.

I glance over my shoulder, catching sight of Duck back on the stage, doing what looks like a line dance.

Of course he is.

I turn back, resuming my counting.

At ninety seconds, the lights flicker and die. The barista swears, fumbling for her phone.

"Sorry—old wiring. Happens sometimes when the square's pulling extra power for events—"

But the cold is already spreading through my chest. That instinct that's kept me alive for twenty years.

Where the fuck is Josie?

"Josie?" I call toward the hallway.

No answer.

I'm moving before the barista can finish her explanation, shoving past the counter into the dark corridor. Emergency lighting flickers on—dim red, barely enough to see by.

The bathroom door is ajar.

I push through, gun already in my hand. Empty. Three stalls, all empty, a tote bag abandoned on the wet floor.

Not Josie's.

I kick through the EMPLOYEES ONLY door at the end of the hall, and in three strides burst into the back alley—

Empty. Nothing but overflowing dumpsters and the distant screech of tires.

A woman is slumped against the alley wall, groaning, just coming to.

"What happened?" I crouch beside her, fighting to keep my voice steady. "There was another woman—brown hair, early forties—"

"Men," she mumbles, her eyes unfocused. "Men grabbed me. They grabbed her. They—" She starts crying.

My world narrows to a single, crystalline point of focus.

They took her.

They took my woman.

I let her out of my sight for less than three fucking minutes.

I hit call on my phone, and Hawk picks up instantly. "Prez? What's—"

"She's gone." The words come out strange. Hollow. "They've got Josie."

"Rally the brothers." My voice doesn't sound like mine. "Get everyone to the clubhouse. *Now.*"

"Stone—"

"NOW."

Less than a half-hour later, the entire club is at the barracks, the lot locked down tighter than a fucking safe.

The Chapel has never felt more like a war room.

Every brother is present, called in from wherever they were, faces grim and ready. Steel and Bones have three laptops running, tracking every camera feed in the county. Tank is on the phone with our contacts in the sheriff's department. Lee stands beside me, silent and solid, the only thing keeping me from putting my fist through a wall.

I can't stop moving.

I pace the length of the table, then back again. My fingers rake through my hair for the tenth time in as many minutes. Every muscle in my body is coiled tight, vibrating with the kind of energy that has nowhere to go. My jaw aches from clenching it.

Where is she?

The question loops in my head like a broken record. I've faced down cartels, corrupt cops, federal agents. I've made decisions that could've gotten my brothers killed and slept fine afterward. But this—not knowing where Josie is, what they're doing to her, whether she's even still—

No. I shut that thought down hard.

She's alive. She has to be alive.

"Stone." Lee's voice is low, steady. "Sit down. You're making everyone nervous."

"I can't fucking sit down."

He doesn't push. He knows better.

The clock on the wall ticks. Every second feels like an hour. Every minute she's out there is another minute I'm failing her.

"We've got a location." Steel looks up from his screens, and my whole body snaps toward him. "The SUV went to the old textile warehouse on Route 9. Same place Caruso's been running his operation."

"That's where the FBI raid is supposed to hit tonight," Hawk says.

"Then we move the timeline up." I pace the length of the room, mind racing. "Steel, get Agent Pilkin on the line. We need federal backup now, not in six hours."

"Already calling."

"What about going in ourselves?" Tank asks. "We've got the firepower. We know the layout."

"And they know we're coming." Lee points out. "They took Josie specifically to draw us out. If we go in blind, we're walking into an ambush."

He's right. I know he's right. But every second Josie is in their hands is a second too long.

I should never have let her go alone. Should have checked the bathroom and hall first. Should have—

"Dad." Lee's hand lands on my shoulder, grounding me. "Stay focused. We'll get her back."

I nod, shoving the guilt down deep where it can't distract me. There'll be time for self-recrimination later. Right now, Josie needs me sharp.

"Pilkin's on line two," Steel calls out.

I grab the phone. "They've got Josie."

"I know. We intercepted their communications five minutes ago." Her voice is clipped, professional, but I hear the urgency underneath. "They're holding her at the warehouse, using her as leverage. They'll want to know what evidence we have on them."

"She won't tell them anything."

"No. She won't." A pause. "Which means they'll escalate. We need to move fast."

The word *escalate* hits me like a sledgehammer to the chest.

I know what that means. I've seen what men like Caruso do to people who won't talk. The images flash through my mind unbidden—Josie's face, her hands, her body broken and bloody because she's too goddamn loyal to give them what they want.

A dark and primal rage claws its way up from the pit of my stomach. The kind that makes men do terrible things.

Anyone who touches her dies.

It's not a threat. It's not even a decision. It's a fact, as certain as gravity. If there's a single mark on her, a single bruise, I will burn that warehouse to the ground with everyone inside. FBI raid be damned. Consequences be damned. They will learn what happens when you take my woman from me.

Lee's hand lands on my shoulder—grounding, steadying. He sees it in my face. They all do.

I force myself to breathe.

"How fast can you get your teams in position?"

"Two hours. Maybe less if I pull some strings."

"Make it less." I grip the phone so hard I'm surprised it doesn't crack. "Whatever strings you need to pull, pull them. That's my woman in there."

"I understand. Stone. We're going to get her back."

"Damn right we are."

I hang up and turn to face my brothers.

"Two hours. FBI takes point on the assault. We'll provide perimeter support, make sure no one gets out." I meet each of their eyes in turn. "This isn't about Summit anymore. This isn't about Caruso or the cartel or any of that shit. This is about family. They took one of ours, and we're getting her back."

"And if she's hurt or...?" Hawk doesn't finish the question.

The rage I've been holding at bay threatens to crack through. I think about Josie—her sharp tongue, her soft heart, the way she looked at me this morning. The way she trusted me to keep her safe.

I fucking failed.

"If she's hurt," I say, my voice deadly calm, "then God help whoever touched her. Because I won't."

I dismiss the men to go do what they need to prepare for the coming battle.

Steel finds me on the roof an hour later.

I don't know how long I've been standing here, staring at nothing, running through every possible scenario in my head. Every way this could go wrong. Every way I could lose her.

The night air is cold, but I barely feel it. All I can feel is the hollow ache in my chest where certainty used to live. For fifteen years, I've been numb. Going through the motions. Running the club, raising my kids, keeping everyone else safe while something inside me slowly calcified into stone.

Then Josie walked into my life and cracked me wide open.

"They haven't hurt her." Steel says quietly. "Their comms are mostly about logistics. They're moving product, cleaning house before the heat comes down. She's leverage, not entertainment."

"Yet."

"Yet," he agrees. "But she's smart. She's keeping them talking, asking questions, probably cataloging everything for the prosecution." He almost smiles. "She's trying to negotiate her own return."

That's my girl.

"The civilian?" I ask. "The woman from the alley?"

"Hawk got her checked out. She's fine—they drugged her, but it's wearing off. She didn't see much, but she confirmed three men, black SUV." Steel pauses. "They planned this, Stone. They knew exactly when and where to grab her."

"Someone's been watching us."

"Looks like it."

I file that away for later. Right now, it doesn't matter how they knew. What matters is getting Josie back.

"Steel." I turn to face him. "When we go in, I need you in a sniper position. Overwatch. If things go sideways—"

"I'll have the shot." He says it without hesitation. "Whatever it takes to get her out."

"You're still a prospect. This isn't your fight."

"Bullshit." His jaw sets, and I see the man he's becoming. "She's one of us. That makes it my fight. And I'm the best shot in the club—we both know it. Put me where I can do the most damage."

I study him for a long moment. The beard. The glasses. The quiet competence that's replaced his early uncertainty. The women call him Fairy Floss, and he lets them, because he's secure enough in himself not to care. But I've seen him on the range. I know what he's capable of.

"Northeast corner of the building next door. You'll have sight-lines on both the main entrance and the loading dock."

"I'll be there."

He turns to go, then stops.

"Stone. We're going to get her back."

"I know."

But as I watch him leave, I make myself a promise.

If anything happens to Josie—if they've touched her, hurt her, done anything to dim the light in her eyes—there won't be a force on earth that'll stop me from burning their world to ashes.

I let her out of my sight, and they took her.

I'll never forgive myself for that.

But first, I'm going to get her back. And then I'm going to make them pay.

Every. Single. Fucking. One.

21

JOSIE

The warehouse smells like chemicals and fear.

They've got me in what looks like a foreman's office on the second floor—glass windows overlooking the main floor, a battered desk, filing cabinets that have seen better decades. My hands are zip-tied in front of me, which is a mistake on their part. Behind would have been smarter. But I'm not about to point that out.

I'm in a metal folding chair, the kind that digs into your spine no matter how you sit. The cold seeps through my jeans, and I can feel my muscles starting to cramp from holding still. I shift slightly, testing the give in my restraints. Not much, but not nothing either.

My heart is pounding so hard I'm surprised they can't hear it.

My wrists ache where the zip ties bite into skin. I'm

thirsty. I need to pee. And underneath the forced calm, rage is simmering—hot and bright and dangerous.

How dare they.

I've spent my entire career putting men like this behind bars. I've stared down murderers in courtrooms, faced threats and intimidation without flinching. And now I'm zip-tied to a chair in a chemical-stinking warehouse because these bastards thought I'd be easy leverage.

They have no idea who they're dealing with.

The fear is still there—I'm not stupid enough to pretend otherwise. But the anger is stronger. And anger, I can use.

Breathe. Focus. Catalogue.

It's the only thing keeping the panic at bay—turning terror into data, fear into something slightly useful. If I let myself feel it all, I'll shatter. So I don't. I shove it down into a box and lock it tight, the way I've done in a hundred courtrooms when a case was going sideways.

There are three men in the room. I watch them, waiting to see where their weaknesses are.

The one by the door is muscle—young, nervous, keeps checking his phone. Probably low-level, likely expendable. The one leaning against the filing cabinet is older, calmer, with the flat eyes of someone who's done this before. He's the one to watch.

The third is the problem. He arrived twenty minutes ago, and the other two snapped to attention like soldiers at inspection. Mid-fifties, silver hair, expensive suit that's out of place in this shithole. He hasn't introduced himself, but I know exactly who he is.

Vincent Caruso.

The FBI's most wanted. The man Stone and I have been building a case against for weeks. And now I'm zip-tied to a chair in his makeshift office, trying not to let my hands shake.

Think, Josie. You're a lawyer. Your weapon is words. Use them.

"You know this is pointless," I say, keeping my voice steady. "Whatever you think I know, the FBI already has copies of everything."

Caruso doesn't look up from his phone. "Ms. Bright. I've been in this business for thirty years. Do you really think I'd go to the trouble of acquiring you if I didn't already know exactly what you have?"

"Then why am I here?"

Now he looks at me. His eyes are flat, reptilian. The eyes of a man who's ordered deaths the way most people order coffee.

"You're here because you're leverage." He sets down the phone. "Your biker friends have been a thorn in my side for months. They've cost me money, product, and now—thanks to your little evidence package—several key business relationships."

"Sounds like a you problem."

His smile doesn't reach his eyes. "It was until now. In approximately—" he checks his watch "—four hours, my associates in the FBI will ensure that raid never happens. The evidence will be lost. The case will collapse. And you, Ms. Bright, will help me understand exactly who else might have copies."

"I'm not telling you shit."

"Everyone says that." He stands, smoothing his jacket. "Ivan will be here soon to begin the questioning. I'm told he's quite... persuasive."

My blood goes cold, but I keep my expression neutral. "Ivan. I heard he's your new attack dog after Carlos disappeared. Didn't that happen after he kidnapped Emma Armstrong? Strange that."

Caruso's jaw ticks, his eyes narrowing.

"You've done your homework."

"I'm thorough." I lean forward, ignoring the way my zip ties dig into my wrists. "Here's what else I know, Mr. Caruso. I know you've been laundering money through Summit Properties for three years. I know you've got at least two federal agents on your payroll—An agent in the Albany field office and someone higher up whose name I haven't confirmed yet. I know about the shipments coming through the port in Jersey, and I know about the warehouse in Scranton where you process the product before distribution."

I'm bluffing on half of this—educated guesses based on patterns in the evidence—but the way his jaw tightens tells me I'm hitting close to home.

"I also know," I continue, "that the FBI agent running this operation isn't one of yours. Alex Pilkin is a straight arrow. Always has been. Which means your four-hour timeline is optimistic at best."

"You're trying to rattle me."

"I'm trying to help you see reality." I hold his gaze. "The club knows where I am by now. They're not going to wait for the FBI. Stone will come for me, and when he does, he won't be interested in arrests or due process. He'll be interested in blood."

"Your biker boyfriend doesn't scare me."

"He should." I smile, and it's not a nice smile. "You've never seen what an MC president does when someone takes his woman. But you're about to find out."

Caruso stares at me for a long moment. Then he laughs —a cold, humorless sound.

"I see why he likes you. You've got fire." He moves toward the door. "Enjoy it while it lasts. Ivan will be here within the hour, and I promise you, Ms. Bright—he's very good at putting out fires."

The door closes behind him.

I let out a breath, my heart hammering against my ribs.

Okay. Think. What do you know?

Four hours until his FBI contacts intervene. That's the timeline. If the raid happens before then, Caruso loses. If it doesn't, he wins and I'm either dead or wishing I was.

Stone knows where I am—Steel tracked the SUV. That means they're already planning a rescue. The question is whether they'll wait for FBI backup or come in hot on their own.

They'll wait. Lee will make Stone wait. Going in without backup is suicide.

But waiting means hours. And Ivan is coming.

I test the zip ties again. They're tight, but not impossible. If I can dislocate my thumb I might be able to slip free. But then what? I'm on the second floor of a building full of armed men, with no weapons and no backup.

You're a lawyer, not a soldier. Stop trying to be an action hero and focus on what you're good at.

Information. I need information.

I scan the office, looking for anything useful. The desk drawers are locked. The filing cabinets too. But there's a laptop on the desk—closed, probably password-protected, but still. And through the glass windows, I can see the main floor of the warehouse.

It's exactly what Steel's surveillance footage showed. Processing tables. Packaging equipment. Stacks of product ready for distribution. A dozen workers moving with the efficiency of a well-run operation.

And guards. I count six on the main floor, plus Tattoo Neck by my door. All armed. All alert.

This is a fortress. Even the FBI is going to have a hard time breaching it.

Unless they have inside help.

I think about the layout. The main entrance is heavily guarded, but there's a loading dock on the east side—I saw it when they brought me in. And the windows on the upper floor are old, probably single-pane. Easy to breach if you've got the right equipment.

Stop it. You're not planning a raid. You're just trying to survive until Stone gets here.

Stone.

I close my eyes, letting myself think about him for just a moment. The way he looked at me this morning, soft and rumpled from sleep. The way he kissed me before we left for the rally.

He's coming and he's going to be so fucking pissed.

The thought almost makes me smile.

The door opens, and my moment of comfort evaporates.

The man who walks in is huge—easily six-four, built like a linebacker gone to seed. His face is a roadmap of violence, broken nose, scar through one eyebrow, the kind of flat eyes that have seen things and enjoyed them.

Ivan.

My stomach curdles. Every instinct I have screams at me to run, to fight, to do *something*—but there's nowhere to go. I'm zip-tied to a chair, and this monster is walking toward me like he has all the time in the world.

I swallow hard, forcing the fear down past the lump in my throat.

Don't let him see it. Don't give him that.

"Ms. Bright." His voice is surprisingly soft. Almost gentle. Somehow that's worse than if he'd been growling. "I've been looking forward to meeting you."

"Wish I could say the same." My voice comes out steady. Thank God for small mercies.

He pulls up a chair, positioning it directly in front of me. Close enough that I can smell him—cigarettes, cheap cologne with a metallic underneath. When he sits, our knees are almost touching.

My skin crawls. I want to recoil, to put distance between us, but I force myself to stay still. Any reaction is a weapon he can use.

"Mr. Caruso tells me you've been uncooperative."

"No, I've been honest. Just because I'm not telling you what you want to hear, doesn't mean I'm uncooperative."

"Doesn't it?" He tilts his head, studying me like a specimen. "In my experience, honesty and cooperation go hand in hand. People who are honest have nothing to hide. People who have nothing to hide don't need to be... persuaded."

"What do you want to know?"

"Everything." He smiles, and it's the smile of a man who enjoys his work. "Let's start with the evidence. Who has copies besides the FBI?"

"I don't know."

The slap comes out of nowhere—a backhanded blow that snaps my head to the side and fills my mouth with the taste of copper. Stars explode across my vision.

"Let's try that again." His voice is still gentle. Still soft. "Who has copies of the evidence?"

I spit blood onto the floor. "Go fuck yourself."

This time, it's a punch. My cheek explodes with pain. The chair tips, and I nearly go over before he grabs my shirt and hauls me upright.

"I can do this all night, Ms. Bright." He's not even breathing hard. "But I don't think you can. So let's make this easy. Tell me what I want to know, and I'll make your death quick. Keep being difficult, and... well." He shrugs. "I have very creative ways of making people talk."

My vision is blurring. Blood drips from my lip onto my shirt.

Buy time. Stone is coming. Just buy time.

"The club," I manage. "The club has copies. They backed everything up to multiple servers. Cloud storage. Encrypted. Even if you destroy everything here, the evidence exists in a dozen different places."

It's not entirely true—I don't know what Steel did with the backups—but it's plausible enough to make Ivan pause.

"Where are these servers?"

"I don't know. The club handled the tech side. I just handled the legal strategy."

Another slap, but lighter this time. Testing me.

"You're lying."

"I'm a lawyer, not a fucking liar." I meet his gaze, refusing to look away. "You want the servers? Go ask Stone. Oh wait—he's probably out there right now planning how to kill everyone in this building."

Ivan studies me for a long moment. Then he stands, pulling out his phone.

"Watch her," he tells Tattoo Neck. "I need to update Mr. Caruso."

He steps out, and I slump in my chair, every inch of my face throbbing with pain.

Bought some time. Not much, but some.

I don't know how long I sit there. Minutes. Maybe longer. The adrenaline is fading, replaced by a bone-deep exhaustion and the steady pulse of pain in my cheek. My lip is swelling. I can feel my eye starting to close.

Stone is going to lose his mind when he sees me.

The thought is almost funny. Almost.

Tattoo Neck hasn't moved from his position by the door. He's watching me with the bored disinterest of a man who's seen worse. I consider trying to talk to him— maybe find a crack in his loyalty—but my mouth hurts too much for conversation.

So I wait.

The sound is so distant at first that I hardly register it. A low rumble that could be thunder, except the sky was clear when they brought me in. It grows louder, closer, and I recognize the sound with a surge of desperate hope.

Motorcycles.

A lot of them.

Tattoo Neck hears it too. He straightens, one hand going to his earpiece.

"Copy," he says. "Understood."

He looks at me, and for the first time, I see something other than boredom in his expression.

Fear.

"What's happening?" I ask, though I already know.

He doesn't answer. He pulls his gun and moves toward the window, peering out at the main floor below.

The chaos starts all at once.

Shouting. Running footsteps. The crash of the main entrance being breached. Gunfire—sharp, staccato bursts that echo through the warehouse like fireworks.

And then the world turns white.

The flash-bang comes through the window, shattering glass and filling the room with blinding light and deafening noise. I squeeze my eyes shut and throw myself sideways, chair and all, hitting the floor hard as Tattoo Neck screams and fires wildly at nothing.

Stone.

He came.

He came, and now all hell is breaking loose.

I curl into a ball, zip-tied hands over my head, and pray that I survive long enough to see him again.

22

STONE

The warehouse erupts into chaos the moment the FBI breaches.

Flash-bangs go first—three of them through the ground-floor windows, turning the night into a strobe of white light and concussive thunder. Then the tactical teams pour in, black-clad figures moving in precise formation, shouting commands that get lost in the roar of gunfire.

I'm not supposed to be inside. Pilkin made that clear.

Perimeter support, she'd said. *Let my people handle the extraction.*

Fuck that.

"Stone!" Hawk grabs my arm as I move toward the loading dock entrance. "Pilkin said—"

"I know what she fucking said." I shake him off. "Josie's in there. I'm going in."

"Then I'm coming with you."

"No. Hold the perimeter. Make sure no one gets out." I check my weapon—Glock 19, full magazine, one in the chamber. "Lee, you're with me. Tank, back up Hawk. Nobody leaves this building unless they're wearing a badge or a cut."

"What about Steel?" Tank asks.

I look up at the neighboring building where a shadow moves into position on the rooftop. The kid found his perch. Now he just needs a target.

"Steel does what Steel does best." I pull my balaclava down. "Let's move."

The loading dock door is already open—FBI cleared it thirty seconds ago. Lee and I slip through the gap, staying low, moving fast. The main floor is pandemonium. Workers scrambling for exits. Guards returning fire from behind processing tables. FBI agents advancing in two-man teams, methodical and relentless.

But I'm not here for the main floor.

"Second level," I shout over the gunfire. "Josie's in the office."

Lee nods, and we break left, heading for the metal staircase that hugs the far wall. A guard steps into our path—young, scared, gun shaking in his hands. Lee drops him with a single punch, knocking him out cold before he can fire one off.

"Keep moving," Lee says. "I've got your six."

The stairs rattle under our boots. Halfway up, I hear it—a woman's scream, cut short. My blood turns to ice.

Josie.

I take the remaining stairs three at a time, bursting onto the second-floor catwalk with my gun up and my heart in my throat. The foreman's office is twenty feet ahead, its windows shattered, smoke still curling from the flash-bang.

Standing in the doorway, using Josie as a human shield, is Vincent Caruso.

He's got one arm locked around her throat, a pistol pressed to her temple. Her face is a mess—swollen lip, blackening eye, blood drying on her chin. But her eyes are alert, fierce, tracking my every move.

She's alive. She's hurt, but she's alive.

"That's far enough!" Caruso's voice is high, tight with panic. Whatever smooth control he had before is gone. He's a cornered animal now, and cornered animals are dangerous. "Drop your weapons or I put a bullet through her brain!"

I stop. Lee stops behind me.

"Not happening." I keep my gun trained on Caruso, but I don't have a shot. Josie's body blocks everything vital. Even a headshot is risky—if he flinches, if I miss by a millimeter, she's dead.

"I'll do it!" He jams the gun harder against her temple,

and she winces. "You think I won't? I've killed a hundred people. One more won't make a difference."

"If you kill her, you've got nothing. No leverage. No way out." I take a slow step forward. "Right now, she's the only thing keeping you alive."

"Stay back!"

I stop again.

Think. Think, goddammit.

The catwalk is narrow—maybe four feet wide, with a railing on one side and a twenty-foot drop to the main floor on the other. Caruso is backing toward the far end, where a door leads to what looks like an exterior fire escape. If he makes it through that door with Josie, we lose him.

I can't let that happen.

"Dad," Lee's voice is low, barely audible over the chaos below. "Steel's in position. Northeast corner. But he doesn't have a shot yet. Not with Josie in the way."

Steel.

If anyone can make this shot, it's him.

But Caruso isn't giving him an opening. He's smart—keeping Josie's body between himself and any possible sniper angle, never exposing more than a sliver of his head.

Unless someone forces him to move.

"Josie." I keep my voice calm, steady, even though my heart is trying to beat out of my chest. "You trust me?"

Her eyes meet mine. Swollen, bloodied, terrified—but underneath all that, I see it. The fire that made me fall in love with her.

"Always," she says.

I lower my gun.

Caruso blinks, confused. "What are you doing?"

"You want a hostage?" I spread my arms wide, making myself the biggest target possible. "Take me instead. I'm President of the Stoneheart MC. I know where the bodies and info is buried, Caruso."

"Stone, no—" Josie starts.

"Hush, sweetheart." I take a step forward. Then another. "Think about it, Vincent. You walk out of here with her, you've got a lawyer. You walk out of here with me, you've got the head of the organization that's been destroying your operation. That's leverage. That's a fucking bargaining chip."

I can see him calculating, weighing his options.

"Stop moving," he orders.

I don't stop. I keep walking, slow and steady, arms still spread. Every step brings me closer. Every step pulls his attention away from the rooftop across the street.

"You're insane," Caruso hisses.

"Probably." I'm ten feet away now. Close enough to see the sweat beading on his forehead. Close enough to see his finger tightening on the trigger. "But I'm also the only chance you have of getting out of this alive. The FBI has you. But they need my evidence. I can get you out of the charges and out of the country, set you up somewhere without extradition."

"You're lying."

"Maybe." I take another step. "But can you afford to take that chance?"

For a moment, nobody moves. The gunfire below has faded to sporadic bursts. The FBI is winning. Caruso's operation is crumbling around him.

He makes his first mistake.

He shifts his aim from Josie to me.

Just for a second. Just long enough to point the gun at my chest, to scream something about how he'll kill us both—

"DOWN!" I roar.

Josie drops.

She goes boneless, dead weight, slipping out of Caruso's grip like water through fingers. He grabs for her, off-balance, his gun swinging wild—

The shot comes from nowhere.

One moment Caruso is standing. The next, his head snaps back, a red mist blooming in the air behind him. The fucker crumples like a puppet with cut strings.

I'm moving before his body hits the ground.

"Josie—"

She's on her hands and knees, gasping, shaking. I drop beside her, pulling her into my arms, running my hands over her body checking for wounds.

"Are you hit? Josie, talk to me, are you—"

"I'm okay." Her voice is hoarse, ragged. "I'm okay. I'm—" She looks up at me, and despite everything—the blood, the bruises, the chaos still raging around us—she manages a weak smile. "Took you long enough."

A laugh tears out of me, half-relief, half-hysteria, "Fuck."

I pull her in, crushing her to my chest. "You said two fucking minutes, Josie Bright."

"I lied." She reaches up, touching my face with trembling fingers. "Sorry."

I kiss her.

It's not gentle. It's not soft. It's desperate and messy, tasting of blood and tears and the overwhelming relief of having her alive in my arms. She kisses me back just as fiercely, her zip-tied hands fisting in my shirt, pulling me closer like she's afraid I'll disappear.

"I've got you," I murmur against her lips. "I've got you. You're safe."

"I know." She's crying now. "I knew you'd come."

Behind us, Lee clears his throat.

"Hate to interrupt, but we should probably move. Building's not secure yet."

I pull back, cupping Josie's face in my hands. Her beautiful, battered, perfect face.

"Can you walk?"

"I can do anything if it means getting out of here."

I cut her zip ties with my knife, and help her to her feet. She sways, grabbing my arm for balance, but she stays upright. My woman. My fierce, stubborn, incredible woman.

Better get a cut on her back before some other fucker tries to take her from me.

"Steel?" I ask Lee as we move toward the stairs.

"He's already breaking down his position." Lee shakes his head. "Hell of a shot. Two hundred yards, through a broken window at a moving target with a partially obscured view. Brother has ice in his veins."

He more than earned his patch tonight.

The main floor is mostly clear when we reach it. FBI agents are handcuffing prisoners, shouting commands, securing the scene. Pilkin spots us and jogs over, her expression tight.

"Ms. Bright." She takes in Josie's injuries, and her jaw clenches. "We need to get you medical attention."

"I'm fine."

"You're not fine. You're—"

"I'm alive." Josie straightens, drawing on reserves I didn't know she had. "Which is more than I can say for Caruso. I assume that was one of yours?"

Pilkin glances at me. "No."

"Anonymous sniper?" I ask smoothly. "Must be a rival organization. These cartel types have a lot of enemies."

Pilkin holds my gaze for a long moment. Then, slowly, she nods.

"Rival organization. Of course." She turns back to Josie. "The medics are outside. I strongly suggest you let them examine you."

"After I give my statement."

"Josie—" I start.

"I have information, Stone. Names, locations, details about his operation that I gathered while they were—" She swallows hard. "While they were questioning me. The FBI needs it while it's still fresh."

They tortured her for information, and she used it to gather intel on them.

God, I love this woman.

"Fifteen minutes," I order. "Then the medics, non-negotiable."

Josie nods, and Pilkin leads her toward a cluster of agents with tablets and recorders. I watch her go, this woman who walked into my clubhouse and turned my entire world upside down.

Lee appears at my shoulder.

"She's something else," he says.

"Yeah." I can't take my eyes off her. "She really is."

"You going to marry her?"

The question catches me off guard. I turn to look at my son—he's grown into a man I'm proud to call mine.

"Damn right, I fucking am."

Lee grins. "About time, old man."

I cuff him on the back of the head, but I'm smiling.

She's alive. She's safe. And as soon as this is over, I'm never letting her out of my sight again.

23

JOSIE

Т he clubhouse is quiet when we get back.

It's nearly 3am by the time we're done with the FBI—my statement, Stone's statement, the endless paperwork that accompanies any federal operation. Alex wanted me to go to the hospital, but after the paramedics confirmed nothing was broken, I refused. I just wanted to go home.

Home. When did the clubhouse become home?

Isabel's waiting in the hallway when we come through the door. She's in pajamas, hair mussed. Her gaze sweeps over me—the bruises blooming on my face, the raw skin at my wrists, the way I'm holding myself like everything hurts.

Because it does.

"Jesus," she breathes. "You look like shit."

"Thanks. Way to make a girl feel good."

We exchange a grin.

"I hope you gave the other guy worse."

A surprised laugh escapes me—rough and painful against my bruised ribs. "Something like that."

We're two women who've faced violence. Two women who found refuge in the same place. She surprises me by reaching out and squeezing my hand. It's brief and fierce, then she drops it and steps back.

"You better go. Your man is about to vibrate out of his skin."

I glance at Stone, who's been standing rigid beside me, barely holding it together. She's right.

"We'll talk tomorrow?" I ask.

"Tomorrow." Isabel nods. "Get some rest, Josie."

Word has spread—I can tell by the way brothers nod at us as we pass, the relief in their eyes, the careful distance they keep. They know what happened. They know what Stone did to get me back.

And they know we need to be alone.

Stone doesn't speak as he leads me upstairs. Doesn't speak as he locks the bedroom door behind us. Doesn't speak as he turns to face me, his expression raw and open in a way I've never seen.

"Boone—"

"I almost lost you." His voice cracks. "Josie, I've never been that scared in my life."

"I know." I cross to him, taking his face in my hands. My wrist aches where the zip ties dug in. My cheek throbs where Ivan hit me. But none of that matters. "I know. But I'm here. I'm okay. You found me."

His fingers trace my swollen lip, the bruise darkening around my eye. His jaw tightens with barely contained rage.

"Who did this to you?"

"Ivan. He's—"

"Dead." Stone's voice is flat. Certain. "If Steel didn't get him, the FBI did. And if neither of them did, I'll find him myself."

"He's dead." I cover his hand with mine. "I saw him go down in the chaos. It's over."

"I put Steel in that position." He closes his eyes. "I ordered him to take a shot that—"

"That saved my life." I pull his forehead down to mine. "You saved my life. Both of you. Don't you dare feel guilty about that."

"I would have killed them all." His hands grip my hips, hard enough to bruise. "Every single one of them. Without hesitation. Without regret. Does that scare you?"

I should probably say yes. A normal woman would be terrified, would run from a man capable of that kind of violence.

But I'm not a normal woman. And he's not a normal man.

"No," I whisper. "It doesn't scare me."

"Josie—"

"I knew what I was signing up for." I hold his gaze. "I'm not some naive girl who thought dating an MC president would be quiet Sunday brunches. I knew there would be danger. I knew there would be moments like tonight. And I chose you anyway."

"Why?"

"Because you're worth it." I pull him down until our foreheads touch. "All of it. The danger, the fear, the 2am emergencies and the canceled plans and the constant worry. It's worth it to be yours."

Something breaks in him—I can feel it, the last of his walls crumbling.

"I might get annoyed sometimes," I continue. "When Church runs long or you disappear without warning. I'll probably roll my eyes and mutter under my breath and give you hell for it later."

"I'd expect nothing less."

"But I'll get over it. Because this—you, the club, all of it—is home. And I'm not going anywhere."

He kisses me then—desperate and hungry and raw.

"I need you," he groans against my mouth. "Right now. I need to feel you, make sure you're real, make sure you're still—"

"I'm here." I pull at his shirt. "I'm real. Take what you need."

He does.

There's nothing gentle about it.

He strips me with shaking hands, his mouth following every inch of skin he reveals—pausing at each bruise, each mark they left on me, pressing kisses like he can heal them with his lips alone. I'm tearing at his clothes just as desperately, needing skin against skin, needing to feel his heartbeat against mine.

"Bed," I manage between kisses. "Now."

He lifts me like I weigh nothing, carrying me across the room, laying me down on sheets that smell like us. And then he's over me, around me, inside me—one long thrust that drives the breath from my lungs.

"God—" He buries his face in my neck. "Josie—"

"Move." I wrap my legs around him. "Please, Boone, I need—"

He moves.

Hard and fast and desperate, like he's trying to crawl inside my skin. I cling to him, nails raking down his back, matching his intensity with my own. This isn't making love. This is claiming. Reassuring. Proving to ourselves that we're both still here, still alive, still together.

"I love you." He pants the words against my throat. "I love you so goddamn much."

"I love you too." I arch into him. "Don't stop. Please don't stop."

He doesn't.

He drives into me relentlessly, hitting spots that make me see stars, one hand gripping my hip while the other slides between us to find my clit. The pleasure builds and builds until I'm sobbing with it, tears streaming down my face from the intensity.

"Come for me." His voice is rough, strained. "Let me feel you come, Josie."

The orgasm crashes through me—sharp and bright and overwhelming. I clench around him, screaming his name, and he follows seconds later with a groan that seems to come from somewhere deep in his chest.

We lie tangled together afterward, both of us shaking.

"I'm sorry," he murmurs against my hair. "That was—I wasn't gentle—"

I shift, wincing as my bruised ribs remind me they exist. "I didn't want gentle." I press a kiss to his chest, ignoring the stinging protest from my split lip. "I wanted you. All of you. No holding back."

"You have all of me." He pulls me closer. "Every broken, violent, possessive part. It's all yours."

"Good." I trace patterns on his skin. "Because I'm keeping it."

We fall asleep like that, wrapped around each other, and for the first time since the alley, I feel safe.

24

STONE

The next forty-eight hours are a blur of logistics and cleanup.

FBI agents crawl over every inch of the warehouse. Statements are given, evidence catalogued, and deals struck. Caruso's body is shipped to the morgue, his organization crumbling without him. Summit's leadership scatters to the wind, their dreams of developing Stoneheart dying with their cartel backing.

We won.

But I know better than to think it's over.

"The cartel's sending an emissary," Agent Pilkin tells me on the second day. "They want to negotiate."

"Negotiate what? Why aren't you arresting them?"

"Because we can't." She sighs, and for the first time I see the frustration behind her professional mask. "Caruso was careful. Most of the evidence ties back to a few underlings and most of Summit's corporate fat cats. His lieutenants have plausible deniability, and the cartel leadership is three layers removed. We push too hard without enough to make charges stick, they lawyer up and we lose any chance of cooperation." She shrugs. "This emissary is their attempt to cut a deal. They're testing the waters."

"So they get to walk?"

"Some of them. For now." Her jaw tightens. "I don't like it either. But sometimes you take the win you can get and live to fight another day."

I let that sink in.

Alex leans against her car, crossing one ankle over the other. "Caruso was their point man for East Coast operations. Without him, they don't have the infrastructure to continue here. They want out—but they want assurances."

"What kind of assurances?"

"That you won't come after them. That what happened here stays here. In exchange, they're offering to leave Stoneheart territory permanently."

It's more than I expected. The cartel cutting their losses, ceding ground without a fight.

"Set up the meeting," I say. "But on our terms. Our territory."

The meeting happens at Devil's Bar.

Neutral ground, recently rebuilt after the fire. The cartel sends a single representative—a gray-haired man in an expensive suit who introduces himself only as Mr. Reyes.

He's smooth. Professional. The kind of man who orders deaths with the same tone he uses to order dinner.

"Your club has caused us significant problems," Reyes says, settling into a chair across from me. "And significant losses."

"Your people kidnapped my woman and beat her face in. They're lucky they only lost Caruso."

"An unfortunate miscalculation." His expression doesn't change. "One that cost us dearly. Ivan was... overzealous."

"Ivan is dead. So is his boss. And the FBI has enough evidence to dismantle every operation you've run through this state for the past five years."

That gets a reaction—a slight tightening around his eyes. "Which is why we're here. To ensure this situation doesn't escalate further."

"Here are my terms." I lean forward. "Your organization stays out of Stoneheart, and away from any Stoneheart MC territory. Not just the town—the entire country. No drugs, no trafficking, no intimidation. If I see so much as a suspicious vehicle crossing our borders, I'll personally deliver the rest of the footage we have to every federal agency in the country."

"That's a significant demand."

"Take it or leave it."

Reyes is quiet for a long moment. I watch him calculate—the costs, the benefits, the risks of continuing a war he can't win.

Finally, slowly, he nods.

"Agreed. The Stoneheart MC is off-limits." He stands, straightening his jacket. "You've made a powerful enemy, Mr. Armstrong. But you've also earned a measure of respect. We won't forget either."

"Just remember our agreement." I don't stand, don't offer my hand. "And don't come back."

He leaves without another word.

When he's gone, Hawk lets out a breath. "Holy shit. That actually worked."

"For now." I stand, stretching muscles tight with tension. "We'll need to stay vigilant. Cartels don't stay gone forever."

"But for now?"

"For now, it's over." I pull out my phone and text Josie.

STONE

Coming home. It's done.

Her response comes immediately.

JOSIE

Good. Hurry, I miss you.

Smiling, I tuck my cell in my pocket, climb on my bike and ride home to her.

25

JOSIE

The nightmares come in fragments.

Headlights. The smell of chemicals. Ivan's soft voice asking questions while his fists delivered consequences. The cold press of metal against my temple and Caruso's reptilian eyes watching me like I was already dead.

I jerk awake with a gasp, heart slamming against my ribs. For one terrifying moment I don't know where I am.

"Hey. Hey, I've got you."

Stone's voice cuts through the panic. His arms are already around me, pulling me against his chest, one hand stroking my hair while the other presses flat against my back like he's trying to hold me together.

"You're safe," he murmurs against my temple. "You're home. I've got you."

I press my face into his neck and breathe him in, panting and gasping. My heart rate slowly returns to normal as the fragments of the nightmare fade, replaced by the solid warmth of the man holding me.

"Sorry," I manage. "I didn't mean to wake you."

"Don't apologize." His arms tighten. "Don't ever apologize."

This is the third night in a row. The third time I've woken up gasping, clawing my way out of nightmares that are far too real. Stone hasn't complained once. He hasn't shown any sign of frustration or exhaustion, even though I know he's not sleeping either.

He holds me. Every time.

"What time is it?" I ask.

"Little after four."

"You should sleep."

"So should you."

"I'm fine."

"Josie." He pulls back just enough to look at me, and even in the darkness I can see the worry carved into his features. "You're not fine. And that's okay. You went through a horrific experience. It's going to take time."

"I know." I do know. Intellectually, I understand trauma responses. I've worked with enough victims to recognize the signs—the hyper-vigilance, the nightmares, the way certain sounds or smells can trigger a flood of memory.

It's been a while since I experienced any of it.

"Have you thought about talking to someone?" Stone asks carefully. "A professional?"

"You mean a therapist?"

"Yeah."

I consider it. I used to see a woman in Atlanta. It started as a workplace health and safety yearly mandated exercise to reduce our insurance premiums, but I'd found talking to someone a few times a year about the material I'd been exposed to helped.

"I saw someone in Atlanta," I say finally. "I'll reach out and see if she has any tele appointments available."

"Sounds good."

"But let me get through the next few days first. The FBI debrief, the election, all of it. Then I'll book it."

"You want me to organize it for you?"

"No, I'm good. Really."

"Okay." He presses a kiss to my forehead. "Whatever you need."

Whatever you need. He's been saying that a lot lately. *Whatever you need, Josie. Just tell me and I'll make it happen.*

The problem is, most of the time I don't know what I need. I feel fragile and vulnerable in a way I've never felt before—like if I move too fast or think too hard, I'll shatter into a thousand pieces. I *hate* it. I've spent my entire adult life being strong, being capable, being the person others lean on. This weakness feels like a betrayal to the person I am.

"You're overthinking it," Stone murmurs.

"I'm not—"

"You are. I can practically hear the gears grinding." He shifts us so we're lying face to face, his hand cupping my cheek. "Talk to me."

"I just…" I struggle to find the words. "I feel broken. I know that's normal, I know it's a trauma response, but knowing something intellectually and feeling it are two different things."

"You're not broken." His voice is fierce. "You survived. You kept your head, gathered intel, stayed alive long enough for us to reach you. That's not weakness, babe. That's strength."

"I don't feel strong."

"I know." He pulls me closer, tucking my head under his chin. "But you are. The nightmares, the fear, the moments when it all comes flooding back—that's you being human. Your body is trying to process stress. We have to ride it out and work through it." He kisses my forehead again. "Your sexy brain needs to recover just like the rest of your body."

"Well when you put it like that…." I sigh, relaxing into him. "The woman they grabbed, is she okay?"

"She's fine. Shaken up, but fine. The FBI got her statement, and she's getting some counseling." Stone pauses. "She asked about you. Wanted to know if the woman they were after made it out okay."

"What did you tell her?"

"That you're the toughest person I know." His hand slides down to squeeze my ass. "And that you're going to be fine. Eventually."

Eventually. I hold onto that word like a lifeline.

"Go back to sleep," I tell him. "I'll be okay."

"I'm not sleeping until you do."

"Stone—"

"Fuck it." He sits up, taking me with him. "I've got a better idea."

I laugh. "We just had sex like three hours ago."

"As much as I love your delectable body, get dressed," he says, already swinging his legs over the side of the bed. "Warm layers. Jeans, not sweats."

"Okay? Where are we going?"

He's pulling on his own jeans. "We're going for a ride."

"A ride." I stare at his back, my sleep-deprived brain struggling to catch up. "It's—" I check my phone. "—4:47 in the morning."

"Best time for it." He turns, and even in the dim light I can see the hint of a smile. "Trust me?"

"Yes."

"Then get dressed. I'll meet you downstairs in ten."

He slips out before I can change my mind.

I sit there for a moment, bemused, before the absurdity of the situation makes me laugh. Here I am, recovering from a near-death experience, plagued by nightmares, and the president of a motorcycle club wants to take me on a pre-dawn joyride.

This is my life now.

I get dressed, chuckling.

The clubhouse is silent as I make my way downstairs—that particular quality of quiet that only exists in the hours before dawn, when even the most dedicated night owls have finally surrendered to sleep.

Stone is waiting by the back door, two leather jackets draped over his arm. One is his—worn and familiar, the Stoneheart patch visible even in the low light. The other is newer.

"Whose is that?" I ask.

He holds it out. "Yours."

"You bought me a jacket?"

He gives me a look that says I'm crazy for thinking he wouldn't have.

Got it.

I slide my arms through the sleeves. It's a perfect fit, the leather is soft, and it smells faintly of wax.

"Ready?" Stone asks.

I strike a pose. "Let's do it."

His grins. "Come on."

His massive Harley gleams even in the pre-dawn darkness. Stone hands me a helmet, adjusts the strap under my chin with gentle fingers, then swings his leg over and settles into the seat.

"Climb on. Hold tight."

The seat is higher than I expected, and I have to use Stone's shoulder for balance as I swing my leg over. The leather is cold against my thighs, but his body is warm where I press against his back.

"Arms around my waist," he instructs. "Lean when I lean. Don't fight me."

"I never fight you."

His laugh rumbles through his chest, vibrating against my palms. "Sweetheart, that's the biggest lie you've ever told. Calling me on shit, is one of my favorite things about you."

Before I can respond, he kicks the engine to life.

The sound is enormous—a deep, throaty roar that shatters the silence and sends a flock of birds exploding from a nearby tree. I tighten my grip, and Stone pats my clasped hands in reassurance.

Then we're moving.

The town is a blur in my peripheral vision—dark houses, empty streets, the occasional glow of a streetlight. But Stone doesn't stay in town. He takes us past the last buildings, past the *Welcome to Stoneheart* sign, and onto a winding road that climbs into the mountains.

The air gets colder as we ascend. I press closer to Stone's back, grateful for the warmth of his body, the solid wall of muscle between me and the wind. The engine's rumble becomes a rhythm, almost meditative, and I find my racing thoughts starting to slow.

This is what he loves. This freedom. The speed. The feeling of the world falling away.

The road twists and turns, following the contour of the mountain. Pine trees rise on either side, dark sentinels against the slowly lightening sky. Somewhere below us, the valley spreads out like a patchwork quilt—fields and farms and the distant cluster of buildings that is Stoneheart.

And then Stone pulls off onto a scenic overlook, kills the engine, and everything goes quiet.

I can hear birds waking in the trees, the rustle of wind through branches, the tick of the cooling engine.

"Look," Stone says softly.

I turn to follow his gaze.

The sun is rising.

It crests the far mountains in shades of gold and pink, painting the sky in colors I don't have names for.

Slowly, the light catches the valley below, turning mist into spun gold, setting the world ablaze with a warmth that seems impossible after the cold darkness of the ride.

It's the most beautiful thing I've ever seen.

"Boone," I breathe.

"I come here sometimes, when things get loud in my head. When the club is too much, and the weight of it all feels like it's going to crush me."

We sit there on his bike—my arms still loosely wrapped around him, his hand occasionally coming back to rest on my knee—and we watch the sun climb higher. The colors shift and change, gold bleeding into blue, the first real warmth of the day starting to cut through the mountain chill.

And slowly, gradually, I feel the fear and grief loosen in my chest.

Not the grief—that's still there, will probably always be there. But the sharp edges of it soften, smoothed by the beauty of this moment, by the man who thought to share it with me.

"Thank you," I whisper.

He doesn't turn around, but I feel his hand squeeze my knee.

"Anytime, sweetheart. I mean it."

We stay until the sun is fully up, until the spectacular colors have faded into ordinary daylight, until the world below has started to wake. Then Stone kicks the engine to life, and we wind our way back down the mountain.

When we pull back into the clubhouse lot, the others are starting to stir—I can see lights in the kitchen, smell coffee brewing through an open window. Stone kills the engine and helps me off the bike, steady hands on my waist.

"You should eat something," he says. "Maggie's probably got breakfast going."

"Okay." I start to turn toward the building, then stop. Look back at him.

He's still straddling the bike, helmet dangling from one hand, watching me with an expression I can't quite read. The morning light catches the silver in his hair, the lines around his eyes, the quiet intensity that drew me in from the very first day.

"Stone?"

"Yeah?"

"Next time the nightmares come, take me on another ride."

His smile is slow and warm and real.

"Count on it."

26

JOSIE

My days become a blur of FBI debriefs and recovery.

Agent Pilkin is thorough—hours of questions about what I saw, what I heard, what Caruso and Ivan said during their "questioning." I give her everything, every detail I catalogued during those terrifying hours, and watch her expression sharpen as she realizes how much intel I managed to gather.

"You're remarkable," she tells me at the end of the last session. "Most people in your situation would have been too terrified to think clearly. You turned your captivity into an intelligence-gathering operation."

"I'm a lawyer," I say with a shrug. "We're trained to observe."

What I don't tell her is that focusing on those details was the only thing that kept me sane. Cataloguing information gave me something to do other than imagine all the ways I might die.

Stone insists on being present for every debrief, sitting in the corner with his arms crossed and his eyes never leaving me. He doesn't say much—this is federal business, not club business—but his presence grounds me.

He's been hovering lately, making sure I eat, making sure I sleep, making sure I don't overdo it. It's sweet. It's also driving me slowly insane.

"I can shower by myself," I tell him when he follows me toward the bathroom.

"I know."

"Then why are you—"

"I can't help it." He runs a hand through his hair, looking frustrated with himself. "You're gonna have to give me a few more days. Every time you're out of my sight, I start thinking about—"

My irritation fades as quickly as it came.

"Boone." I close the distance between us, taking his face in my hands.

"I let you out of my sight for a second, and they took you. If I'd followed you in—if I'd been faster—"

"Then they would have waited for another opportunity. This isn't your fault."

"It feels like my fault."

I rise on my toes and kiss him—soft, gentle, trying to pour all my reassurance into the contact. "The only people responsible are Caruso and his men. And they're dead or in federal custody. It's over."

"I'm trying to give you space. But after everything—"

"I know, and I appreciate it." I smile at him. "But I really can shower alone. I promise not to drown."

His mouth curves reluctantly. "I make no promises about not checking on you."

"One check. After five minutes. Deal?"

"Two minutes."

"Four."

"Fine. Four." He kisses me again, harder this time, then steps back. "Go. Before I change my mind."

"Promises, promises."

I'm laughing as I close the bathroom door behind me.

STONE

Church convenes a little before 9AM.

Every brother is present—a full table for the first time in weeks. The air is different today. Lighter. The shadow that's been hanging over us since Summit first appeared in our lives has finally lifted.

We won. Against all odds, against a cartel with connections stretching across the Eastern Seaboard, against everything they threw at us—we won.

But that's not why I called this meeting.

"Before we get to regular business," I say, standing at the head of the table, "we've got an important issue to discuss."

The brothers exchange glances. They know what's coming.

"Steel." He jerks upright from where he was leaning against the wall at the back of the room. As a prospect, he can be invited to observe, but only full members have earned the honor to sit at the table. I gesture at the empty chair at the far end. "Take a seat."

He looks confused, but he sits. He's young, but he's proved he can handle himself, and do what needs to be done for the club.

It's time.

"You all know what happened," I say, keeping my voice steady despite the emotion threatening to crack it. "My woman was taken. Kidnapped by a cartel boss who intended to use her as leverage against this club. Against all of us."

The room goes silent. Every man here knows the story, but hearing it laid out in Church gives it weight.

"We planned a rescue operation in coordination with the FBI. Tactical teams, coordinated assault, the works. But when we breached that building, Caruso had Josie at gunpoint. There was no clear shot for anyone."

I look around the table, meeting each brother's eyes in turn.

I turn back to Steel. "Except Steel took the shot."

Hawk whistles low. He's seen the aftermath. He knows what that shot required.

"Two hundred yards," I continue. "Through a broken window. At a moving target partially obscured by a hostage. One chance. One bullet. And this prospect—" My chuckle, correcting myself. "This *brother* put that bullet exactly where it needed to go. He saved Josie's life. Saved mine too, probably."

Steel is sitting straighter now, his shoulders back, his jaw set. But I can see the hope in his eyes.

"There are a lot of things that make a man worthy of wearing our colors," I say. "Loyalty. Courage. The willingness to do whatever it takes to protect this family. But more than any of that, what makes a brother is simple. When the moment comes, when everything's on the line, you show up. You do what needs to be done."

I walk around the table until I'm standing in front of Steel. He lumbers to his feet, bracing himself.

"You did what needed to be done. I trust you with my life—with any of our lives—without hesitation."

I pull the patch from my pocket. I've been carrying it since yesterday, waiting for this moment. The full colors of the Stoneheart MC, ready to replace the prospect patch on his cut.

"You've earned this," I tell him. "Not just for that shot—but for everything. For the surveillance work that cracked Caruso's operation. For the evidence that brought the FBI on board. For standing watch over this club through every threat we've faced." I hold out the patch. "Welcome to the brotherhood, Steel."

He takes it with trembling fingers, his throat working.

The brothers are on their feet, crowding around, slapping Steel's back, pulling him into rough embraces. Bones is grinning ear to ear. Tank looks like a proud parent. Even Duck is nodding with respect.

Steel takes the patch with hands that aren't quite steady. When he looks at me, his eyes are bright.

"Thank you, Prez," he says. "I won't let you down."

"I know you won't." I grip his shoulder. "You're one of us now. That means when you're in trouble, every man in this room will ride for you. It means when you need help, you've got the full weight of the brotherhood ready to drop everything for you. We got your back, kid. Welcome to the Club."

I let that sink in, then turn to address the table.

"That's what this club is about. Not the bikes, not the leather, not the reputation. It's about family. About having people in your corner no matter what. About knowing that whatever comes, you don't face it alone."

I think about Josie upstairs, still recovering from her ordeal. About Isabel and Lily, finding safety within our walls after years of abuse. About every person this club has protected, every battle we've fought, every sacrifice we've made.

"We've been through hell these past few months," I continue. "Summit tried to buy our town out from under us. The cartel tried to break us. And we're still standing because of the men in this room, and the women out there."

I meet each of their gazes again—Hawk and Tank, Lee, Bones, Cash, Duck, Axel, and the rest—every single one of them has bled for this club.

"I don't say this enough," I admit. "Probably because I'm a stubborn bastard who doesn't know how to express emotions properly."

A ripple of laughter goes around the table.

"But I want you all to know—I'm proud of you. Every single one of you. There's no one I'd rather have watching my back. No one I'd rather call brother."

The room goes quiet. It's not often I get sentimental in Church. Not often I let them see beneath the president's mask.

Hawk breaks the silence first. "Getting soft in your old age, Prez?"

"Fuck off," I say, but I'm smiling. "You assholes will only be hearing this once. Don't get used to it."

"We love you too, Stone," Tank says, making kissing sounds in my direction.

"Alright, alright." I wave them off, settling back into my chair. "Enough feelings. Let's get to business. We've got an election to win and a town to rebuild. Steel—" I nod at him. "First order of business as a full patch, you're leading the surveillance rotation for Duck's security detail."

Steel's eyes widen. "Me?"

"You've got the skills. Time to use them." I lean back. "Anyone have a problem with that?"

No one does.

We spend the next hour going over details—security for today's election, the ongoing federal investigation, the steps needed to ensure the cartel's remaining allies don't try anything stupid. By the time we adjourn, the mid-morning sun is streaming through the windows and the clubhouse is filling with the sounds of life.

"Alright, go vote for Duck. Dismissed."

Steel hangs back as the others file out.

"Prez? Can I have a minute?"

"Of course."

He waits until we're alone, then takes a breath. "I wanted to thank you. Not just for the patch—for everything."

"You earned it," I tell him. "I didn't do shit."

"Still." He looks down at the patch in his hands, running his thumb over the embroidered colors. "This means more than I can say. I never had... I mean, before the club, I didn't really have people. A family. You know?"

I do know. Group homes, foster care, a military stint that gave him skills but not community. He came to us hungry for something he couldn't name.

But I knew. He needed to belong.

Now he has his place, his family, his club.

Now he belongs.

I clap him on the back. "Go on," I tell him. "Put that patch on. The women are planning some kind of celebration tonight—there was talk of a banner and confetti. You might want to brace yourself."

Steel groans. "Ginger?"

"Who else?"

"She's going to make it embarrassing, isn't she?"

"Almost certainly." I clip him over the ear, playfully. "Welcome to the family, brother. For better or worse."

He's laughing as he heads for the door, the patch clutched in his hand.

We've still got a long road ahead—for Josie, for the club, for all of us, but we're going to walk it together.

27

E lection day dawns bright and clear.

My bruises have faded to a sickly yellow-green, easily covered with makeup, and my lip has mostly healed.

The town is buzzing with energy—people heading to polls, campaign signs everywhere, a sense of anticipation that's almost tangible. After everything we've been through, this feels like a victory lap.

And when the results come in, it's not even close.

Duck wins by a landslide.

The "PUBIC Servant" incident, it turns out, only made him more popular. The man who could laugh at himself was the man they wanted running their town.

The clubhouse erupts in celebration. Music blasting, drinks flowing, brothers cheering like they've won the

Super Bowl. Duck is mobbed by well-wishers, his face splitting in a grin that might be permanent.

"Can you believe it?" Kya appears at my elbow, practically bouncing. "A biker for mayor. The town council is going to have a collective aneurysm."

"That's half the fun." I clink my beer against hers. "Here's to aneurysms."

Stone finds me in the crowd, pulling me against his side. "Hell of a day."

"Hell of a week." I lean into him. "Hell of a year, really."

The women cluster on the deck outside like groupies at a concert, waiting for Steel to exit.

"You do this for every new patch holder?" I ask Ginger.

She laughs. "Yep. What goes on in Chapel is their business." She waggles a finger at me. "But what happens outside of that male dominated room is our responsibility. It's good these new boys know we're the boss from the beginning."

I tilt my head back to smile up at Stone. "Is that right? Am I the boss?"

"Everywhere but the bedroom, sweetheart."

Inside the clubhouse, I can hear muffled voices. Then laughter—a lot of it.

"That's either very good or very bad," Kya observes.

"With this club? Could be both."

Ginger checks her watch. "The banner's going to fall if they don't hurry up. I rigged it with fishing line and prayer."

The doors swing open.

Steel emerges first, looking dazed, his cut now sporting full colors instead of the prospect patch. The brothers behind him are grinning, slapping his back, clearly having given him hell in there while Maggie officially sewed on his patch.

"SURPRISE!" Ginger yanks a cord.

The banner unfurls—WELCOME TO THE FAMILY, FAIRY FLOSS—just as the confetti cannons explode.

Steel gets a face full of glitter.

"Who—" He's sputtering, trying to look dignified while covered in sparkles. "Who approved this?"

"I did," Stone chuckles, raising his beer in toast.

Ginger shoves a bottle into Steel's hand. "You're getting a party. Shut up and enjoy it."

Isabel watches from the edge of the crowd, Lily on her hip. When Steel catches her eye, he lifts his beer in a small salute, taking a deep drink.

She doesn't smile, but she nods.

I catch Brick watching them from across the yard, his jaw tight. .

"That's going to be interesting," Stone murmurs.

"You mean the 'who's got the bigger dick energy' those two are throwing off? Yeah, you're telling me."

The party kicks into high gear—food, drinks, music, dancing. Duck gives an impromptu speech about community and gratitude that has Ginger crying. Steel gets passed around for congratulations and kisses until he's pink-faced and overwhelmed.

And through it all, Stone never strays far from my side.

Until suddenly, he's gone.

I look around, confused, and find him standing by the bar, whistling for attention.

The music cuts, and everyone turns.

"One more piece of business tonight," Stone says. His voice carries across the suddenly silent yard.

My heart stutters. *What is he—*

"Josie. Get over here."

The crowd parts. I walk toward him on legs that don't feel entirely steady.

He's holding a fold of leather. A vest. And on the back—

PROPERTY OF STONE

The room erupts. Cheers, whistles, and Ginger starts crying again.

"This isn't asking," Stone says, loud enough for everyone to hear. "This is telling. You're mine, Josie Bright. Have been since you walked into my clubhouse and told me my legal strategy was shit."

"It was shit," I manage, my voice cracking. "You were planning to threaten a judge."

"And you showed me a better way." He holds out the vest. "Put it on."

My hands are shaking as I slide my arms through the sleeves. The leather settles against my shoulders like it was made for me.

Because it was.

Stone pulls me against him and kisses me in front of everyone—deep, claiming, nothing held back.

When we break apart, I'm breathless and dizzy and happier than I've ever been.

"You know," I say, loud enough for the crowd to hear, "if you're going to claim me as property, you should probably make an honest woman of me first. Legally speaking."

"Josie—"

"I'm a lawyer, Boone. I believe in contracts." I grin up at him. "Vegas has twenty-four hour chapels. Just saying."

The crowd goes absolutely silent.

Stone stares at me for a long moment. Then his face splits into the biggest smile I've ever seen on him.

"You want to marry me?"

"I want you to make it legal before you go around branding me with leather goods, yes."

"Vegas." He's laughing now. "You wanna get married by Elvis?"

"Obviously."

He kisses me again, then turns to the crowd. "Looks like we're going to Vegas!"

The clubhouse shakes with the roar.

"I'm booking you the honeymoon suite!" Ginger is already on her phone. "Don't even try to stop me!"

"Wouldn't dream of it," Stone says, not taking his eyes off me. "When do we leave?"

"First light?"

"First light."

Lee raises his beer. "To the President and his Old Lady!"

"TO THE PRESIDENT AND JOSIE!"

Stone pulls me close, his mouth against my ear. "You sure about this?"

I press my hand against the leather vest. His name is on my back. His ring will be on my finger soon.

"Absolutely."

28

STONE

The party eventually winds down.

Brothers drift off to their rooms, to their women, to whatever sleep they can grab before tomorrow. The clubhouse settles into that familiar late-night quiet—the creak of old wood, the hum of the refrigerator, the occasional burst of laughter from somewhere down the hall.

Josie is already upstairs when I finish locking up. I find her standing by the window, still wearing the property vest, looking out at the darkness.

"Hey." I come up behind her, wrapping my arms around her waist. "You okay?"

"More than okay." She leans back against my chest. "Just... taking it in."

"Having second thoughts?"

"About marrying you?" She turns in my arms, facing me. "Never. But I might be having thoughts about the order of operations."

"Meaning?"

"Meaning—" She rises on her toes, pressing a soft kiss to my lips. "—I think we should consummate the marriage before the wedding."

"How very untraditional of you," I gasp in mock horror.

"Objections?"

"Not a one, Counselor."

I kiss her slow and deep, savoring the knowledge she's mine.

"Take off the vest," I murmur against her mouth. "I want to see you."

She slides it off her shoulders, setting it carefully on the chair. Then, piece by piece, she undresses—shirt, jeans, bra, underwear—until she's standing before me in nothing but the moonlight.

"Your turn," she says.

I strip quickly, then take her hand and lead her to the bed.

"Tonight," I tell her, "I'm going to worship you. Slow and thorough. The way you deserve."

"Boone—"

"Let me."

I lay her down against the pillows and take my time kissing every inch of skin. I'm relearning her body, finding the spots that make her gasp, the touches that make her moan, the words that make her shake.

By the time I finally slide inside her, she's trembling with need.

"Look at me," I say, holding still despite every instinct screaming at me to move. "Stay with me."

Her eyes meet mine—dark with desire, soft with love.

I move slowly, deliberately. Deep strokes that drag against every nerve ending, building pleasure like waves rolling toward shore. Her hands grip my shoulders, her legs wrap around me, but neither of us looks away.

"I love you," I tell her. "Everything I am. Everything I have. It's yours."

"I love you too." She arches into me. "God, Boone, I love you so much."

The orgasm, when it comes, is slow and deep and endless. She comes with my name on her lips, and I follow seconds later, spilling inside her with a groan that feels like it comes from my soul.

After, we lie tangled together, her head on my chest, my hand tracing patterns on her back.

"That was..." She trails off.

"Yeah." I press a kiss to her hair. "It was."

"We have forever now." She sounds almost wondering. "Don't we?"

She falls asleep in my arms, and I lie awake a while longer, just watching her breathe.

Forever. I like the sound of that.

29

JOSIE

The Love Me Tender Wedding Chapel is as tacky as I imagined.

There's an overwhelming abundance of red velvet, not to mention the gold trim on things that have no business being gold-trimmed. A painting of Elvis on black velvet hangs behind the altar, and the carpet is the kind of pattern that was probably designed to hide stains. The whole place smells faintly of roses and beer.

It's perfect.

"You sure about this?" Stone murmurs, his hand warm in mine. "We can find somewhere classier. The Bellagio does weddings."

"I don't want classy." I grin up at him. "I want Elvis."

He presses a kiss to my head "Then that's what you'll get."

The chapel is packed—well, packed for a 2am Vegas wedding, anyway. The entire club road tripped to Vegas to watch us get hitched. Even Brick and the Ridgeline crew came, all of them looking wildly out of place in a wedding chapel.

Even Isabel agreed to come. She and Lily stand in the back, looking as if they're unsure exactly what they signed up for.

Don't worry. You'll get used to it.

"Dearly beloved," Elvis—or rather, a man in a white sequined jumpsuit who looks like Elvis's less successful cousin—intones, "we are gathered here today to witness the union of Boone Armstrong and Josephine Bright in holy matrimony."

I catch Stone's eye, and we both struggle not to laugh at the Elvis impersonators horrible impression.

"Marriage," Elvis continues, striking a pose, "is not to be entered into lightly." He twirls. "It is a sacred bond," a hip thrust, "a promise made not just to each other," he gyrates, "but to all those gathered here today." He finishes with another twist. "It is a promise to love, to cherish, to stand by each other through the good times and the bad."

I'm trying not to giggle as Stone squeezes my fingers, his lips pressing together as if to keep his own laughter in.

Somewhere in the audience, Ginger sniffles loudly.

"For god's sake woman," I hear Tank whisper. "Again?"

"I love weddings."

Stone's shoulders begin to shake, and I try desperately to swallow another laugh.

"Now, I understand y'all have written your own vows?" Elvis asks.

Stone nods, turning to face me fully. He takes both my hands in his, and suddenly the tackiness of the chapel, and the humor of the situations fades away.

There's only him.

"Josie." His voice is rough, unsteady in a way I've never heard. "When you walked into my clubhouse that first day, I knew you were trouble. The best kind of trouble— the kind that makes a man question everything he thought he knew about himself."

I squeeze his hands.

"I spent fifteen years believing I wasn't built for love or partnership. You made me realize that was bullshit." A soft laugh ripples through the audience. "You made me realize I was waiting. For you."

He reaches up, brushing his thumb across my cheek.

"I can't promise you easy. Our life is complicated, sometimes dangerous, and I know there will be days when you wonder what the hell you got yourself into. But I can promise you this. I will love you every single fucking day. I will protect you, support you, argue with you when you're being stubborn—"

"I'm never stubborn," I mutter, and the audience laughs.

"—and I will cherish you until my last breath." His gaze holds mine. "You're my home, Josie. The only one that's ever felt real."

I take a shaky breath. It's my turn.

"Boone." I have to stop and compose myself. "I came to Stoneheart looking for boring. Quiet. A life where nothing would ever hurt me again." I laugh. "Instead, I found you."

His hands tighten on mine.

"You are the least boring person I've ever met. You're infuriating and protective, and so goddamn stubborn it makes me want to scream sometimes. You make decisions without consulting anyone, you think you always know best, and you have a pathological inability to delegate!"

"This is supposed to be complimentary," he murmurs as our friends and family roar with laughter.

"I'm getting there." I smile. "You're also the kindest man I've ever known. The most loyal. The most fiercely loving, even when you pretend you're not. You make me feel safe in a way I haven't felt since I was a child. You make me feel seen for exactly who I am."

I step closer, until there's barely any space between us.

"I didn't come to Stoneheart looking for love. But I found it anyway. I found you, and your crazy family, and this life that's nothing like what I planned but everything I didn't know I needed." I reach up, cupping his face. "I love you, Boone Armstrong. All of you. I love you, and I choose you, and I will keep choosing you every single day for the rest of our lives."

Elvis clears his throat. "Well, now. That was... that was beautiful." He dabs at his eyes with a sequined sleeve. "The rings?"

Lee steps forward, producing two simple gold bands from his pocket. He hands them to Elvis with a grin.

"By the power vested in me by the state of Nevada and the King of Rock and Roll," Elvis proclaims, "I now pronounce you husband and wife." He strikes another pose. "You may kiss the bride, baby."

Stone doesn't need to be told twice.

He kisses me like we're alone, like there aren't a truckload of people watching, like the rest of the world has simply ceased to exist. His hands cup my face, his mouth claiming mine with a tenderness that makes my knees weak.

When we finally break apart, the chapel has erupted in cheers.

"Ladies and gentlemen," Elvis announces over the noise, "may I present, for the first time anywhere, Mr. and Mrs. Armstrong!"

Ginger is openly sobbing now, Tank awkwardly patting her shoulder. Lee is grinning so wide it looks like it hurts. Emma is recording everything on her phone, tears streaming down her face. I even catch Isabel smiling.

Elvis breaks into song, crooning a shockingly excellent rendition of Love Me Tender as we walk down the aisle.

"We did it," I whisper to Stone.

"We did. Any regrets?"

"Ask me in fifty years."

"Is that a challenge?"

"It's a promise." I rise on my toes to kiss him again. "Now come on, husband. I believe there's a honeymoon suite with our name on it."

"Best wedding ever," he murmurs against my lips.

"Just wait until you see what I'm wearing under this dress."

His eyes darken. "Josie..."

"The answer is nothing." I wink. "Absolutely nothing."

He grabs my hand and practically drags me toward the exit.

STONE

The honeymoon suite at the Bellagio is excessive.

A king-size bed with approximately four thousand pillows dominates the bedroom. Floor-to-ceiling windows with a view of the Strip line one wall, and there's a bathtub big enough to swim in. Champagne chills in a bucket that probably cost more than my first bike.

I don't care about any of it.

The only thing I care about is currently standing by the window, her back to me, the lights of Vegas casting her silhouette in gold.

My wife.

My wife.

The words still don't feel real.

"You're staring," Josie says without turning around.

"I'm allowed. You're my wife now."

She turns, and the smile on her face makes my chest ache. "Say that again."

"My wife." I cross to her, pulling her against me. "Mrs. Armstrong. My old lady. Mine."

"Possessive, much?"

"Absolutely." I brush my lips against her temple. "Is that a problem?"

"It's really, *really* not."

I kiss her—slow at first, savoring, but it quickly turns heated. Her fingers thread through my hair, pulling me closer. My hands find the zipper at the back of her dress.

"You weren't lying," I murmur as the fabric falls away. "Nothing underneath."

"I'm a woman of my word."

I lift her, and she wraps her legs around my waist as I carry her to that ridiculous bed with its four thousand pillows. I lay her down in the center, taking a moment to savor the view.

Josie Bright. My wife.

The woman who walked into my life and refused to leave. Who challenged me, changed me, made me want to be better than I ever thought I could be.

"I love you," I tell her, settling over her. "I don't know if I say that enough."

"You show it." Her hand traces down my chest. "That's better than saying."

"I want to do both." I kiss her collarbone. "I love you." Her shoulder. "I love you." The curve of her neck. "I love you."

"Boone..."

"Let me worship you." I meet her eyes. "Let me show you what it means to be loved by me."

"You already have." But she arches into my touch when my hand slides between her thighs. "A thousand times over."

"Then let me show you a thousand more."

I take my time. We have all night. We have forever.

I explore every inch of her body. I bring her to the edge again and again, drawing out every sensation until she's begging for release.

"Please," she gasps. "Boone, please—"

"Please what?"

"I need you. Inside me. Now."

I slide home in one long stroke, and we both groan at the connection. She's tight, wet, perfect—everything I never knew I needed.

"I love you," I tell her again as I start to move. "My wife. My everything."

"I love you too." She arches up to meet me. "Husband."

We move together, finding a rhythm that builds and builds. The pleasure coils tighter with every thrust, every gasp, every whispered declaration. And when we finally fall over the edge together, it feels like the beginning of everything.

Afterward, we lie tangled together, sweaty and satisfied, watching the lights of Vegas through the window.

"So," Josie says, tracing patterns on my chest. "What now?"

"Now we go home." I press a kiss to her hair. "Build a life. Take down the occasional cartel. Host holiday dinners that Ginger will inevitably take over."

"Sounds boring."

I can hear the smile in her voice. "You love it."

"I love *you*."

"Same thing."

She tilts her head up to kiss me, soft and sweet.

"Thank you," she whispers against my lips. "For giving me this life I never knew I wanted."

"Thank you for letting me." I pull her closer.

We fall asleep as the sun starts to rise over the desert, wrapped around each other, exactly where we belong.

EPILOGUE
JOSIE

THREE MONTHS LATER

The clubhouse is fucking chaos.

Ginger has taken over the kitchen, directing traffic like a sequined general. Maggie is arranging flowers on every available surface. Duck—Mayor Duck now, which is a still fucking hilarious—is attempting to help and mostly getting in the way. The twins are running circles around everyone while Andi tries unsuccessfully to corral them.

It's Thanksgiving, and apparently that means the entire extended Stoneheart family has descended on the clubhouse for dinner.

"Is it always like this?" Isabel asks, appearing at my elbow. Lily clings to her leg, watching the chaos with wide eyes.

"Pretty much." I smile at her. "You get used to it."

"Really?"

"Eventually." I crouch down to Lily's level. "Hey, sweet. Want to help me set the table? I need someone to put the napkins in the right spots."

She considers this very seriously, then nods.

"I'll be right here," Isabel tells her. "Just in the next room."

The fact that she can let Lily out of her sight for even a moment is huge. Stone finds me in the dining room, Lily carefully folding napkins beside me.

"Looking good in there," I tell him.

"You're the ones doing all the work."

"I meant you." I rise on my toes to kiss his cheek. "You look happy."

"I am happy." He wraps an arm around me. "I have everything I've ever wanted."

"Even the chaos?"

"Especially the chaos." He watches Lily arranging napkins with intense concentration.

Ginger appears in the doorway. "Turkey's ready! Everyone to the table!"

What follows is the loudest, messiest, most wonderful meal I've ever been part of. Food is passed in every direction. Conversations overlap. One of the twins knocks over a gravy boat. Duck tries to make a toast and gets heckled by literally everyone.

And through it all, Stone's hand stays in mine under the table.

When the plates are cleared and the pie is served, Lee stands up, tapping his glass.

"I'd like to make a toast," he announces. "To family. The one we're born into, and the one we choose."

"To family!" everyone echoes.

I look around the table—at Ginger and Tank, at Hawk and Andi, at Lee and Emma, at Duck and Maggie, at Isabel and Lily, at all the brothers and their partners who've become my people over the past year.

My family.

Stone squeezes my hand.

"Happy?" he asks quietly.

I think about the road that brought me here. The pain, the loss, the years of believing I wasn't built for this kind of love. I think about what I've found on the other side of all that fear.

Home.

"Yeah," I tell my husband. "I really am."

He kisses me—soft and sweet, right there at the table, earning a chorus of cheers and groans from the assembled family.

"Get a room!" Tank hollers.

"We have one," Stone calls back. "Several, actually. It's my clubhouse. Get the fuck out."

The laughter that follows washes over me.

I'm home.

BONUS EPILOGUE
STEEL

Duck's Thanksgiving whiskey has gone straight to my head.

Not that I'm complaining. After the last few months, I figure I've earned a little celebration of my own.

I'm a full patch member. Finally.

I trace the rocker on my cut as I stumble down the hallway toward my room. Even after three months the leather feels heavier.

Fairy Floss, the women call me. I let them. Doesn't matter what nickname they give me—what matters is the colors on my back and the brothers who put them there.

The clubhouse is quiet now, most everyone either passed out or paired off. I should probably drink some water, eat something, be responsible.

Instead, I'm heading to my room to collapse face-first into my pillow and deal with the hangover tomorrow.

I push open the door to my room, already reaching for the light switch—

And freeze.

Someone's inside.

The moonlight through the window catches her first—a silhouette leaning against the far wall, arms crossed, completely at ease in my space like she belongs there.

My hand drops from the light switch. The drunk haze clears faster than it should, survival instincts kicking in despite the whiskey sloshing through my veins.

I let my gaze drift up. Taking inventory.

Boots first. Black leather, knee-high, with a heel that could double as a weapon. The kind of boots a woman wears when she wants to fuck—or fight.

Thigh-high stockings disappear under a skirt that's more a suggestion than fabric. She's got thick thighs that make my mouth go dry despite the alarm bells ringing in my head.

My gaze lifts higher still to curves that could stop traffic— full hips, a waist my palms itch to hold, breasts that strain against a top that's doing the Lord's work keeping them contained and perky.

And the weapons.

Jesus Christ, the weapons.

A knife is strapped to one thigh. Another at her hip. The telltale bulge of a shoulder holster sits under the jacket she's wearing. This woman is a walking armory dressed up in seduction.

My gaze finally reaches her face.

Long dark hair tumbles over her shoulders. Full lips curve in a smile that's equal parts invitation and threat. Her eyes catch the moonlight and throw it back—dark, knowing, amused.

She's gorgeous. The kind of gorgeous that gets men killed.

I kick the door closed behind me, the click of the latch loud in the silence.

She pushes off the wall, moving toward me with the fluid grace of someone who knows exactly how dangerous she is. Each step is deliberate. Calculated. The moonlight catches the glint of her knife, the curve of her smile.

She stops inches away. Close enough that I can smell her perfume—dark and expensive, nothing like the cheap stuff the women I grew up around wore. She's close enough that I can see the gold flecks in her brown eyes.

Close enough to kill me, if that's what she's here for.

Her hand comes up, fingers tracing along my jaw. Despite every instinct screaming at me to move, to fight, to run—I don't.

I can't.

Because I know that touch. Know it like I know my own heartbeat, even after three years of trying to forget.

"Hello, husband," she murmurs, her smile turning sharp. "Have you missed me?"

THE END.... FOR NOW.
Want some more Stone and Josie, and a sneak peek of the next series?

Check out EvieMitchell.com for the bonus chapter!

ACKNOWLEDGMENTS

First, to my readers—you absolute legends. You bought the books, left the reviews, joined the Facebook group, and slid into my DMs demanding to know when Stone was getting his happy ending.

Your enthusiasm for this grumpy, overprotective, emotionally constipated man kept me going through every late night and looming deadline. This book exists because you wanted it.

Thank you for loving Stoneheart as much as I do!

To Megan Wade, my partner in fictional crime. Thank you for helping me build this world and these characters. Stoneheart wouldn't be what it is without your brain, your talent, and your willingness to brainstorm motorcycle club chaos at unreasonable hours! Maybe we forever be pubic servants within the motorcyle club of our dreams!

And finally, to everyone who's been screaming for Steel since the moment he appeared on the page...

You saw that epilogue, right?

You're welcome, and I'm NOT sorry!

—*Evie*

ABOUT EVIE MITCHELL

Fierce Romance

Evie Mitchell is a USA Today bestselling romance author based in Australia who specializes in steamy, inclusive, body-positive romance. As an author living with disability, Evie Mitchell champions authentic disability representation and #OwnVoices storytelling in romance fiction.

She's a thirty-something woman (she/her/hers) who believes in inclusion, accessibility, and fierce romance for every body. When she's not writing, Evie loves curling up with an excellent book, a cup of tea, and her sausage dogs.

Visit Evie's website for her current booklist
www.EvieMitchell.com

Follow Evie on all socials
@EvieMitchellAuthor

Or join her Greedy Reader Facebook Group

ALSO BY EVIE MITCHELL

All Access Series

Knot My Type

Love Flushed

Darn Knit All

Larsson Siblings

Thunder Thighs

Clean Sweep

The X-List

Reality Check

The Christmas Contract

The A-List

Capricorn Cove

The Shake-up

Double the D

Muffin Top

The Mrs. Clause

New Year, Knew You

Double Breasted

As You Wish

You Sleigh Me

Meat Load

9 781923 610101